BAD
HAND

PAULA ASTRIDGE

WOODSLANE

Woodslane Press Pty Ltd
10 Apollo Street Warriewood NSW 2102 Australia
Email: info@woodslane.com.au
Website: www.woodslane.com.au

First published in Australia in 2015 by Woodslane Press
© 2015 Woodslane Press, text © 2015 Paula Astridge

The information in this publication is based upon the current state of commercial and industry practice and the general circumstances as at the date of publication. Every effort has been made to obtain permissions relating to information reproduced in this publication. The publisher makes no representations as to the accuracy, reliability or completeness of the information contained in this publication. To the extent permitted by law, the publisher excludes all conditions, warranties and other obligations in relation to the supply of this publication and otherwise limits its liability to the recommended retail price. In no circumstances will the publisher be liable to any third party for any consequential loss or damage suffered by any person resulting in any way from the use or reliance on this publication or any part of it. Any opinions and advice contained in the publication are offered solely in pursuance of the author's and publisher's intention to provide information, and have not been specifically sought.

National Library of Australia Cataloguing-in-Publication entry

Author: Astridge, Paula, 1958-
Title: Bad Hand : The untold story of Christian, Bligh and Macarthur
Edition: 1st
ISBN: 9781922131898 (paperback)
Notes: Includes bibliographical references.
Subjects: Christian, Fletcher, 1764-1793 – Fiction.
            Bligh, William, 1754-1817 – Fiction.
            Macarthur, John, 1767-1834 – Fiction.
            Bounty Mutiny, 1789 – Fiction.
            New South Wales – History – 1788-1851 – Fiction.
            New South Wales – History – Rum Rebellion, 1808-1809 – Fiction.
Dewey #:   A823.4

Cover Design and layout by Pen Astridge

Printed in Australia

To my three exceptional sisters:
Jacqueline, Delphine and Susan,
for a lifetime of inspiration.

Other books by Paula Astridge

Kill The Fuhrer

Golden Boy

In The Way Of The Reich

Waltzing Dixie

Everything is preordained, even our mistakes.

– Mel Gibson

PROLOGUE

He was God for a day, but now Captain James Cook was dead; murdered by the Hawaiian natives who once revered him.

Their eyes had narrowed with killer intent when the island drums began to beat. Yet, with the inimitable resolve of an Englishman, Cook turned his back on them and strode towards his ships moored in the bay.

He heard the spear whistle through the air towards him and at the explosive agony of it penetrating between his shoulder blades, he fell, face-first, into the surf, its bloodied foam frothing pink from his mouth.

He struggled to raise his body, but like suction cups, the swirling sand swallowed his hands whole and pinned him ripe for the kill. There, the natives beat him to a bloody pulp, while the wielder of the lethal spear put his foot on Cook's back and removed it with a twist.

Under the command of Lieutenant John Williamson, the sailors in the waiting row boat pulled hard on their oars to escape, while those on board Cook's ship, HMS Resolution, watched on in stunned disbelief; shocked by the savagery of the scene, but more so by their inability to do anything about it.

The first among them to snap back to action was the young ship's master, William Bligh.

"*Damn you* for a coward, Williamson!" he cursed, as the lieutenant clambered from the row boat back on board. "Why didn't you stand and fight? Why didn't you *save him*?"

"He was dead…*he was dead!*" Williamson raved back in panic.

Although his feet were now safe on deck, he was still running on adrenaline and far too terrified to take exception.

For speaking to his superior officer in such a way, Bligh should have been flogged, but in the dismay of the moment the entire ship's company stood still, their stony silence confirming young Bligh's accusation.

They were mortified by what they had seen, but it was nothing compared to the horror of the next day.

With their killing spree over, the Hawaiian chief came to pay homage.

"We are sorry that we killed our Great White Father," he said, handing a peace offering to Resolution's new captain, Charles Clerke.

He reeled back in revulsion at its contents, for beneath the ritual palm frond was Cook's severed head, heart and hands.

"It is an *honour*," the chief explained.

Clerke gagged, disguising his mouthful of vomit with a discreet cough into his handkerchief. It was protocol enough to send the chief happily on his way, while Cook's remains, draped in the naval ensign, were committed to the sea.

He is gone. He's gone, thought Bligh, as he braced himself against the southerly wind and even colder reality of his loss. *This man, who was not only my mentor, but the closest I ever had to a father.*

Cook, one of the world's greatest navigators was dead. And deep in mourning, William Bligh was destined to be the next.

- BAD HAND -

ONE

While Cook was making the ultimate sacrifice in the South Seas, England and France had declared war. As participants in the American Revolutionary War, they had recently locked horns at the Battle of Ushant and for the foreseeable future, the oceans were theirs – a blue battlefield on which to kill or be killed.

"With one exception," the French nobly decreed. "If our ships should encounter Cook's expedition, it shall be spared in deference to a great man."

The French did not baulk at chopping off the heads of their fellow countryman, but they were intent on placing a crown of laurels on Cook's, now formally their enemy. Little did they know that that revered head rested barnacled and bloated at the bottom of an island lagoon.

This was the gruesome image William Bligh found impossible to forget, because he, above all, loved and respected his captain.

"I want that young man on my ship," Cook had said when plans were underway for his third Pacific expedition some months earlier.

His mandate this time round was to find the elusive North West Passage through the Arctic Ocean, a shorter route to the east which would expedite travel time and side-step the treacherous Cape of Good Hope.

"As soon as Bligh is done with his lieutenant's exam, send him to me."

In response to this remarkable compliment from the naval hero of the day, 20-year-old Bligh passed his exams with flying colours. Finishing in half the time of his fellow candidates and achieving twice their marks, there was a certain swagger to his step when he entered the captain's office.

Cook stood up to shake his hand, taking a moment to weigh up the short, slender man approaching with his air of confidence. "Well, congratulations Lieutenant. Distinctions in mathematics and science … precisely why I've singled you out."

"Thank you, sir," Bligh replied, returning the handshake with a firm enthusiasm and broad, white smile which almost made him handsome. But to Cook, it was more his mind that mattered.

"Tell me, Bligh, exactly how much actual experience have you had at sea?" he asked as he poured them both a glass of Madeira and offered his recruit a seat.

Bligh accepted both, working hard to steady his hand when, with easy familiarity, the great man sat down in the armchair opposite.

"I was on the Monmouth as captain's servant when I was seven, sir."

Even by stoic English standards, that was very young to be ripped from family and friends and Cook looked at him with some sympathy for the small, frightened child he must have been.

At the sharp recall of that fact, Bligh's body language briefly gave him away. Nervously, he swept a strand of his thinning fair hair from his forehead and scratched at his round, clean-shaven chin.

"My mother died when I was five," he explained, suddenly to his horror, having to blink back the wet film that clouded his clever blue eyes. "When my father remarried soon after, it was apparent that one of us had to go. As it turned out, she proved more essential than I."

Cook cocked a cynical eyebrow and put his empty glass down on the desk.

"Well, what must have been extremely difficult for you back then, Bligh, now stands you in good stead. Your practical experience at sea is exactly what I'm after. I want to offer you the position as sailing master on my ship, Resolution. Are you fit for the challenge?"

Bligh's rubicund face lit with excitement. Not only was it a prestigious promotion, but one made by the man he admired most.

"I've been keeping my eye on you for the last few months," Cook continued. "You have a flair for cartography and navigation."

"A passion, sir," Bligh corrected with an audacity only such a passion could instil.

"I share that passion and need the back up of intelligent, young men to carry on my work. Those to whom I can teach all I know."

All Cook knew was vast – as vast as the night sky which he used as his tool to steer his ships into the unknown. Where Bligh had a talent for facts and figures and an excellent grasp of map making, it was Cook who opened his eyes to the stars and their infinite possibilities.

For such a man of vision, however, Cook was short-sighted in selecting a second lieutenant to share in his tuition process. That role fell to Lieutenant James King to whom, during their service together on the Resolution, Bligh had taken an instant dislike. Jealousy had nothing to do with it. Bligh simply saw King as a weak man of innate cruelty; one who was dedicated to the bad treatment of those he considered beneath him; most particularly, men of lesser rank, social or in the service, who were not in a position to fight back.

Unfortunately for King, Bligh was … and did.

– oOo –

"Blast your eyes!" he swore, snatching the whip from King's hand. "The boy's done nothing to deserve such brutal treatment."

"Stand aside, Bligh and let me finish the job," King spat back. "He's slovenly at his work and needs the laziness whipped out of him."

In a fit of rage, King had bypassed the formality of strapping the 15-year-old gunner's mate to the mast for punishment and was inflicting it on the spot. The boy was already reduced to crawling on all fours, his back ripped raw and mouth dripping saliva, grateful only that the squabble between the lieutenants was giving him a brief reprieve.

During their shared few months at sea, Bligh and King were at daily loggerheads, but now their differences came down to the physical. Trying to wrestle the whip back from Bligh, King met with firm resistance and the sudden humiliation of Bligh slapping him hard across the face.

The brawl brought the ship's crew to a standstill and Captain Cook, to the end of his tether. An argument between warrant officers was unpardonable and deserved a public lashing, but not wanting to make a spectacle of their punishment, Cook ordered them below deck. There, he swung round on them in savage rebuke, incensed that his two protégés had embarrassed him.

"You are officers and gentlemen," he concluded, having hauled them over the coals, "and will henceforth conduct yourselves as such."

Suitably contrite, they saluted and turned to leave, but Cook held Bligh back to say:

"And Lieutenant, you must learn to curb that tongue and temper of yours. It does you a disservice when you have right on your side."

I am his favourite, Bligh thought with satisfaction as he continued his duties. To him, these duties were a feast of navigational delights, with he and Cook forever bent over maps, charting new lands that loomed on the horizon.

However, it was not all plain sailing and those tasks became far more demanding when Resolution and its consort ship, Discovery, tackled the notorious Cape of Good Hope.

"Man Overboard!" came the distress call from the crow's nest when the sky suddenly darkened around them. Thunder rumbled, jagged fingers of lightning clawed the sky and gale-force winds whipped the ocean into a fury. Heaving at the uproar, that black, convulsing sea pounded their ship into submission, pushing it hard towards the rocks.

All hands were on deck fighting for their lives, but more importantly, the survival of their ship. The loss of one soul overboard was regrettable, but a necessary evil compared to the sacrifice of the entire crew. Or what was worse: the desertion of one's post.

Bligh took that risk to rush to the man's rescue. With waves crashing on deck and his footing tenuous on its slippery slant, he fought his way portside, reaching the gunwale just in time to fish the sailor's hand from the pounding sea.

Hanging on for what was left of his life, the old salt screamed through the storm: "Don't let go! For the love of *Christ ... don't let go!"*

Bligh didn't. The strength he brought to bear was unfathomable when the weight of the man was double his own. With clenched teeth and every fibre of his being burning under the strain, he clung on ... and clung on until finally the man managed to find a foothold and scrambled back on board.

Slapping Bligh's back, he said: "Thank you Lieutenant" and got back to business, moments before a blast of wind blew out the mainsail and made Bligh bellow in pain.

The rope that secured the sail snapped clear of the cleat. Breaking free from its constraints, its ghost-white canvas flapped furiously in the wind, before its belly billowed and strung its tethering rope taut. In a savage whiplash, that six-inch thick hemp cable strapped Bligh to the side of the ship – there for him to experience the agony of rope-turned-razor slowly slicing his flesh down to the bone. If not for the quick thinking of the ship's carpenter, who slashed it through with a machete, Bligh's left leg would have been severed.

A good ship's surgeon made sure that it was not – another bonus of Cook's captaincy and his insistence on the finest of crew and conditions. Fresh food, scrupulous quarters and the physical hygiene of his men took priority, assuring a near-perfect survival rate. It was a lesson learned and always practised by Bligh. This day, the system saved his leg.

Yet still, Cook felt he was to blame. For two weeks, Bligh hovered on the brink of death, fighting to recoup from his chronic blood loss and the threat of gangrene. They were restless days for the captain as he came to grips with the prospect of losing his young friend. When the colour came back to Bligh's cheeks, Cook breathed a sigh of relief and wanted to celebrate.

"I'm naming it Bligh's Cap," he announced on Christmas Eve, having ordered that his convalescing lieutenant be carried up on deck.

The stretcher-bound Bligh winced at the intrusion of sunlight as Cook pointed to the high, round rock jutting from the sea.

He handed Bligh his telescope. "My gift to you Lieutenant, for courage under fire."

TWO

Like Cook, all good things had to come to an end and having traversed the oceans of the world, the ships of his third and last mission turned on starboard tack and sailed home without him. They carried news of new lands for their English Empire, cargo holds bulging with treasure and a ship's log attesting to the loss of their leader.

How do you follow an act like that? Bligh asked himself when the Resolution docked at The Nore in the Thames Estuary.

The answer was that he could not. To sustain the excitement of such a monumental, four-year odyssey was impossible. And soon, his emotional and physical high deteriorated to the daily humdrum of looking for a new job and overcoming his unholy rage.

"If Cook had lived, I wouldn't *be* in this position," he hurled angrily at his friend and sponsor Joseph Banks.

As always, in times of strife, Bligh had gone to Banks' home in Soho Square to thrash out the problem in regard to

British Admiralty's decision. *Why*, Bligh wanted to know, had they failed to promote him? Was it a mere oversight or a direct insult?

If any man could answer the question, it was Banks who, as a botanist, had been on the Endeavour when Cook discovered Australia 10 years before. Banks had named Botany Bay and in honour of his work there – collecting and categorising a plethora of unknown species – was made president of the Royal Society. Revered by all, he was ever true to England, but his heart and lifetime dedication held fast to Cook, the Endeavour and Australia.

Not only did he share Cook's adventure, but also his liking for Bligh. A young man, they agreed, who showed enormous potential. Admiralty, however, did not seem to share their opinion and Banks sympathised, to an extent, with Bligh's outburst.

"Cook would have seen to it that my promotion from warrant to commissioned rank was guaranteed. Surely, I proved myself worthy of it?"

"There's no question of that, William. You're a first-rate officer and navigator. Perhaps it's just a question of red tape."

"Not true," Bligh snapped back.

Forgetting himself and the extent of Banks' patience, he continued to rant.

"It's not fair. After four years at sea, I've returned as I left … a ship's master, when midshipmen, Harvey and Lanyan, are both now commissioned lieutenants. Lanyan's my own master's *mate*, for heaven's sake and has been promoted over my head! I don't know what I've done or *not* done to deserve such an insult."

Nor did Banks, but whatever it was, he had every confidence in Bligh and was determined to compensate for

Admiralty's oversight. He said as much when they parted, sending Bligh on his way in a much better frame of mind.

It would have sufficed had Bligh not returned to his London lodgings and found another piece of bad news:

> *Your father is dead,* his stepmother wrote in a letter. *He died of pneumonia in Plymouth and has left you nothing. All his worldly goods were willed to me.*

As a customs agent, those worldly goods did not amount to much, but still it cut Bligh to the quick to know that he was forgotten. It was a matter of pride when he wrote back:

> *It is of no consequence, madam. As far as I am concerned, you are welcome to them, for my real father died in the Sandwich Isles, leaving me rich in all that matters.*

He had taken the moral high ground, but his finances were at an all-time low.

When he had first returned to England, he supplemented his "sailor-on-shore" half-pay by preparing the charts for the official history of Cook's voyage. The public was hungry to hear the story, but once their appetite was sated and party chat complete, Bligh slipped quickly back into obscurity. He was at a loose end and in a very bad mood, because despite Banks' best efforts on his behalf, Admiralty still had not issued him either a commission or new orders.

It was extremely puzzling to Bligh, when England was in dire need of every good man it could get.

At war with France, America, Spain and Holland, Britain's boasted superiority at sea had also stirred Russia and other European countries to join a league of "Armed Neutrality" against it.

Not for the first time or the last, England stood alone. It was frantically building new ships and dragging out the old from Rotten Row, plundering that farthest corner of Portsmouth Harbour to re-rig and make ready for battle every tired hulk that had gone there to die. To further fill naval ranks, England risked ruining the country's economy by hiring press gangs to scour the land and rip men from their families and more fruitful employ. Yet still, Bligh, fully trained and chaffing at the bit to help, was left in limbo. It was an unendurable place to be for such a vital man at a time of war.

"I'm *sick* of sitting round twiddling my thumbs," he told Banks, once again using his old friend as a sounding board as he threw his clothes into his timber travel chest.

Calmly puffing on his pipe, Banks asked:

"But where will you go?"

Much as he did not blame Bligh for being angry, he only wished he could control his temper. It was his one downfall; that and his tendency to lace his language with expletives when riled. Clearly, his young friend was suffering another of those migraines which plagued him. Along with his anger, it flushed his cheeks red, matted his fair hair with sweat and glazed his blue eyes with a mad intensity.

"Up north to the Isle of Man," Bligh replied belligerently. "Perhaps there's something for me there."

There was: not only the woman who was to be the love of his life, but the start of his extraordinary career and the man who would go to the ends of the earth to destroy it.

THREE

Fletcher Christian never begrudged his older brother Edward his success. It was just a matter of bad timing. With 12 years between them Edward was fully grown and able to take advantage of the family fortune before it was lost. When their father had died, Edward was 22, had finished his law degree at Oxford and was well on his way to a brilliant future.

Fletcher, however, was not. Only 10 when he lost paternal support, his upbringing fell to his frivolous mother – a pretty, pampered woman who had no concept of money, other than to spend it in lavish amounts at phenomenal speed. After just one year with her at the helm, their Cumbrian estate was bankrupt. All liquid assets and land holdings had been drained on dresses, dinner parties and a spectacular array of jewels. The money ran through her manicured fingers like water, leaving the Christian family drowning in debt.

Edward was furious.

"It's a disgrace! Our family is of Manx nobility," he complained to his fellow barrister. "We can trace our ancestry back to William the Conqueror, but now we are nothing … *nothing!*"

On top of his resentment and guilt for having escaped his family's fate, he was embarrassed by it.

"My dear chap," his colleague replied with courtroom calm. "You are honour-bound, of course, to do the best you can for them, but there are ways of dealing with such a situation without being implicated in it."

Edward moved fast on the adfvice, seeing to it that his family was not thrown into the streets and that their new-found poverty did not reflect on him. Quietly, he arranged a modest annuity for his mother and exchanged their impressive Eaglesfield manor house for a little cottage on the Isle of Man. A haven of stone and thatch, nestled away with their heritage, well out of reach of the creditors who were hammering at their old mansion door.

Their new home was quaint enough to pass social muster without straining his purse strings and in putting a roof over their heads, he fulfilled his moral obligation. It was with a clear conscience that he turned his thoughts back to his stellar career, not letting them linger on the reality that their thatched roof leaked and that no-one who lived under it had the means to mend it.

None of which mattered a scrap to young Fletcher, who knew that his face was his fortune. Handsome, genial and with an inscrutable charm, he never went wanting. His knack of winning friends and influencing people was elusive and irrevocable. Once won, they were his for life, forever held captive under his spell.

Certainly, his scholastic ability did not suffer from the absence of private tutors and having Ancient Greek under his belt. He and his sisters attended the local free school and did well under its strict system; their reading, writing and arithmetic learned all the faster for being taught to the tune of a hickory stick.

Despite the teacher's sadistic streak, however, he never really enjoyed giving Fletcher six of the best. Not when the boy would bravely bear his punishment and then thank him for inflicting it. Whether Fletcher was truly ingenuous or exercising ingenuity was never quite clear, but by the time he was ready to graduate, he had beguiled all around him and they were sorry to see him go.

There was a tight lump in the headmaster's throat when he sent him on his way with a glowing reference.

"He has excelled and is now poised to follow in his brother's footsteps."

But a career in law did not appeal to Fletcher. To a degree, the calamity of his family's genteel impoverishment suited him. It stripped him of the social restraints of a starched, structured existence, leaving him free to go to sea and live a life of adventure.

It started on the HMS Cambridge.

"We can take you on as ship's boy," Captain John Holloway said as he scribbled Christian's name on the ship's muster roll and told him to sign his mark.

Christian hesitated.

"Wouldn't you prefer my signature, sir?" he asked.

His cultured voice and broad smile was a pleasant surprise and put the captain instantly on side.

"I would indeed, Mr Christian," he replied, handing him the quill.

He signed his name under that of the man who had done the same only an hour before. Glancing at the entry, he was impressed by the handwriting's bold flourish: *William Bligh, Sixth Lieutenant.*

The name resonated as if inexplicably linked to his own; which was pure vanity on his part, when the proximity of words on a page was likely to be as close as he would ever get to the man during their tenure on the ship. Ten years his senior and streets ahead of him in naval rank, it was doubtful that this faceless lieutenant would seek his company or even deign to address him, unless barking out an order.

Bligh did neither because his attention was focused on their mission. Having served a boring few months on the port-bound HMS Berwick and Princess Amelia, he had finally been transferred to the Cambridge. As part of Lord Howe's 1782, 65-ship-strong relief fleet to Gibraltar, this new ship came good on its promise of action, battling its way through the aggressive French-Spanish Armada to deliver troops, supplies and ammunition to their beleaguered British garrison on the peninsula.

They were successful, but during the process, Bligh hardly noticed the young Fletcher Christian whose job was to keep his head down and work hard. On the one occasion he briefly lifted it and looked in Bligh's direction, however, he did make an impact of sorts. With his black hair wet with sweat and eyes brilliant blue against bronzed skin, he threw Bligh a radiant smile. A smile that said: *So you're the man who signed up on the same day I did.*

The intimacy of that short moment of recognition caught Bligh's attention.

"Who is that young man?" he asked Lieutenant Jack Collingsworth. "He looks at me as if I know him."

"Christian ... Fletcher Christian," he answered. "Blue blood gone bad. Poor wretch will have to *work* his way back up the ranks."

Mildly curious, they watched as he went about his work, both impressed, when with split-second initiative, Christian suddenly leapt into action to save another sailor's life.

There was no warning when the block and tackle broke free from its bollard and swung with savage speed towards the ship's gunner. Inches from fatal impact with his skull, Christian lunched to catch it in full flight. At his own peril, falling with a bone-cracking thud to the deck, the missile stopped and secured at his chest. It was an astonishing piece of quick thinking and agility that roused a cheer from the rest of the crew.

As if pleased by a friend's achievements, Bligh smiled and said: "Oh, he may just make good. He appears to have a winning way about him."

And that was the last he said or saw of Christian for some time. When their ship returned to England in January, 1783, they both went their separate ways: Bligh to spend a short, restless time in London, while Christian made his way home to the Isle of Man.

Fletcher was now 18 and flying headlong into life. Convinced of his boundless capacity to succeed, he was too proud for his own good and primed for a fall. Fate was happy to oblige.

"I never hold others accountable for their faults and I am jealous of no man," he boasted, with the confidence of youth and inexperience.

Yet he was sincere and completely surprised when his open attitude suddenly pinched to petty envy of his brother and men of his kind.

It was not their money he wanted, but for the first time he bitterly resented what his own lack of it cost him – the love of the beautiful Isabella Curwen. She was a young woman whose heart, nowhere near as big as his own, could only be won by the status and wealth which men of Edward's ilk could offer.

Despite Fletcher's admirable attributes and the fact that she actively desired him, he did not stand a chance. Apparently, it was not enough that she was an heiress in her own right. Priorities won out.

"But you *can't* marry him!" he said as Isabella fought to pull from his embrace; an embrace which she had welcomed during their waltz on the ballroom floor and encouraged to grow more intimate later on the balcony outside. Yet, it was at this romantic moment that she had chosen to break the bad news.

"There's no point trying to talk me out of it," she replied, flicking open her fan to cool her flushed face and ardour.

He was shocked. It had never crossed his mind that she would reject him. No one ever had before. This was a new experience for him and he didn't like it. The bottom fell out of his world.

"But you love *me*. You *know* you do."

To this, she had no answer because it was true. For a fleeting moment, her resolve wavered and he took advantage of the window of opportunity.

"Isabella. You *know* you do … and you *know* I feel the same."

That window slammed shut.

She turned and wandered to the other side of the balcony; her every step changing his disappointment to disdain.

"You don't honestly think that he'll make you happy?"

The man who had stolen her money-hungry heart was Fletcher's cousin Henry. He was 22 years her senior, a reputed fop and as plain as a pikestaff. Yet, he was a man of consequence and that was all that counted.

Suddenly seized by burning jealousy, Fletcher was fit to kill. The thought of her wrapping her limbs around another man was enough to drive him mad, particularly when she had denied *him* as much only minutes before. At that fever-pitched moment of passion he was sure their love was forever, but he was wrong.

"There are many kinds of happiness," she lifted her implacable, brown eyes to say. "And ours is not to be."

With her dainty mouth set firm, these were to be her last words to him. She walked back into the ballroom, her blue satin gown hugging the sensuous curve of her hips and her golden hair hanging long and glorious under the glow of the candle-lit chandeliers. It was a picture of beauty that he framed in his memory forever, putting it on a pedestal whose heights were never to be reached again.

She disappeared from view and so went the strength of his hot-blooded resentment to be replaced by a lifetime of unrequited love.

His heart was broken.

FOUR

Bligh's heart, however, burst with joy when he met and married the woman of his dreams.

When he was introduced to Elizabeth Betham, daughter of a Scottish customs collector, he fell quickly in love and even faster on his feet for having attached himself to one of the Isle of Man's most prominent families. Their wedding was an impressive affair, attended by guests from near and far, the most important of whom was Elizabeth's uncle, Duncan Campbell, who made a special trip from London for the occasion.

As a wealthy trader with West Indies plantations and a fleet of merchant ships, he was a man of great influence in the community and a most opportune contact for Bligh. Such a stroke of luck aroused the suspicion that the young lieutenant contrived the situation for his own ends.

The night before the nuptials, Bligh set the record straight.

"On that question, sir," he said to Campbell, "you must

trust my integrity. I know how much you love your niece, but I promise you that I love her more."

Campbell believed him, having put Bligh under close scrutiny for some weeks. The shrewd businessman knew how to ferret out fortune-hunters and he had taken a hard line with this man betrothed to his niece. After running extensive background checks on Bligh, he found nothing but an impeccable record that gave him no reason to doubt his veracity.

"You have my blessing," he replied, shaking Bligh's hand. "But mind you treat her well or you'll have me to answer to."

The warning was unnecessary. From the instant they met, he and Elizabeth adored each other, sharing a love that embraced both passion and the closest of friendships. With looks and stature that only measured up to mediocre, Bligh knew he had the better end of the deal. For she, with her wit, warmth and pretty presence, exceeded all expectation and satisfied his every need.

"Tell me about your sea battle," she said, with her humorous, dark eyes dancing at the thrill of being in love and the certainty that it was returned.

"Oh Betsy … *not again!*" Bligh groaned, as much at ease with the use of her pet name as his assurance that she was his forever.

He had told her the story of his part in the Battle of Dogger Bank a hundred times over, but she never tired of it. As Ship's Master on the Belle Poule during the Fourth Anglo-Dutch War in 1781, he'd had his first taste of action pre-dating that on HMS Cambridge. He performed well enough for Betsy to glow with pride at its repeated recounting.

Truth be known, Bligh was just as proud of his performance and secretly thrilled to have the chance to relive it without being accused of boasting. Holding her hand, he leant forward in his seat to tell the tale; from force of habit, changing his voice from character to character to add colour, while doing her the courtesy of omitting the expletives.

She knew the story by heart, but listened with avid interest as if its every sentence came as a revelation; less enthralled by the sequence of events, perhaps, than the sound of her fiancé's voice.

"I gave the order to *draw and lash the yard in to the mast*," he began, knowing his script by rote. "In the confusion of the smoke and cannon fire, the crew were in disarray, so I ran to help them. Together, we roped in that rogue spar and the panic subsided."

He took a moment to catch his breath and continued:

"We were now running broadside to broadside with the enemy, both ships having the same number of guns and manpower, but we finally outfought her. She backed her topsails and the white flag of France fluttered down.

"*Belay there. Cease fire!* our Captain Patton bellowed. And all fell silent, bar the waves lapping loud at our timbers as our ships edged nearer. Patton put a congratulatory hand on my shoulder as he climbed onto the lee bulwark and shouted to the French privateer: *"La Cologne – Heave to and prepare to take our ship!"*

"My pardon m'sieur," the French captain shrugged and said. "This has all been a frightful mistake. We mistook you for a merchantman. It wasn't until you opened your ports and revealed your cannon that we realised we had taken on an English ship of the line. *Mes apologies abondantes.*"

At this point in the story Betsy laughed out loud as she always did; as much delighted by their victory as her husband's funny French accent.

"And Captain Patton thanked you, *in particular*, for your part in it?" she asked, knowing the answer was *yes*.

"He did indeed, my love and promised me the highest commendation."

That commendation came in the form of Bligh being instated as 5th lieutenant on the HMS Berwick and then 6th on the Cambridge. It was a decent promotion and an active couple of years of service, during which Betsy gave birth to Harriet, the first of their six daughters. The baby girl came equipped with dark hair and eyes like her mother, just as William wanted.

All was going well, but when the French surrendered at the end of The American Revolutionary War, money was tight. Now officially on the "inactive" list, Bligh was earning a paltry two shillings a day. Both he and America had achieved their independence at a cost – America, by war and Bligh, by that war's regrettable absence. It was a worrying time for him with a family to support and he could not have been more grateful when Duncan Campbell stepped in to help.

"I'm offering you the command of my merchantman Lynx," he announced over dinner.

It was as much an act of kindness as business acumen. He had come to greatly respect Bligh's ability and had absolutely no doubt he was reliable.

Lynx was Bligh's first command and he did his job well. For four years, he sailed Campbell's ships, Lynx and Britannia, between the West Indies and Britain without incident. Near the end of his merchant navy career, his experience was extensive and his pockets full.

"Let's move to London," Betsy suggested, full of hope for her husband's future.

And within weeks, they bought and moved into 3 Durham Place, Lambeth -- a family home of solid brown brick with a blue front door. It was Christmas and their second daughter was newly born. They called her Mary in deference to the season and the fact that she was destined to be the child in whom Bligh put all his faith.

FIVE

Set on putting the past and Isabella behind him, Christian had signed on to the 24-gun HMS Eurydice and sailed to Madras. It was a slow, 19-month voyage during which he devoted himself to his job. His single-minded determination had him quickly promoted from midshipman to master's mate and then to acting lieutenant. All augured well for his brilliant career, but like Bligh, the negotiated peace between nations put his feet back on dry land and stalled his impressive climb up naval ranks.

He was low on cash and casting round for something to do when he and his family were invited to dinner at the Bethams. Theirs was a fast friendship cemented by their similar social status on the Isle. Although Betsy was well acquainted with the mother and two Christian daughters, she was keen to be introduced to the long-absent Fletcher and was only sorry that her husband could not be there, busy as he was readying his ship for the West Indies.

"You should apply for a berth on the Britannia," Betsy volunteered as she passed Fletcher the pepper and salt. "It belongs to my uncle, you know, and is captained by my own husband. I'm sure they'd both be glad to have you on board."

She looked over expectantly at her Uncle Duncan who was put out by the presumptuous offer made on his behalf. None other but Betsy could get away with it, and loathe to contradict her, he nodded his gruff assent. It was fortunate that Christian had won him over too.

"We really must see what we can do for him," Betsy continued, skimming over the surface of her uncle's concerns. "Britannia's setting out again in a few days. I'm sure William won't say no to having another able-bodied seaman on board."

Bligh wouldn't dare! Even though he already had a full complement of crew and it was a nuisance finding room for another, he could never deny a request from Campbell, who was always so good to him ... and certainly not, when Betsy was behind it. He and Campbell were putty in her hands and she had sweetly engineered them into hiring a man about whom they knew nothing.

Although, that was not entirely true. When Christian came to his cabin the next day to be interviewed, Bligh did a double take.

"Don't I know you?" he asked.

"Yes sir. We served together on the Cambridge at Gibraltar."

Bligh hesitated before his eyes, narrow in recollection, lit at the memory of Christian's heroics.

"Ah yes, I remember. And a sterling show you made of it too."

Bligh was pleased. Not only to have recalled the connection, but to have re-established it. He'd liked the look of Christian back then and suspected he would grow to like him even more. The man had an intrinsic charm that bordered on addictive. Even now; his easy smile showed the promise of true friendship, which was an invitation Bligh was keen to accept.

"You know, at the time, I had a strange feeling our paths would cross again," he confessed.

Christian's response was eager and immediate.

"I too … when I saw your name signed above mine on the ship's muster."

The reality was, however, that they were strangers, separated by several rungs in naval rank. Accordingly, Christian pulled back.

"I do beg your pardon, sir. I'm taking liberties addressing my prospective captain with such familiarity."

"That you are," Bligh agreed, "but I'm not offended by it."

He stood up and showed Christian to the door.

"A long voyage is made more tolerable with people we like. Put your kit below deck, Christian. Good to have you on board."

That long voyage they shared to Jamaica turned into two. From just an ordinary seaman on the first, Bligh promoted Christian to second mate on the next. He took him under his wing and played mentor, as had Cook, putting an emphasis on mathematics and astronomy.

"On a man-o'-war or merchantman, they'll never go astray," he advised.

Christian's aptitude for the subject did not match Bligh's, but he proved an avid pupil whose knowledge and ego were boosted by his captain's attention. Ten years his junior in age and experience, Christian had a lot to learn. He did it fast, drinking in all Bligh had to offer, while polishing up his flair for public relations.

There was no doubt that he was the most popular man on board. The fact that he was handsome and congenial was part of his appeal, but it went beyond that.

He is a gentleman. An honest and forthright man, Bligh noted in the ship's log. *I would not be sorry to sail with him again.*

By the time they returned to England, their friendship and credentials were firmly established. Bligh was 32 and an experienced ship's commander and Christian, at 22, had proved capable of taking on the role of lieutenant thanks to his promotion on the Eurydice. Both men were primed to take on the world, or at least, its next naval mission.

SIX

It was the opportunity of a lifetime and Banks could not wait to tell Bligh.

"Campbell and I have sponsored you to take charge of another South Pacific expedition. You're to be lieutenant in command of His Majesty's Armed Vessel, Bounty."

Bligh was thrilled, but had three questions:

"What is the mission? Why me … and why only lieutenant instead of captain?"

"To collect breadfruit plants from Tahiti for the cheap sustenance of our West Indies slaves," was Banks' answer to the first.

To the second:

"Because you're the best man for the job."

But when it came to the third, he was less succinct.

"I've petitioned Admiralty on your behalf in regard to this, but they won't budge. They say the promotion lacks precedent."

"That's rubbish!" Bligh said indignantly. " Lieutenant Moorsom has just been advanced to post captain for a much simpler assignment."

There it was again -- that flash of hot temper which worried Banks so much. For all Bligh's fine attributes, he had a very short fuse, a personality flaw that in men of lesser sensibility often made them great, but in Bligh's case, tarnished an otherwise impeccable character and rendered him vulnerable to criticism. As far as Banks could make out, it was Bligh's migraines which were to blame. They triggered a touch of schizophrenia, which accounted for his streak of brilliance, but also for the fact that, in a split second, he could snap from the best of humour to red rage.

For those who did not know him well, these sudden mood swings were alarming. More so to Bligh than anyone else, because as a man of integrity, he never knew why his good intentions were so often misunderstood.

"All bark and no bite," Banks once said in his defence, unwittingly choosing a maxim which reflected Bligh's very name being derived from the Cornish "*wolf*". Despite his faults, Banks admired him and would always remain faithful -- except at this moment when he was not about to debate Admiralty's ruling.

"Why worry about the finer details?" he answered. "The ship's yours. The mission and honour are yours. Make the most of it."

There was no doubt Bligh would do that, but a bit more of the glitter rubbed off the glory when he set eyes on his ship. Fresh from its navy refit, it came as a major disappointment.

"But it's only a cutter," he complained to Banks, who quickly reassured him.

"Small but fast."

"*Much* too small for such a dangerous trip," Bligh shot back, for the second time annoyed by Admiralty's lack of foresight. "How am I expected to convey a fragile cargo of living plants halfway around the globe in that?"

Bligh had good reason for concern. At only 215 tons and 90 feet in length, the small ship was destined to be swamped by high seas. The crew numbered just 46 and Bligh was to be the only commissioned officer on board. That meant he would be starved of good company and lumped with double the responsibility. The one botanist to come along was of some consolation, but with no marines to provide protection from hostile natives or to enforce ship's discipline, it was a tall order.

"I have no doubt you'll succeed," Banks said. "I've yet to see you back away from a challenge."

That was true and with Cook having shown him the way, Bligh was proud to follow in his wake. The best way to do it was to throw himself into the hell-fire expedition, never mind its obstacles. It was with this in mind that he helped supervise the conversion of the Captain's Great Cabin into a hot-house for potted breadfruit plants.

"Commanding *Lieutenant's* cabin," he mumbled belligerently as his final piece of defiance before he obligingly quartered himself in a cramped cabin next to the crew.

Having sacrificed his own comfort for his cargo, he saw to the fitting of glazed windows to the upper deck and arranged for lead lining and an ingenious system of pipes to carry surplus water to his plants. Not forgotten, his crew received every bit as much of his care and attention.

"I must have a fiddler on board," he insisted.

Banks looked puzzled, so Bligh explained.

"The provision of fresh food and daily exercise for my crew is essential. Not only does music soothe the soul, but a fiddler's provision of it will inspire the men to dance. And dance they will … whether they like it or not."

The picture of the rough old tars joining in a jig made Banks laugh out loud.

"You may have problems enforcing that," he jibed.

But Bligh saw no humour in the situation.

"If we are to survive this dangerous duty, they will dance when I tell them, eat what I tell them … do *whatever I damn well* tell them."

Banks' brow furrowed.

"I see sense in discipline, but for your own sake, William, you must learn to loosen the reins a little. Don't be so hard on yourself and others."

"Loosen them and the horse bolts," Bligh replied, convinced of the need to restrain bad habits, most of all, his own. "It is exactly what Cook taught me and I will follow it to the letter."

"Minus the expletives, I hope."

Banks' sarcasm promptly put him in his place. Swearing came easily to Bligh and on this occasion made him fall short of Cook's standards. He was ashamed that Banks had to remind him of them.

"I may have a sharp tongue, but I'm not a cruel man," Bligh came back defensively. I won't abuse my authority or the whip, but I'm determined to make this expedition a success. You can rest assured that whatever I say or do will be for my crew's sake, even if they don't understand it."

– oOo –

Fletcher Christian believed he had no trouble understanding Bligh and was looking forward to working with him again. Having firmly ensconced himself in Bligh's and his family's affections during the course of their mutual merchant navy service, he was first to sign up as master's mate.

"Our little Mary adores him," Betsy said.

And as much under Christian's spell as his daughter, Bligh agreed.

"It would appear that everybody does."

Already, Christian felt like a brother and Bligh was pleased at the prospect of having him in his life forever. But friendship aside, it was a good career move for Christian. Such a long voyage would complete his time as a midshipman and if the mission were a success he would have no problem securing the permanent rank of lieutenant on their return.

For Bligh, Christian was his answer to three major concerns: his presence solved the problem of companionship, his popularity with the crew propped up Bligh's own, and his capacity to take on the role of acting lieutenant in an emergency, as he did on the Eurydice, ended Bligh's worry about being the sole commissioned officer on board.

This, of course, would not sit well with Bounty's sailing master, John Fryer, who was first in line for such a promotion. But Bligh was in two minds about him. At first, he had found Fryer impressive and stated as much in the ship's log:

The master is a very good man and gives me every satisfaction.

A month later, however, his opinion changed. There was something about the man he found disturbing. No question that Fryer was competent, but there was always a look of cool assessment in his eyes when issued an order. Constantly subjected to his scathing scrutiny, Bligh's words turned sour.

> *Fryer has served in the Royal Navy since 1781 and risen to Master of the Third Rate. Given that his performance is nothing else but, that's exactly as far as he'll go.*

Even as he wrote it, Bligh knew he was being unfair, but he was in a bad mood and his head was pounding. They were coming close to rounding Cape Horn and the weather, like his temper, was foul.

"If Admiralty hadn't delayed our departure from Spithead for three weeks, we wouldn't *be* in this position," he railed at Christian across the captain's table.

At his comment, the Bounty heaved high, its bow lifting clear of the ocean to thump down hard into the deep trough of a wave. It sent their dinner plates skidding across the table, with none of those seated around it able to catch them before they crashed to the floor. But content that he had held tight to his wine glass, Bligh continued his tirade.

"*Three weeks* they held us back while all other ships took advantage of fair winds to clear the Channel. They jinxed us right from the start by making us set out in stormy weather, with the promise of worse at The Horn."

To this bad tempered rambling, there was no answer other than Fryer's quiet control which only served to highlight Bligh's lack of it. Eyeing his sailing master with mild disdain, Bligh swilled the rest of his wine and called an end to the meal.

"I don't know what's worse … the storm or that man's temper," Fryer yelled to Christian through the wind and rain when they climbed back on deck.

Steadying himself against its dangerous pitch, Christian secured the main topsail and called back.

"Aye, but I'd rather be under his command than any other on a voyage like this, because I know he'll see us through it."

Christian's confidence in Bligh was complete; as was Bligh's in him. The crew described their relationship as water-tight, but in Christian's case it wasn't exclusive. Whereas Bligh's side of the friendship was focused and intense, Christian's was less committed because of his liberal liking of all. He was everybody's best friend, but tied to no-one in particular; and it was this intangible quality … this mastering of the superficial, that incited others to vie for his attention and attach kudos to its achievement.

For the time being, though, Bligh had his unerring support and would have been pleased to hear his compliment, had other matters not been preying on his mind. Below in his cabin, his head was in the vice-like grip of blinding pain. Midway through charting their course, he suddenly dropped his compass and collapsed to the floor.

"*Hell's teeth!*" he yowled, calling urgently for his personal servant, "Fetch me a cool cloth and vinegar … and get me to bed."

With rat-like efficiency, John Samuel scurried to do his job. His quick movements and whispered words of compliance made him a man who did not appeal to many, but to Bligh at this agonising moment, his services were invaluable. When Samuel lay the wet rag on his forehead, Bligh breathed its vinegar fumes in deep and closed his eyes against the crippling pain.

"God ... won't it ever *stop?*" he said in place of his prayers as he rubbed his throbbing temple and turned on his side to find respite in sleep.

When he woke in the morning his headache was gone, only to be replaced by one far worse.

It was their third attempt to round The Cape. In the atrocious weather, they had been trying for a solid month, without success. The freezing winds had turned to blizzard and like icing on a cake, snow now capped the barren rocks that formed the coast of *Terra Del Fuego*. Against all odds, their muscle-wrenching efforts were not so much to affect a sail past, as to pull the Bounty free from the magnetic grip of the treacherous headland.

Both ship and crew were exhausted and weighing up the continued risk, Bligh came down in favour of his men's survival.

"Turn about and proceed east. We'll round the Cape of Good Hope instead," he ordered the ship's master.

"Africa!" Fryer exclaimed in dismay. "But that will mean four months of hard sailing across the Indian Ocean."

Bligh swung round on him ferociously.

"Do I *look* as if I'm happy about it? That for all our effort, we are *still* on the same parallel of longitude as we were two weeks ago? My men are ill, my ship is leaking. As commander, I have no choice but to see to their welfare."

The crew was fed up, but Bligh was doubly so. For all his strategic planning, they were still as far away from

Tahiti as they were when they left England. Not only was this infuriating, but it came as a blow to his pride. Secretly and as a self-imposed discipline, he was pacing himself and his ship against the exploits of his fellow seafarer, Governor Designate Captain Arthur Phillip, who was on his way with his convoy to colonise New South Wales.

Although Phillip's First Fleet had a few months' lead, the Bounty was crossing the oceans at much the same time and it was a private vanity of Bligh's to keep up with Phillip's achievement and add to it his own. But by now, he was sure Phillip had reached his destination and cemented his name in history, whereas he, commanding lieutenant of the little Bounty, seemed destined to be omitted from its pages. Despite wanting to make a sterling show of it, he was still fighting the elements and working even harder to keep the respect of his crew.

Slapping his thigh in frustration, he strode away, but then turned abruptly to say:

"And Fryer … don't you *ever* question my orders again."

Christian looked over at the sudden, savage exchange. He was tempted to intervene but the look on Bligh's face told him not to dare.

It was the first of many bouts of Bligh's bad temper to come. His tantrums were short-lived and of little consequence in the broader scheme of things, but they began to alienate the men, most of whom were no longer sure that his good points outweighed his bad.

He could be the best and worst of men. Clever and courageous, he was also fiercely competitive and did not like to be crossed; a complex personality, who, although inclined to the vindictive and use of bad language, had equally valid moments of kindness and good humour. What his crew failed to comprehend was that in either mood, his intentions were invariably good and married unequivocally to the rulings of English law.

"Quick to temper, quick to forgive," was boatswain William Cole's sensible summation of his commander's character.

And had his astute analysis been shared by the rest of the men, they would have seen Bligh for his true worth and not taken his angry outbursts to heart.

SEVEN

For now, with Good Hope their destination and fresh state of mind, the crew felt more kindly towards him. The weather and their health were better and Bligh was in high spirits, feeling that all was well with the world and his Bounty.

My men are all active, good fellows. I haven't been obliged to punish any one of them, he wrote to Campbell and Banks.

After putting in at the Canaries for supplies, we are now sailing nonstop to Tahiti and will need to ration our food. I will compensate by ordering three watches instead of the customary two, so the men can get more rest. I'm sure they will benefit and see the good sense in it.

All of them did, except Fryer, who wasn't worried about the rations, but cared very much indeed when Christian, his own master's mate, was promoted over his head and put in charge of the new third watch.

"We are still faced with a long, hard voyage," Bligh announced from the quarterdeck.

"I mean to make good use of every hour of sailing time. To assist me in this, I am replacing Mr Fryer with Mr Christian, who will now act as executive second in command with the rank of acting second lieutenant."

Those were fighting words, as were the many that followed.

"This is an *outrage!*" Fryer objected. "In all my years at sea …"

"Your years at *sea?*" Bligh lashed back contemptuously. "Good Lord man. If I'd known your nature, I wouldn't have accepted you as boatswain of a river barge!"

At this, Fryer hurled down his telescope and strode away.

"*Mr Fryer, sir!*" Bligh yelled out after him. "*Come back here!* I will dismiss you when I have done with you, sir. Do you hear me?"

With a face of stone, Fryer returned and stood stiffly before him.

"Must I suffer this before the men?" he hissed.

"You will suffer my correction whenever you are at fault, sir."

"*What* fault?" he demanded in disgust.

"*God damn your eyes, sir,*" Bligh shouted. "You turned your *back* on me."

Fryer relented.

"Well for that I apologise."

"Very well."

"But I still protest."

"You protest, do you?"

"I am *master* of this ship, Lieutenant."

"And I, sir, am its commander and your better. *Now* you are dismissed, God damn you."

By right of superiority, Bligh won the first round, but the fact that Fryer questioned his authority and was spared the whip, opened the way for others to do the same. Rather than like Bligh for his leniency, it was construed as weakness and led to disrespect. But oblivious to the crew's simmering contempt, Bligh still believed he ran a happy ship and recorded as much in his log.

> *In the morning I ordered a sheep slaughtered to serve to the ship's company as a pleasant meal.*

Satisfied with himself, he put down his quill at much the same time that James Morrison, the boatswain's mate, picked up his. With a snort of contempt, he scribbled down a very different account:

> *One of the sheep died. Lieutenant Bligh ordered it to be served instead of pork and peas. It was just skin and bones.The bulk of it had to be thrown overboard. We had dried shark for Sunday dinner.*

It was a fair complaint, when early in the piece, Bligh had decided to ration their food to counter difficult times ahead. He hadn't done it to inflict unnecessary hardship on his crew, but to ensure that they and their supplies lasted the distance.

Unfortunately, without Bligh's insight or experience of real deprivation, the men were incensed by his harsh measures. They did not appreciate the fact that his strict regimen was keeping them free of starvation and scurvy. *That* was a considerable achievement on such a marathon voyage. Yet there was only a handful of intelligent men on board who recognised it.

"Bligh should gain much credit for his resolution and perseverance," said surgeon's mate Thomas Ledward. "And also for the extreme care he takes of his company."

But even *his* amenable attitude eroded over the issue of cheese.

"Where is it?" Bligh demanded when it was discovered that two blocks of Edam were missing from the storage casks.

"Beggin' your pardon, sir," ship's cooper Henry Hillbrandt stepped in to explain. "They were removed by Mr Samuel and taken to your own house before we left England. We assumed it was at your order."

Caught out, Bligh flew back on the attack.

"*Keep quiet and don't lie!* How *dare* you accuse your commander of theft, when it's you who are a pack of thieves … the lot of you."

The accusation roused an angry rumble among the crew. One which grew louder and more dangerous when Bligh added:

"And say one more word like that Hillbrandt and I'll have you flogged."

That two small chunks of cheese could warrant such harsh punishment was outlandish. So Christian intervened to quell what promised to be the crew's hostile reaction.

"Our apologies, sir, for pointing the finger of blame at you. There's obviously been some misunderstanding here, but please let me assure you that we, too, are all innocent of the crime."

Sure of their friendship, he spoke with confidence and was shocked by Bligh's bitter response.

"I accept no assurances from *you*, Mr Christian, now that you have betrayed my trust."

Considering that he was Bligh's favourite, it was a statement that shocked them all. None more so than Christian, who thought he had Bligh wrapped around his little finger and could get away with anything. Given that he had never pushed those boundaries, he could not imagine what he had done to lose his commander's regard.

As to that, Bligh could not say. Firstly, because he had nothing tangible to hold against Christian, but more so, that he was unable to put into words the peculiar, envy-based emotions that Christian's subtle shift in allegiance of late stirred. It was jealousy, pure and simple, but he wasn't about to admit it.

Between men it seemed absurd, so it was better explained as him being deprived of a valued possession. Christian was *his* protégé and confidante, but when their tight bond was extended to include midshipman Peter Heywood, Bligh found himself suddenly excluded from it and saw green. A vibrant hue that deepened in intensity each time he saw them with their heads together.

It's natural, of course, that they should seek each other's company, Bligh told himself. Heywood and Christian had a lot in common. They were both of an age and shared an aristocratic Manx lineage. No one really was at fault. It was just that Bligh was lonely and mourning the loss of a loved one.

EIGHT

By the time they reached Tahiti, they were at constant loggerheads. With Christian unable to understand and Bligh unwilling to explain their new-found enmity, it escalated out of control. Heywood's ever-encroaching presence on the equation left Bligh dangerously isolated. The fact that his friendship had been swapped for another's came as a blow to his pride and he was hell-bent on making Christian suffer.

As the crew's spokesman, it was Christian's duty to address all concerns to their commander. But each time he confronted Bligh it added fuel to the fire. He blamed Christian for all that went wrong, persistently and very publicly abusing him to achieve optimum humiliation.

"*Fool!*" he called him in front of the crew. "I'd have you whipped if I thought that *anything* could get through that thick skin of yours."

These were the milder of words passed between them. Bligh with his acid tongue won each exchange. Yet, with every right to despise him, Christian refused to desert him completely.

"Love him or loathe him, he's ours for the duration," he told the crew. "We could do worse in our task master and certainly no better in regard to his navigational skills."

"Ah, you're as weak as piss Christian. Stop holding the man's hand and give him what he deserves," able-bodied seaman Matthew Quintal snarled back.

He was in no mood for half measures, having just received his third flogging for insolence and mutinous behavior. His 24 lashes were well deserved, but as a brutal troublemaker, feared by all on board, he was itching for a fight and his mind was set on murder.

Bligh had hesitated to inflict his punishment. He was not whip-happy, but his hand was forced when Quintal blatantly refused to obey an order and exposed his heavily tattooed backside to illustrate his point.

"I'll *shoot* you if you don't do what you're told!" Bligh screamed, approaching hysteria.

He was a proud man standing alone, unable to control his temper or the mob and his predicament at the time piqued Christian's sympathy.

"You gave him no choice," he explained to Quintal, still of a mind to defend his old friend.

But the truth was that that friendship had collapsed. Although they missed each other's company, they were both too proud and angry to admit it; Bligh only doing so when he was out of his wits.

"Get Christian … I want *Christian*," he raved at the peak of one of his migraine deliriums.

But like an increasing number of Bounty's crew, his servant Samuel ignored the order and fetched him a glass of water instead.

"Now there's no need for that, sir," he insisted. "You'll feel better in the morning."

He wasn't worried that Bligh continued to thrash about in distress. These fits of physical weakness were Samuel's golden opportunity to put his commander under obligation and he worked them for all they were worth.

"You can lean on me," he continued, with an agenda all his own. Racked as he was with resentment for all men better than himself, this was his only time to shine and he wasn't about to share it with Christian.

So that cry for his friend's help went unheeded, which killed all hope of mending their rift and changed the course of history. For had Christian known that Bligh needed him, he would have rushed to his side without question, all wounds healed.

Instead, that festering wound was left raw and wide open for the 10 months, three days and 27,086 miles it took to reach Tahiti.

– oOo –

"*Land Ho!*" came the call from the crow's nest.

At the wonderful news, Bligh rushed from his cabin up on deck.

"Over *there*, sir," Christian said excitedly.

Beaming from ear to ear, he pointed to the misty blue outline of a mountain range on the horizon. "Well done, sir. *Well done.*"

With the instinct of good friends, they shared the moment, quite forgetting the trouble between them. But it would not be long before they remembered themselves.

As soon as they downed anchor at Matavai Bay, Bligh set the rules. It was a case of wishful thinking on his part when they were bound to be broken after such a long trip; and certainly when his men caught sight of the carnal delights on offer.

"Steady boys," Quintal said provocatively as the natives paddled their canoes towards them, each boat laden with friendly faces and a bevy of beautiful, bare-breasted women.

Midway through Bligh reading his rules, the men broke ranks and rushed to the rails, chorusing a round of wolf-whistles and lewd remarks: each of them urging the native girls, with their flower-bedecked hair and radiant white smiles, to dive into the warm water and swim towards them. It was a man's fantasy come true, but at the shrill General Call of the boatswain's pipe, they reluctantly fell back into line.

Bligh eyed them in reprimand, but then said with that cool humour they enjoyed:

"Under the extenuating circumstances, gentlemen, I will overlook this breech and continue."

But by now the natives were scaling the sides of the ship and his men were straining at the leash. Inhibited by time and their insatiable lust, Bligh talked fast:

"These rules are to be followed to the letter and are punishable by flogging:

All natives, without exception, are to be treated with kindness and respect.

*If they steal, no man may retrieve said goods by
violence, unless under threat of his life.*
*It is imperative that none of Bounty's arms are
stolen. Their cost will come out of your pay.*
*All bartering will be conducted by one man,
nominated by me and by none other.*
*But most important: Under no circumstances
must any man reveal that Captain Cook is dead
or that he died at the hands of natives.*

The mention of Cook's name left a tight lump in Bligh's throat, a silent tribute that he kept to himself.

It was impossible, however, to conceal his emotion when he went ashore to greet the local chieftain.

It was a hundred degrees in the shade and he was sweating profusely in his full-dress uniform when he trudged up the beach to be welcomed by a ceremonial parade sporting a portrait of Cook as their standard.

At this gruesome reminder of his severed head being flaunted by Hawaiian natives in the same way, Bligh stopped dead in his tracks, his face ashen. It was a reaction that surprised Chief Tynah, who had expected thanks and a smile.

"Our Great White Father left this for our protection," he explained. "He told us to carry it out to every captain who came so that they would be our friend."

Now that Bligh understood, he said his silent thanks to Cook for continuing to watch over him and got back to business.

"In his name, you can be sure of our friendship and help," he confirmed. "We only request the same of you."

Having asked, he received. Not only did the Tahitians lavish them with their good-natured labour in cultivating the breadfruit plants England wanted, but they were doubly generous in their provision of hospitality and wholesale sex.

The men were in seventh heaven. Overjoyed that all was free for the taking, they took it over and again, their constant requiting of their sexual appetite leading to a marked decline in morality and their enthusiasm to carry out King George's wishes. With breadfruit on the backburner, there was nothing Bligh could do but roll up his own sleeves and set an example with his own manual labour, while countering the hot sun and sensuality with a good dose of discipline.

"Muspratt, Thompson and Quintal have gone swimming. They've left their clothes and tools untended on the beach," John Fryer reported.

This was Bligh's pet peeve and a cardinal sin when the natives stole everything in sight. But with the bigger picture in mind, he kept his cool.

"Five lashes when they dry off," he responded, taking a brief respite from his back-breaking work to stretch his body and wipe the sweat from his face.

Realistically, it was impossible to maintain rigid control over his crew and their raging hormones, so he had to compromise. The punishment was lenient for these three men who were base characters at best. Licentious and entirely without principles, their vulgar behaviour came as no surprise, but Christian's shocked him.

"You've gone to the dogs, Mr Christian," Bligh remarked with calm reproof as he strolled past his second-in-command writhing in a sandy sex romp. "It is a pity when I once knew you to be a gentleman."

Ashamed, Christian got to his feet. Quickly putting on his shirt to cover the name "*Isabella*" tattooed on his chest, he saluted his commander. He had nothing to say in his own defence and was further embarrassed when ship's surgeon Thomas Huggan staggered over with a bottle of rum in hand, to say it for him:

"It's not his fault, sir," he slurred. "The women are crazy for him."

Bligh's reply was caustic.

"You're drunk again, doctor. If you wish to address your commander, do so when you are sober."

Huggan was an alcoholic and on-going problem. Already one sailor was dead from gangrene as a result of his misdiagnosis and neglect. By the time Bligh had been told, it was too late.

"He was an asthmatic, you imbecile!" he berated, nowhere near choosing his words carefully "What in God's name possessed you to bleed him and leave him untended?"

The fact that *anyone* was still alive in sickbay was a miracle and due solely to the competent services of surgeon's mate Thomas Ledward, who Bligh had the sense to recruit as back-up.

In *any* scenario, Huggan's inebriated support was detrimental and, in this instance, was something Christian neither wanted nor deserved. For like the doctor, he chose to run with the pack and embrace decadence. Here in paradise, it was in copious supply and available to all men of weak character.

Bligh had every right to condemn him, when he, as their young commander, was every bit as virile as they, but did not succumb to temptation. For this, Christian admired him, but more so, envied him his woman back home who killed all need for another.

NINE

For Christian, it was a case of compromise. If he couldn't be with the one he loved, he had to love the one he was with; albeit a pale imitation of his dream.

"Why you call me that?" asked Maimiti, the woman he chose from the throng of Tahitian beauties at his disposal.

Fresh from diving for pearls, she looked up at him with dark-eyed devotion, her breasts and long black hair glistening with beads of liquid silver.

"Because Isabella is a pretty name for a pretty girl," he replied, whitewashing his real reason for keeping a memory alive.

A tear ran down her cheek as she pulled a series of pearls from the oyster shells fished from the sea.

"You no go," she cried, not content with his lie or what little of it she could understand.

"I have no choice. We must all go home at our king's order."

They'd had this conversation over and again and always with the same result. Her love was not enough to stop him leaving, so she had to offer him something more valuable. Despite her tenuous grasp on the English language, she knew what it meant when the sailors' eyes lit with greed at the sight of their black Tahitian jewels. And though, to her, they were nothing more than pretty pebbles, she used them to her advantage.

"If I give these, you stay?"

Her plea was sad and unnecessary. For neither he, nor the rest of Bounty's crew needed pearls to tempt them to remain when their every instinct was to cling to Tahitian shores forever. The breadfruits were potted and loaded on board, however, and there was no need to linger any longer; already their mission had extended well beyond its parameters.

The crew had been on a "go slow" campaign for five long months while they cavorted with the natives. Time and familiarity had dissolved their depravity to domesticity and rounded the flat bellies of their Tahitian women with pregnancy. The once philanderers, were now would-be fathers, fond of their island families and reluctant to leave.

Bligh's tolerance was at an end with their incessant schemes to delay departure. He fought hard to keep his crew's respect, but because they didn't return the favour, he was forced to use the whip to make himself understood.

"Twelve lashes!" he ordered inflicted on able-bodied seaman John Adams for neglect of duty.

A rudder gudgeon was stolen from one of the ship's lifeboats on Adams' watch and to Bligh that was reprehensible. The cat-o'-nine-tails was applied in full view of the

Tahitians who wept as they witnessed the act. Their distress made Bligh all the more uneasy for it matched his own. He took no pleasure in enforcing the law, but without it there lay chaos. Yes, his men hated him for it, but no more so than he hated himself.

"And *why*, Mr Heywood, do you look at me with such reproof?" he demanded at the stroke of the last lash.

There was no need for another man's censure, when Bligh imposed it on himself. As much repulsed by the primitive process as they, he cringed at the sight of the bleeding strips of flesh ripped from Adams' back.

"Because … if I may speak freely, sir," Heywood hesitantly replied. "I think it was unwarranted."

Bligh's reply came crisp with sarcasm.

"Do enlighten me."

"It's just, sir … that we, as Englishmen, can't abide to think of others as our betters. Unlike us, these Tahitians have an extraordinary swimming ability and we and our boats are at their mercy. Not only can they hold their breath for three minutes underwater, but they can do it at night. No matter how vigilant a man is on guard, he can't detect them. I believe this is how they stole our rudder gudgeon and also sabotaged our rowboats the other day. It was not Adams' fault."

"Thank you, Mr Heywood."

Bligh never liked conceding an argument and particularly not to Heywood to whom he had already conceded a most valued friend. To find him commendable, in any shape or form, was objectionable and this was the second time in as many weeks that he'd had to do so.

"What took you so long?" he had demanded of

Christian 10 days earlier, when he and Heywood returned late from shore duty.

Far from being apologetic, Christian was excited at the prospect of gaining Bligh's approval.

"Heywood, sir, is compiling a Tahitian dictionary. He hopes it will prove helpful to future English visitors: missionaries and the like."

With the work of God being brought into play, Bligh held his tongue. He was impressed by Heywood's initiative, but refused to admit it. Instead, as was now his practice, he turned aggressively on Christian.

"Why am I last to know?"

To this Christian had no answer, as he had no explanation for Bligh's shabby treatment of him over the past few months. It seemed that nothing he did pleased him and the harder he tried, the worse it got.

He turned and walked away in a dark mood contrary to his nature, which came as a concern to the crew.

Boatswain William Cole shook his head as he watched after him.

"Whatever fault there is to be found," he said, "our poor Mr Christian is sure to bear the brunt."

Which was wrong, when Cole was next to come under fire.

"A new set of sails … you've allowed *a brand new set of sails* to mildew and rot!"

Bligh was beside himself with rage.

"I'm sorry, sir. I know it's my fault, but I didn't realise what terrible damage the extreme humidity here could cause."

In speaking the truth, he effectively passed the buck to Bligh, who with his experience of the tropics should have known better. Although he was not in the mood to make concessions, he knew he must.

"You should be horse-whipped!" he couldn't resist saying before he made them.

"That I should, sir," Cole agreed, hanging his head.

"But this time, it shall go with just a warning."

Surprised and relieved, Cole looked up at his commander with thanks. He had been let off the hook, but others were not as fortunate.

Seaman John Williams was given six lashes for his pitiful performance in "heaving the lead", while Robert Lamb received 12 for allowing a native to steal his cleaver. But when Isaac Martin was sentenced to 24, the word "mutiny" was mumbled among the men.

"So I'm damned if I do and damned if I don't," Martin shouted defiantly at the first sting of the leather lash.

His torture was in two parts: 12 lashes for allowing a native to steal and an additional 12 because he hit the man who did it.

"Striking a native is strictly against the rules and cannot go unpunished."

Bligh was emphatic. England had standards and it was up to him to enforce them.

His bigger mistake, however, came two days later when he accused the natives of cutting the Bounty's hawser. Had he examined the thick mooring cable more closely, he would have seen that the clean cut which severed it was not made by a crude native tool, but by the keen-edged blade of an English sabre. Done in desperation by one of his crew to set the ship adrift and maroon them on their island paradise forever; or at least until British Admiralty got wind of it.

Unable to accept that any of his men had the courage to commit such a crime and accept its "death by hanging" consequence, Bligh blamed the Tahitians and held their Chief Tynah accountable.

The smile fell from Tynah's face. He did not like being called a criminal. And now, having put the chief offside, Bligh had nowhere else to turn his attacks but back on Christian.

"It was *your* watch and *your* fault that the cable was cut."

"I *refuse* to take the blame!" Christian, for the first time fought back, already so often in Bligh's bad books that he had nothing to lose. "It was *impossible* to see through the black night and heavy rain."

In sympathy with Fletcher and needing to prove a point of his own, Chief Tynah grabbed a token Tahitian culprit and dragged him before Bligh.

"*Here's* the offender – *kill him!*"

Bligh baulked at the man's cold-blooded brutality towards his own kind.

"Twelve lashes," he commanded instead at the risk of showing himself to be weak.

Seeing him as just that, Tynah turned away in disgust, but Bligh refused to resort to murder to appease him. Lack of discipline was rife and he knew they had to set sail soon if there were to be any chance of restoring it. He would have done so immediately had the habitual troublemakers, seamen Muspratt, Millward and Charles Churchilll, not stolen a boat and eight muskets to desert to a nearby island.

It was the last straw. When their whereabouts was discovered, Bligh fetched them himself. Walking boldly up to their grass hut, he flung open its bamboo door, grabbed Muspratt by the scruff of the neck and booted him up the rear.

Never before had Bligh abandoned decorum. Watching him do so made Millward and Churchill quickly surrender and march down the beach with their guns carried high above their heads.

Among their belongings left behind were bottles of rum and a bag of pearls. But when Bligh stumbled on the scribbled plans for their desertion, he was shocked to see the names Heywood and Christian among them. Whether scribbled in the *hope* of their participation or the certainty of it, Bligh could not tell, but either way it was betrayal of the first order and it cut to the quick.

"The punishment for desertion is 100 lashes," Fryer reminded him.

The severity of the figure worried Bligh when the application of as many was as good as a death sentence.

"Forty-eight," he said instead, and with a view to making those licks of the lash more tolerable, added: "To be received in two installments."

So far, over their 16-month mission, the floggings totaled 210 for desertion, disobedience, neglect of duty, striking natives, insolence and contempt.

"I'm not proud of the score," Bligh admitted to Fryer, who despite his personal animosity towards his commander, always remained true to his job and the respect due his superior.

"But you should be, sir," Fryer replied. "Compared to other captains, the tally is remarkably low. On my last ship, the commander averaged over 1200 floggings in a quarter of the time and didn't flinch at having 12 men whipped per day."

Grateful for Fryer's unexpected support, Bligh pushed for more.

"So you don't think I've served the navy ill by being unnecessarily harsh?"

"Indeed not, sir. Under the circumstances, you have been extremely lenient. You know as well as I that Cook, himself, would never have been so merciful. They say his own sailors got more floggings than compliments."

From first-hand experience, Bligh knew this was true and often wondered about it.

Why, he asked himself, *could Cook be so harsh and command such respect when he, who was half as hard-handed, commanded so little?*

"He roused enough fear among his men to ensure their admiration," Fryer continued, as if reading his mind; "Whereas you, sir, with your rash anger and prompt forgiveness, have proved yourself vulnerable. The latter doesn't inspire enough dread to hold them in check. I mean this as a compliment."

It was said with such good sense and sincerity that Bligh could construe it as nothing less. Short of saying that he was weak, it almost inferred that at times, he could be likeable. So, he quit while he was ahead and changed the subject.

"We'll leave on the morning tide," he said, confident in his decision.

With a fresh rush of resolve, he took a deep breath of island air, so thick and intoxicatingly sweet that it had made his men sick. What they needed was a good dose of salt air to bring them to their senses.

"Yes …" he said. "All will be better when we're back at sea."

TEN

That was not the consensus. Their fond farewell more closely resembled a funeral, with the natives beating their chests and wailing from the beach. In a frenzy of mourning, the multitude of pregnant women among them mutilated themselves in grief, slashing their wrists and abdomens with knives and painting their faces red with their own blood.

From the ship, the sailors watched in distress and yearning. Hanging over the rails and from the rigging, they waved goodbye as the Bounty sailed slowly out to sea, its white sails glowing golden-pink in the crimson dawn.

"Well that's that then," seaman John Williams said as he slid glumly down the halyard back to deck. His feet hit the planks with a dull thud that echoed the mood of all on board.

"Take heart," Bligh encouraged, as one of the few among them free from emotional stress. "I know it's a hard haul to the West Indies, but I promise that after a few days, you won't be sorry you left."

But they were … very sorry indeed and with Bligh constantly nagging them to overcome their flagging spirits and improve efficiency, nothing augured well.

"It's just that their lethargy and basic stupidity drives me mad!" Bligh confided to Fryer, for one unguarded moment, mistaking the master's sense of duty for friendship.

Fryer's tight smile in response came as a reprimand of sorts that told Bligh to keep his thoughts to himself.

He only wished he could, but being supremely efficient and blessed with boundless energy, he found it impossible to tolerate the opposite in others. His every instinct was to boot them into action, but he made do with a series of verbal incentives:

"Trust me. I push you for your own good. Hard work is its own reward and will help you forget your woes."

But it didn't.

"I wish the son of a bitch would just shut up!" Quintal snarled.

They were all finding it difficult to fall back into line after their euphoric five months. None more so than Christian who ruled the roost back on Tahiti and was not too keen to hand back the reins or listen to anything Bligh had to say, even if it were said for his own safety.

"Stay away from the natives as much as possible," Bligh warned when they made their last stop at Nomuka Island and Christian was put in charge of foraging.

"Fresh food and water take priority," he continued. "Leave all firearms in the boat and only use them in an emergency. We can't risk any of the men getting trigger-happy and inciting a massacre."

Ironically, the natives on this *Friendly Isle* were far more aggressive than their Tahitian counterparts and with memories of Cook's demise, Bligh was concerned for his men's safety and particularly Christian's, loathe as he was to admit it.

With a nod of compliance, Christian and his party set out for the beach. The second they set foot on it, a horde of excited natives crowded around them, distracting them from their work and stealing everything in sight. The shore party was swamped and Christian made an on-the-spot decision to forfeit their tools in favour of food. It was a strategic call that made Bligh furious.

"What in the *hell* does he think he's doing?" he cursed, peering through his telescope from the quarterdeck. "*God damn it …* if you want something done right, you have to do it yourself."

Scrambling into a boat, he rowed to shore to take over proceedings.

"Are you *mad?*" he yelled as he stormed up the beach.

Christian pushed his way through the swarm of islanders to explain.

"There's too many of them, sir. They're stopping us doing our job and I thought it safer to divert them."

"*Damn you* for a coward!" Bligh screamed back. "Why would you be afraid of a pack of savages when you've got *firearms?*"

Smarting at the public scolding, Christian didn't hold back:

"And what good are firearms when you order them *not to be used!*"

Too angry to worry about the consequences, he strode away along the beach. Bligh watched after him, seeing the validity of the man's argument and his own shame for having railed against it. But it was too late to say he was sorry and Christian was way beyond accepting his apology.

Now that Bligh was without the option of backing down, he had nowhere else to go but deeper into bad temper.

"But surely, sir, the loss of one anchor to the natives is not so great?" was Fryer's response to his next outburst. "We have plenty more on board."

The master's casual attitude did more to fuel Bligh's tantrum than the theft itself.

"If it is not great to *you*, it's *certainly* great to me!" he fired back in a tone savage enough to take Fryer aback. "One way or another, I'm going to put a *stop* to this!"

The way he went about it was to make sail as soon as the island chiefs came to visit them on board.

"You are my guests," he assured them when their eyes widened with fear, "but none of you are free to go until our anchor is returned."

"*Stand at arms!*" he then ordered his crew, but the slovenly way they went about it, made him bellow:

"*Damn your eyes* for a parcel of lubberly rascals! If I had four more reliable men with me I could disarm the lot of you with sticks!"

Well past the point of no return and seeing that one of his crew was not paying attention, Bligh drew his pistol and aimed it straight at the man's face.

"You're a *dead man* if you don't listen while your commander is talking."

It was a tense standoff allayed by approaching canoes carrying news that the thieves in question came from another island. Bligh had to backtrack fast.

"I'm so sorry," he apologised, immediately kneeling down to untie his hostages' hands. Frightened and not understanding the white man's ways or words, the natives were sweating and sobbing profusely.

"I don't know what I can do to make amends," Bligh rambled on as he cast round for compensation, finding it in a glut of gifts he loaded into their canoe when he sent them on their way.

His heartfelt apology was almost enough to win back Christian's allegiance, but then came the trouble over coconuts.

"Who's stolen them?" Bligh fumed when they were back at sea."I left them here under your watch. Explain yourself."

Christian was at a loss. When he had seen the mound of coconuts stacked on deck, it had never occurred to him that Bligh had earmarked them *sacred and only to be used for survival.* For months, they were free for all on the islands and of little intrinsic value.

"I was thirsty, sir. I must admit I took one."

"*You liar!* More than *half* of them are missing."

"I *swear*, sir, that I'm not. Had I known of their importance to you, I wouldn't have dared touch even that one."

"A liar *and* a fool," Bligh raved on, deaf to Christian's defence. "How could you not understand them as security against our dying of thirst? *God damn you* for a scoundrel and a thief. But I'll make you sweat for it … you and your men. I'll have half of you wanting to jump overboard before we get through Endeavour Straits."

His accusation and threat were outrageous; both made worse when just half an hour later he sent his servant Samuel to Christian's quarters.

"The commander sends his compliments, sir," Samuel relayed, "and wishes to invite you to dinner."

For a split second Christian's astonishment outstripped his contempt.

"He's gone stark staring mad," Quintal interrupted, only to be put quickly back in his place.

"*Don't* say that!" Christian hissed, angry with his subordinate, but more so with himself for wanting to defend his old friend when that friend had turned enemy. At this sudden clarity of thought, he replied.

"Please extend my apologies to Lieutenant Bligh, but I'm afraid I'm feeling too unwell to attend."

Samuel scuttled away to deliver Christian's message, not so much convinced by the truth of his excuse as by its motivation. Trouble was brewing and he was not quite sure which side offered him safety.

Quintal did not care. He looked hard at Christian, his eyes glassy with conviction.

"It's up to you," he said. "We have to do something about it."

ELEVEN

Bligh woke with a start and a cutlass at his throat.

"Get to your feet and surrender your ship!"

He sat bolt upright in bed. In the dense dark of pre-dawn, he was unable to make out the shadows surrounding him, but was sure that the cold blade pressing on his neck meant murder. Christian was holding it fast to his flesh; so tight that the drawn blood was dripping on his nightshirt.

"Mr Christian …," he said in dismay. "what *is* all this?"

"Say one more word and you're dead!"

His threat was underscored by the click of muskets cocked to kill. A three-man firing squad was at his disposal, their eyes trained down the barrel of their guns.

Bligh leapt to his feet.

"*Mutiny!*" he screamed, calling for the support of any loyalists left on board.

He was sure Fryer, Samuel or at least Ledward would run to his rescue, but whether out of earshot or sympathy, no one came.

"You're on your own," Christian informed him. "I've put sentries at their door. So be quiet and do what you're told."

Barefooted and in his nightshirt, Bligh was dragged up on deck and strapped to the mizzen mast – there to suffer the indignity of being only half clad, while his hands were tied so tight that both arms lost circulation. Alone and at the mutineers' mercy, he quickly cast his eye around the ship in search of support. It appeared that all loyalists were confined below, but there was a ray of hope in that those on deck who were not among the ringleaders of the revolt stood stunned, not knowing what to do. Here was his chance and he took it.

"Come on now my lads," he cajoled, working on their ambivalence. "You've had your fun. This has all been one big misunderstanding. Just let me go and we'll say no more about it. You won't suffer for it. I promise."

That seemed fair and a few of them moved to set him free.

"That's right boys," he coaxed. "It's the best thing to do. Stop this now and all will be well, but persist and you'll all be strung up to the nearest yardarm when news of this reaches home. And it will … you can be sure of it."

He was talking them round and alarmed, Christian rushed over and rested the tip of his sword on Bligh's chest.

"This is your last chance to live. Say no more."

His voice was on the brink of hysteria, but it was the crazed look in his eye that told Bligh to back off and resign himself to the loss of his ship.

The first loyalist to witness his commander's dire straits was boatswain William Cole.

"Hoist out the jolly-boat!" he was ordered when Quintal brought him up on deck.

"Fryer has requested that he be allowed to come topside too," Quintal reported to Christian. "I told him *no*."

"Well go back and tell him *yes*. It's inevitable that he should see what's going on at some point. It may as well be now. And bring Purcell with you while you're at it."

To both mutineers and Bligh, Fryer was an unknown quantity, capable of swinging either way. He loathed Bligh as much as any man on board, but Christian suspected that his sense of duty to the Crown was stronger. Either way, it was a gamble both sides had to take.

"Will you let me remain on the ship?" the master stood before Christian and asked.

"No!" came the resounding response from the rest of the rebels, but for a moment, Christian was undecided.

In that strategic second, Fryer edged closer to Bligh.

"Have you any orders Commander?" he whispered, waiting for instructions.

He had picked his side, so Bligh quickly whispered back:

"Knock Christian down and cut me loose."

But Fryer's brief hesitation was long enough to alert Christian to the danger. Now that he knew which way the wind blew, he put an abrupt end to their collaboration.

"Take Fryer back below!" he ordered.

Seamen Mills and Burkitt tied their ship master's hands behind his back and shoved him on his way.

"I'm sorry, sir," Fryer looked over his shoulder to say. "God be with you."

Wary of the sympathy those words stirred among the crew, Quintal lunged towards Bligh.

"*Shoot him* and all his friends now and let's get back to the island."

Christian stayed his hand.

"I'll not be responsible for the murder of innocent men," he replied. "We'll put them in the boat and leave justice to The Almighty."

"It'll be a rum sort of justice in *that* jolly-boat," loyalist carpenter William Purcell dared say. "It's too small and leaks from every crevice. With the weight of more than a dozen men, we're sure to drown."

On closer inspection, Christian agreed and ordered the larger launch to be made ready.

In it went Bligh and most loyalists on board, except carpenters McIntosh and Norman and armourer Joseph Coleman, who were held back for the basic maintenance of the Bounty.

"Please know, sir, that we didn't choose to stay," they yelled down to Bligh in the launch. "We're being kept on board against our will."

"Never fear my lads," Bligh called back. "You can't all come with me, but I'll do you justice if ever I reach England."

Their courage in speaking out of turn under such volatile circumstances was commendable and tolerated by the mutineers only because their skills were so essential. But when midshipmen Thomas Hayward and John Hallett burst into tears and begged Christian to keep them safe on board, the feeling of the crew was unanimous.

"Get rid of them!"

Christian hesitated. Although both the young gentlemen were universally disliked for their laziness and cruelty towards their subordinates, he felt sorry for them. They had proved to be cowards and for a man, that was a fate worse than death.

Quintal took the decision out of his hands and pushed the pair, at gun point, into the launch.

The only other to resort to tears was near-blind fiddler Michael Byrne. His was a terrifying experience in the dark when he was left on his own in the boat rejected for Bligh's banishment. It was still tethered to the ship, but assuming himself forgotten, alone and adrift, he wept copiously for some hours before the mutineers remembered to haul him back on board.

"Now where's that other little rat we want be get rid of?" midshipman Tom Ellison said.

They all hated Bligh's servant Samuel with a passion and reveling in the thrill of new-found power and bloodlust, Ellison's eyes scanned the ship for any sign of him.

True to the rodent he resembled, Samuel had darted from sight – not as an act of cowardice, but of shrewd, forward thinking. He raced to his commander's cabin to grab the ship's journal, along with spare uniforms, and tried his luck at absconding with Bligh's maps. Those, however, were ripped from his hand when he was found and thrown into the launch.

"You won't be needing these," seaman Matthew Thompson said, depriving the exiles of what was certainly their last hope of survival. "If our clever commander is such a great navigator, he can find his *own* way home."

"I'll be damned if the bastard doesn't do just that," Ellison added contemptuously, as his finger twitched on the trigger of his musket. "We should kill him now while we've got the chance."

He aimed his gun to shoot, but Christian knocked it off its trajectory.

Having paled at the prospect of imminent death, Bligh quickly regained his composure. He was grateful for Christian's mercy and despite his own dire predicament, was strangely flattered by Ellison's confidence in his navigational skills when the chances of him making his way back to England, or in fact, surviving beyond even a few days at sea, were negligible. The food and water the mutineers were loading onto the launch would sustain them no longer than a week and as the last of them was winched down to Bligh and his fellow exiles, confusion broke out on Bounty's deck.

"I don't want anyone kept on board against their will," Christian was insisting,

In this, he was at odds with the other mutineers and a ferocious argument ensued, settled only after the remaining loyalists locked in their cabins were brought up on deck.

"For right or wrong, It is our duty to accompany our commander," all the petty officers among them agreed with a loyalty intended to shame Christian.

It did and was a shame made more acute when the bulk of the other ordinary seamen opted to stay with him on board the Bounty; their support effectively relegating Christian and his actions to the ranks of lesser men of lesser minds.

In a last-minute rush of guilt, Christian grabbed up his own sextant and book of nautical tables and tossed them down to Bligh.

"They are my own, sir, and of good quality," he called out as they landed with a dull thud in the launch. "They should be sufficient for every purpose and give you a fighting chance."

"That they will," Quintal laughed, "if they don't first die of starvation and thirst."

At this reality, Christian looked distressed and Bligh took advantage.

"Will you not think on this again my old friend?" he called up. "I am prepared to forsake my honour and never speak of this again if you will relent. By your action, you are condemning me and nearly 20 of your shipmates to death. Remember our friendship and my family … those children of mine who adore you so and who you have happily danced on your knee."

At this outrageous piece of emotional blackmail, Christian's eyes burned hot with the threat of tears. He was already suffering from his own inner struggle and had just been hit with another massive dose of self-reproach. Incensed, but desperate to explain himself, he slammed his fists down hard on the ship's rail.

"Can't you *see*, sir. that I'm in hell … *I'm in hell!*"

"I can, my friend," Bligh replied with calm indulgence. "So relent now before you condemn yourself to it for eternity."

At this curse of damnation from the one they considered the devil himself, Christian's resolve hardened.

"Cut them loose!" he suddenly ordered, sending his captain and condemned comrades to their fate; as penance, watching them disappear into the morning mist before he turned the Bounty due east to Tahiti.

TWELVE

"So what now?" ship's gunner William Peckover asked as he shifted his sore rear from one uncomfortable spot in the launch to another.

All eyes were on Bligh. They were adrift in the middle of nowhere, floating on an ocean that rarely saw a European ship. There was next to no chance of rescue.

"I don't fancy waiting it out on the Friendly Isles," Bligh answered, "Without the back-up of Bounty's guns I wouldn't count on them living up to their name."

He was taking the matter in hand and that was reassuring.

"The other option," he continued, "is to try to make it to the nearest East Indies trading post. Dutch Timor would be our best bet."

"Well then let's go," quartermaster Peter Linkletter chimed in.

But Bligh quickly curbed his enthusiasm.

"It's not that simple," he said. "We've no maps and only a compass and sextant to guide us through three-and-a-half thousand miles of uncharted waters. I'm not a miracle-worker."

"We all have complete faith in your ability, sir," young midshipman Robert Tinkler replied.

Considering their dire circumstance and its cause, Bligh cocked a cynical eyebrow.

"Would that I had inspired such confidence before."

At this, the men fell silent, shamed for ever doubting their commander's capacity. For *now* they were all too keen to lay the entire responsibility for their lives on his shoulders. Deep in thought in regard to that burden, Bligh continued:

"There's a third option. We could try to make it to New South Wales. By now, Captain Phillip and his First Fleet should have arrived at Botany Bay and established their settlement."

"That's a dangerous gamble," Fryer contested. "We've had no news of his success while we've been at sea. For all we know, they could have all died en route."

It was a gloomy view, but nonetheless a very real possibility, and loathe to commit himself and his men to a trip that, from the onset, promised an uncertain end, Bligh negated the thought.

"Well the East Indies it is then," he confirmed with a conviction that gave his men reason to hope.

Their lives were in his hands and, for the most part, safe to be there. Because if true grit could not do it, then Bligh's gut determination to get back to Britain and bring Christian to justice would.

His men, however, were out of condition after living a life of luxury in Tahiti. Just to take up the oars again was a feat in itself, but to row over 3000 miles would be a Herculean ordeal. But row they did, with a dedication second only to their dread of drowning.

First stop: the island of Tofua to replenish supplies. It was 30 miles away, reached in a boat just 23 feet long, six feet wide and loaded within seven inches of its gunwale. That was a considerable achievement and Bligh breathed a sigh of relief when at nightfall, eleven hours later, the slice of land appeared in silhouette on the horizon.

"There it is," he said, recognising the ring of smoke that circled its steep, volcanic peak.

New energy went into reaching its shore before the dark settled in. They failed and with strong winds threatening to smash their boat against its treacherous coast, they lay low under the lee of the isle and spent a grossly uncomfortable night in the launch.

By morning, a few of the men were hungry enough to scale the precipitous cliff looming over them. Their incentive was the sole palm tree growing on its crest. It was a dangerous, disappointing venture which reaped only a few coconuts as reward for risking life and limb. Within minutes, they were devoured and washed down with a meagre spoonful of rum.

"Well thank God for that," Fryer exclaimed when they rowed a little further around the coast and found a more inviting cove to moor their boat.

Cheered by the feel of solid ground beneath his feet, Bligh doled out a few ounces of pork and as a generous afterthought, gave each man two bananas and half a glass of wine to sustain them for a full day of foraging.

"We found a small cave up there," Purcell said, when he and his small party returned to the beach that afternoon.

He put down the two casks of fresh water they managed to fill and pointed to the small aperture high up in the rocky headland.

"It's warm and dry and there's room for a few of us to sleep tonight if you want more space in the boat."

This was the second time that the ornery old salt, Purcell, had helped out with cool-headed logic. The first was at the height of the mutiny when Christian's friend Peter Heywood had grabbed a gun and in the confusion didn't know which way to point it. Despite the fact that he was a loyalist, he hadn't wanted to use it against his mutineer friend and standing so close to Bligh with a loaded weapon at that critical moment of indecision posed a problem.

"*What in the name of God,* Heywood, are you doing with *that?*" Purcell demanded when he was brought up on deck with Fryer. "Put that gun down *immediately!*"

Shocked by the sheer audacity of the carpenter's command, Heywood had obeyed and Bligh drew a sigh of relief.

And here, again, was Purcell stepping in to save the day; or more succinctly, the anticipation of another dreadful night.

"Capital idea!" Bligh agreed, full of praise for the man's initiative.

It had been a long day and with many more to come, none of them relished the prospect of spending another night in such cramped, wet quarters. With the luxury of being able to stretch out his legs, Bligh slept like a log in their lifeboat until Fryer shook him awake.

"Get up, sir! Natives approaching."

There were three of them, near naked and curious: a man, woman and child, who although cautious in their welcome, seemed extremely eager to share their new found friends with the rest of their tribe. Within an hour, Bligh and his crew were surrounded by a multitude of a hundred or more, all keen to draw close and establish their visitors' worth.

"Buttons and beads should do it," Bligh decided, not realizing that among their number were a few fine young cannibals keener to feast on their flesh.

Composed in his ignorance, Bligh spread his bagful of loot on the sand and sat down to barter.

At the sight of the shiny trinkets, the natives' eyes lit with wonder. Thanks to the English navy and its uniform requirements, Bligh had enough brass buttons and bright, enamel pieces to keep the savages happy until his men returned with provisions. In the meantime, he instructed those who remained on the beach with him, to keep calm, but on alert.

All went well until the baubles ran out and the Chief of Tofua asked:

"Where's your ship?"

The delicate question was translated by Peckover, who spoke fluent Tahitian. Its answer required great tact, but to Bligh's horror, quartermaster's mate George Simpson took the lead.

"It sank," he implied with the downward tilt of his thumb.

Proud of himself for skirting the mention of mutiny, Simpson had no idea that he had just put his small band of unarmed Englishmen in mortal danger.

"So you are all alone?" the chief confirmed, as his eyes curved in the direction of his warriors to issue silent instructions.

Although unvoiced, those instructions came across loud and clear.

Instantly, Bligh leapt to his feet and with cutlass in hand strode bravely towards the natives who had started hauling their launch onto the beach. It was pure bluff on Bligh's part, but it worked. For a short time, the natives were scared off, but minute by minute, were growing more aggressive. Already, they were knocking stones together as a prelude to attack and with vivid memories of this same overture to violence preceding Cook's death, Bligh had to act fast.

"Do it casually," he whispered to boatswain Cole, "but get the supplies onto the launch as fast as possible."

That was easier said than done when high tide was rolling in. Its soaring waves were crashing hard on the beach and waist high in wild water the sailors struggled to get their cargo aboard.

"You stay the night," the chief said to Bligh in a tone suddenly more hostile than hospitable.

To which Bligh replied with premium British aplomb.

"That's extremely kind of you, but I never sleep out of my boat. In the morning we'll trade again, because we can't leave until the weather is better."

Unconvinced by the charade and considerably less practised at keeping up appearances, the chief dropped all pretence.

"If you not sleep on shore, we kill you."

All bets were off, and in a sudden, skilled move, Bligh had him in a head lock and was dragging him back to the boat as hostage.

The natives' percussion of stones stopped.

"*Peckover!*" Bligh yelled to his ship's gunner through the ominous silence. "As fast as you can, run back to the cave and fetch our ship's log."

That was a tall order when the natives were now armed with spears and smelling a massacre. Yet, despite the fact that Peckover never cared for Bligh, he cared even less for being called a coward. Boldly, he pushed his way through the pressing throng of bronze-skinned warriors, fighting off each in turn as they tried to tear the book from his hands.

"Good man," Bligh commended him, for he had saved this most valuable of possessions.

But rude as he ever was to Bligh, Peckover shrugged off the praise and spoke his mind.

"What I do, I do only for Captain Cook, because I was with him on his every voyage and know that for *some* reason he loved and trusted you. It's for his sake *alone* that I continue to stand at your side."

This dire moment wasn't the time to take offence and casting the insult aside, Bligh opted for any help he could get. The natives were closing in around them and suddenly the chief broke loose from his grip.

"*Run for your lives! Get to the boat!*" Bligh shouted to his men.

He did the same, splashing into the rough surf to feel the eye-crossing agony of razor-sharp coral slicing through his boots into the soft under flesh of his feet. But now that the natives had revealed themselves as cannibals and were stampeding towards him with blood in their eye and shrunken heads strung around their necks, Bligh's stark terror outweighed the pain.

"They've got hold of the *hawser*," he spluttered in panic as his men dragged him on board. "Don't let them pull our boat aground!"

It was quartermaster John Norton who made the supreme sacrifice and slipped his rotund self back into the water.

"*Release the rope!*" he called out, hoping to bully the natives into submission, but their answer came back in a barrage of stones.

One struck him in the temple and stunned, Norton collapsed to his knees in the sand. There, he was knocked down and beaten to death, his splattered blood colouring the water red, while the sound of his moans were silenced by the thud of rocks pummeling his flesh.

There was nothing they could do to save him and with the natives still trying to drag their launch ashore, Bligh lunged for a sabre and slashed the rope through. The boat broke free, giving its crew a short, gruesome moment to witness Norton's corpse being butchered and divvied up among the human vultures descending upon it.

"And what precisely do you propose to name this little piece of paradise?" asked Fryer in revulsion.

Gagging at the horrific sight and the pragmatic thought that the loss of Norton's weight would help speed them on their way, Bligh could not speak.

"*Bloody Murderer's Cove,*" Tom Ledward said for him, not realising the name would stick.

But Bligh was no longer listening.

"Oh my God," he gasped with fresh alarm. "They're coming after us!"

They thought themselves safely away, but now the natives were paddling their canoes in hot pursuit. As experienced oarsmen, they were quick to make ground and were soon alongside, hurling stones and brandishing spears.

There was nowhere to hide. Cornered and frantic, the sailors could do nothing but hurl back the rocks that landed in their boat, their inexperience at primitive warfare having them miss their mark.

Bligh's quick thinking had him scream the order:

"*Forget the stones ... throw the clothes!*"

Over into the ocean they went: those uniforms that Samuel had so sensibly stowed on board. He meant them as protection from the cold and never dreamed they would otherwise save their lives. At once, the natives were in the water, forsaking the promise of fresh prey for dinner in favour of Bligh's blue coats and brass buttons.

The men of the Bounty left them to their feeding frenzy and rowed back out to sea. They had survived the first of their Herculean labours and now had only 3470 miles to go.

THIRTEEN

Bligh's freezing hand was on the tiller when the big wave hit. In the dead of night it curled over the stern and crashed into their tiny craft. The rush of wild water swept quarter master Simpson screaming into the black oblivion, and in a blind attempt at his rescue, Bligh cast out a rope. It was a hundred-to-one shot in the dark and nothing short of a miracle when he felt the drowning man's tug at the end of it. They dragged him back on board and shaking from fear and the ocean chill, Simpson silently took his place again next to his friends, all of them drenched to the skin and sitting knee-deep in salt water.

"*Bail! Bail!*" Bligh ordered, as he helped bucket the brine from the boat -- a routine they had perfected since being set adrift.

With the immediate emergency over, they let out a communal sigh and relaxed back in their seats. Ten days into their odyssey and only a quarter of the way to salvation, the constricted muscles in their legs and bowels ached from malnutrition and the enforced immobility of their cramped quarters. Beset by chronic constipation, rheumatism and exposure, most of them were close to dying of thirst and the rest, of starvation. Not one day had passed without a deluge of rain and the bone-numbing cold had them curled up like contorted embryos to keep warm.

"Strip off and rinse your clothes in the sea," Bligh commanded.

With their teeth chattering in the icy wind, it was the last thing the men wanted to do, but it worked. The salt saturating the fabric formed a crusty protection from the elements and offered some relief.

"Who would have thought?" young Robert Tinkler remarked to Fryer through parched, blue lips, not for the first time impressed by his captain's ingenuity.

It seemed odd to him, though, that Bligh, nearly twice his age, was so resilient, when he, a strong young man of 17, was on the brink of death. "You can only wonder where the man gets his strength."

"From the devil," Fryer replied dryly, as he spoon-fed Tinkler his daily allowance of rum and then shaded his own sun-burnt eyes to look up at Bligh.

There he was, standing at the prow of their small launch as it plunged precariously into the sea. With sextant and soggy map in hand, he was making sketches and charting their course with a precision and optimism that was a wonder to them all. Nothing, including the fury of Neptune, seemed to dampen his spirits.

"If my calculations are correct, we're right on course," Bligh said, as he picked his way back to his seat. "I do believe that we're the first Europeans to pass from east to west through this Fiji archipelago."

The primitive, wooded islands to their starboard, were proof of it and Bligh pointed to them with pride. While his men were silently debating his questionable source of power, Bligh had been seeing to their welfare by drawing a map of their approximate position in relation to New Guinea and New Holland. If he should die, he hoped it would give them at least a fighting chance of survival.

Unaware of his captain's noble intent, Fryer's next comment was facetious.

"You are truly a credit to British navigation, sir."

Bligh baulked at his tone.

"Do I detect a note of sarcasm, Mr Fryer?"

"Not at all, sir," he came back with his usual, detached calm. "We are all in awe of the way you are handling our dire situation."

This came as news to Bligh, when only hours before he was berated by two of his crew. Harking back to his bad treatment of them on the Bounty, their words had stung and shocked him.

"But I went to so much trouble to provide you with a fine supply of wholesome food," he said in his own defence when young Hallet and Purcell accused him of past abuses. "Had I not taken such great pains for the benefit of all, you would not be here."

His words were wide open to innuendo, and taking advantage of both them and the even playing field on which he and his captain now co-existed, Purcell replied:

"Yes, if you hadn't taken *such* great pains with us, we should *never* have been here!"

That was the sad truth, but incapable of losing any argument, Bligh reciprocated with a low blow to put Purcell back in his place.

"I'm afraid I'm going to have to requisition your tool box, Purcell."

This much-touted, metal box was the carpenter's pride and joy and off limits to all but him.

"You will not!" he dared contest, but here, Bligh reasserted command.

"My dear fellow, we have precisely 150 pounds of biscuits remaining on which to survive. If they get wet, we're dead men. That box of yours is the only dry compartment left available. If you deny us of it, you'll be guilty of murder."

The harsh indictment struck a chord and Purcell handed him the rusty, iron key.

"Good man, I shall take special care of it."

Purcell let out a surly hiss.

"Well, I'm a better man than *you'll* ever be."

At this, Bligh seized his cutlass: dire circumstance or not, this was gross insubordination and an insult of the first order.

"Arm yourself, sir!" he demanded, as he got to his feet and set the boat swaying. "We'll see who's the better man right here and now."

But fast, Fryer secured a firm grasp on Bligh's wrist to restrain him.

"If you dare interfere with me," Bligh swung round on him to say, "I'll run you through."

"I beg of you, sir … regain your control," Fryer rose to say to him face to face. "We will be lost without you. Purcell is a rude pig. He does not speak for us all."

His good sense had Bligh relent and settle back in his seat. But with one storm passed, he still had to contend with the string of others -- those squalls which continued night and day, leaving them half drowned and frozen to the bone. Their clothes were in shreds and with only the scraps of their ripped canvas sail to cover them, there was no shelter from the raging elements.

In the incessant downpour, Bligh doled out their daily allocation of rum and mouldy biscuits, one day adding to the menu the two small seabirds that landed and lingered too long on the gunwale. In one fell swoop, he snatched them and snapped their necks, cutting the raw kill into 18 equal portions to divide among them. Every skerrick was devoured: bones, entrails and flesh, while their blood was given to Tom Ledward and sail master Lawrence Lebogue, who were in bad shape. Seeing their suffering, Bligh topped up their intake of the thick red fluid with what little was left of the wine.

"They are worse off than the rest of us," he explained, when the others questioned this preferential treatment.

Why waste good wine and food on those who are about to die? their dark-ringed eyes all looked at him to say.

But Bligh said back: "They're not dead *yet* and this little extra may just be enough to turn the tide and secure their survival."

Ashamed as they were, however, for wanting to deny their dying comrades an extra sip of alcohol, the crew was outraged when Bligh helped himself to the same. Thinking them all asleep, he drank it down as he scribbled in the ship's log:

Being constantly wet, it is with the utmost difficulty that I can open a book to write. We experience cold and shivering scarce to be conceived. Now little better than starving, we struggle to surmount our chronic hardships. However, I thank God for this blessing of cold, wet weather, when hot weather, more typical of this region, would have had us die raving mad with thirst. Although we sleep covered with rain and sea, we have been spared that torment.

Ever the optimist, he believed that The Almighty was on his side and would remain there until justice was served. For his part, all he had to do was stay alive to see it done.

"You cheat!" Purcell sat bolt upright to say when he woke to see Bligh swallow the extra mouthful of rum.

He was caught in the act and the sound and seriousness of the accusation roused the other men. Bligh's only defence was to tell the truth, but although it was based on good sense, it did not go down well.

"I humbly beg your forgiveness for taking more than my share," he apologised. "But it is imperative that I stay alive."

"Why?" Purcell demanded. "Because you think your life is so much more valuable than ours?"

"No ... but it is essential if I am to *ensure* yours. Without my skills, you won't survive. As your captain, I have watched over you as you sleep and have worked while you rest. This has been my dedication and duty, but it has demanded extra energy. You rightly blame me for succumbing to temptation, but know now that this is the first and last time that I shall allow myself any such luxury."

They were happy to have chastised Bligh. Deep down, however, they knew that he was right and felt uneasy when, from that point on he abstained from even his fair share. To make amends, he cut his rations in half, causing them to watch his deterioration with a keen, concerned eye.

"You go too far, sir, to prove a point," Fryer struggled to sit erect and say. "You must eat and drink enough to sustain yourself, else we'll all die."

They had been at sea for 49 days and for all of them death hung heavy on the horizon. Lying with their eyes fixed vacantly on that line that separated sky from sea, they prayed for landfall before the sun set on them forever.

It was Bligh who focused on it first. In his weakened condition, he supposed it to be a mirage and had to squint through the tropical mist to define the jagged outline of Timor.

"*Land ho!*" he cried in a feeble voice, as tears of relief streamed down his cheeks.

The weight of the world rolled from his shoulders, for he was only a young man who had been put through an initiation of hell and high water. At the onset of his naval career he had taken on the most taxing of missions, perhaps the most extraordinary that the world had ever known. Against all odds and the contempt of his crew, he achieved what, by rights, was impossible. In little more than a row boat he steered a steady course through disaster, navigating his way over thousands of miles of hostile, unchartered waters to save most of his men and give them a second chance to live on and loathe him.

It was Wednesday, the 12th of June, a day emblazoned on the men's minds as one of pure joy.

With Timor's surf too high to facilitate a landing, however, they had another day of rowing ahead of them before they anchored in a small cove and were greeted by a group of Malay villagers. The natives were used to the sight of Europeans, but were fascinated by this group of emaciated sailors who staggered from their small boat and collapsed on the beach at their feet.

"You've landed South West of Coupang," one of sarong-clad men said, as he offered the starving castaways food and water. "The Governor of Timor lives there."

Relieved at the news of civilization, but exhausted at the prospect of having to travel further to find it, Bligh looked up at him, bleary-eyed:

"Is it far?" he rasped through cracked lips, trying to stop his voice from wavering.

"No, not far," the Malayan reassured, putting his hand on Bligh's shoulder. "We'll help you row the distance."

The next morning found them in their weather-worn launch at the entrance of a small harbour. To Bligh's relief, its tranquil waters were dotted with square-rigged ships from around the world and its shore populated by the busy Dutch settlement of Coupang.

Despite their dire straits, however, Bligh was still a stickler for the rules and resisted the urge to row fast towards the town. Instead, he ordered his men to down oars and hoist the "signal of distress" flag to their battered masthead.

"What on earth for?" Fryer questioned in frustration, figuring that their wretched state on arrival would speak for itself."

"Because, Mr Fryer," Bligh replied. "It would not be proper for us to land without leave."

"Bring her in!" a Dutch soldier called out from the quay. Seeing the state of the ex-Bounty crew and their boat, he motioned with some urgency for them to do so.

With swollen, cramped legs, Bligh hauled himself ashore to be welcomed by a group of locals. On hearing an English voice among them, he struggled to straighten his shoulders and fumbled to do up the one remaining brass button that was hanging by a thread to his tattered blue jacket.

"Lieutenant?" the English stranger queried as he approached Bligh.

Bligh returned his salute and promptly collapsed to the ground, coming to, moments later, in the arms of the English sailor who introduced himself as able seaman John Croft from the Dutch merchantman Walcheren.

"If you can get to your feet, sir, I'll take you to my Captain Spikeman," Croft said. "I'm sure he'll see to you and the welfare of your men."

Spikeman was an English officer in the Dutch service and was just as astonished as Croft by Bligh's sad state and story of survival.

"It's nothing short of a miracle," he said, giving Bligh the support of his arm as he helped his fellow commander to a chair and sent his staff running for food, water and bandages.

Bligh downed the glass of brandy he was offered, but in his half-starved state it went straight to his head.

"My men," he said urgently, as he leant forward in his seat to stop from fainting.

"No need to worry," Spikeman replied, leaping from his own chair to tend to him. "I've put them under the care of our local surgeon, Mr Max. He's seeing to them as we speak, so put your mind at ease."

As soon as Bligh had had a chance to eat a little food and pull himself together, Spikeman took him to the Governor of Coupang, Willem Adrian Van Este.

"God knows, sir, you're a man in a million," Van Este said, greeting Bligh with warmth and respect. "Let me offer you the large house up there on the hill. You deserve a little luxury in which to recoup after all you've been through. I'm sure Captain Spikeman will be happy to accommodate your men on his ship in the meantime."

"No, I'm sorry, sir, but that won't do," Bligh surprised the Governor by saying.

"I will not be separated from my men. They deserve no less than I and after all we've shared I insist on continuing to do so until my mission is complete and I've seen them safely home to England."

"As you wish, Lieutenant Bligh," Van Este agreed, having had his high opinion of the man confirmed.

After making sure that his men were comfortable in their rooms, Bligh went to his own and made an entry in his log:

> It is over – the nightmare that lasted from Tuesday, 28th April to Sunday, 14th June, 1789; a journey covering a distance of 3,618 unchartered miles.

With his hand shaking from weakness and head pounding with pain, he wrote the last words.

> *Thus happily ended, through the assistance of Divine Providence, without accident, a voyage of the most extraordinary nature that ever happened in the world.*

He finished with a full stop and too tired to walk to his bed, put his head down on the desk and fell sound asleep.

– oOo –

"I *suppose* he saw us through it all right," surgeon's mate Ledward of the Bounty reluctantly admitted.

Having shared Bligh's journey and indulged in a few days of good food and rest in Coupang, he felt revived and well within his rights to be begrudging.

"But nonetheless," he added, "I will always think of Bligh as being a petty man."

Considering the circumstances and Bligh's genuine concern for his crew, the comment was grossly unfair and turned out to be of little account when Ledward drowned during his voyage back home on the Dutch merchantman Welfare. The ship went down with all hands under the command of a much lesser captain than the one he condemned.

FOURTEEN

"Well we can't stay here!"

It was a decision Fletcher Christian had to make.

Since he and his mutineers anchored at the island of Tubaui, they had suffered a series of vicious native attacks and a multitude of problems posed by fellow rebel Matthew Quintal, whose wild antics were putting all their lives in peril.

"I'll do what I damn well like!" the troublemaker barked back when Christian reprimanded him for going ashore without permission.

It was getting harder to keep a grip on the reins and deluged with the complexities of command, Christian was beginning to sympathise with Bligh.

"And who are *you* to tell me what to do now that we're all meant to be our own masters?" Quintal argued, as he stepped aggressively close and hammered his finger hard at Christian's chest. "We finally got rid of that bastard Bligh and now you're sounding just like him."

With this, many of the mutineers agreed. Much as they liked Christian, they thought he was getting a little high-handed and so they slapped him in irons.

"You can stay there until you learn your lesson."

"All hail the joys of democracy," Peter Heywood said wryly when he was sent to unlock his friend's shackles later that evening.

"Where's Quintal?" Christian asked, rubbing his red raw wrists.

"Drunk, but in a better mood. Apparently you've been forgiven."

Nevertheless, Christian approached him with caution.

"You've made your point, Quintal," he said. "But we've got to get away from these island barbarians and find a haven from what we both *know* is going to be the most brutal of British justice to come. Whether you like it or not, we sail for Tahiti tomorrow."

"Well, why didn't you just say that in the first place?" Quintal slurred, before promptly vomiting up the barrel load of rum he had imbibed.

At the sight and stench of it flowing over the captain's table, Christian bristled with rage.

"*Because*, you imbecile," he snarled, with the same scathing sarcasm he'd found so offensive from Bligh "It'll be the first place Admiralty will look for us."

Once they returned to its sand-white shores, however, they still had a few months of freedom to frolic before the long arm of the law reached them.

It was enough time to impregnate more women and for familiarity to breed contempt. Within only three weeks, two of the mutineers were murdered.

A combination of lust and greed resulted in one shooting another dead, and then suffering the same fate himself by being stoned to death in a fine example of savage, Tahitian-style revenge.

The bloodied rocks that littered the shore were vivid proof that the Bounty rebels had worn out their welcome. Now that they had taken advantage of the island's delights, it was time to leave and steal a few of them away.

"We can't stay here any longer," Christian told his island wife Maimiti. She was carrying his unborn child and he would not leave her behind. "You must come with me in search of our new home."

She was willing to follow him to the ends of the Earth, unlike the 11 other women who were kidnapped to venture there; theirs being a one-way ticket that came at the cost of having to extend sexual favours to all mutineers who requested them.

Despite that enticing prospect, only eight of Bounty's rebels were prepared to be pioneers, trail-blazing their way into the unknown. For the 16 others assembled on deck, it was time to speak out.

"We've decided to risk the hangman's noose and stay here in Tahiti," they informed Christian.

The four loyalists among them, who had been held against their will when Bligh was banished, were smug in their certainty that they would avoid punishment for the mutiny.

More scornful of them than the rest, Quintal spat up a glob of yellow saliva on Bounty's deck: "It's *your* neck," he said, but then abruptly dragged Joseph Coleman from their ranks. "But we'll be needing *you*."

"I'll not go!" Coleman protested.

Jerking his arm free from Quintal's fierce grip, he ran the length of Bounty's deck, dived over the side and swam back to the beach.

"Let him go," Christian said calmly. "Each man's fate is his own."

Christian was superstitious and not at all convinced that they had got away with committing the crime of the century. They were setting sail for a new life with little hope that it would be a good one. It was a sentence they imposed on themselves, which they had no right to inflict on others. Suddenly afraid of a justice higher than man's, Christian reached for the comfort of his wife's hand.

For why should God, he asked himself, *reward us with good for bad?*

It was in this cynical frame of mind that he sailed at Bounty's helm for the four days it took to sight land.

"Our sanctuary from sin," he announced when the rocky silhouette of Pitcairn Island appeared on the horizon.

Shrouded in the midst of a tropical thunderstorm, it emerged like a mythical titan from the sea, its craggy shoulders lifting free of the wild waves crashing at its stone sides and its symmetry of palm trees lining the shore like prison bars through the grey mist.

FIFTEEN

All in all, 1789 was a big year: for right or wrong, Bligh and Christian had made their mark in history and the French Revolution had begun. The storming of the Bastille and the liberal lopping off of aristocrats' heads, however, had nowhere near the impact of Bligh's trial when it hit the headlines.

"You must leave for England as soon as possible," Bligh was instructed by the Dutch doctor stationed In Coupang. "You're suffering from malaria and won't survive unless you get out of these Indonesian tropics."

Bligh agreed with that, but had one stipulation:

"Only if the rest of my crew can follow on the next available ship under Mr. Fryer's care."

"What there is left of us," Fryer mumbled as he watched a sheet being draped over quartermaster Linkletter's body.

That made seven of them dead in all -- a sad irony, that after surviving the indescribable hardships of their marathon voyage, four of them succumbed to fever since reaching safety.

"But 12 of us survived," Bligh said with some satisfaction at his court martial on the HMS Royal William at Spithead. There, he was summoned to account for the loss of his ship.

The case was eight months in coming, during which time Bligh enjoyed celebrity status throughout Britain. The tales of his epic trip inspired the nation, a box-office bonanza of a play and the awestruck respect of English Admiralty. For reasons of protocol alone, their representatives were seated at a long table, ready to hear the evidence and pronounce judgment.

Almost a year had passed since Bligh had set eyes on his Bounty companions. As they filed in to submit their testimony, he looked at each with perverse nostalgia. For despite the trouble many of the men caused him, there existed a strong bond between them. After all they went through together, their lives were inextricably linked.

From most of them came a tight smile of greeting, but Fryer's face was as inscrutable as ever. When he stood to give evidence, however, Bligh was surprised and felt a twang of guilt at his generous words. At last he realised that Fryer's allegiance should never have been in doubt because it was always to the truth. Fryer had long since overcome his resentment of Christian's promotion before his own and did not see it as the trigger to the mutiny. Certainly, he believed it was a move that Bligh lived to regret and one over which he had suffered enough.

"So you don't think that Lieutenant Bligh acted inappropriately when in command?" one of the naval judges questioned.

"No sir, I do not," Fryer answered. "The reality is that as ship's master, I would never be promoted to lieutenant at sea. Our commander advancing Mr Christian to acting lieutenant was not without precedent when Captain Courtney of the Eurydice previously did the same. I have no doubt in my mind that it was a result of Mr Christian's competence, rather than Lieutenant Bligh's favouritism. I lodge no complaints."

At this point, Admiral Samuel Barrington spoke out with authority.

"Before we continue with the trial, Lieutenant Bligh," he asked as the reflection of his dazzling gold epaulettes danced on the ship's wooden walls. "Have you anything to say against these men regarding the mutiny."

"I do not, sir."

Nine hours later, the verdict was in: *Not guilty!* Bligh was completely exonerated.

"But do *you* hold me accountable?" Bligh asked of his newly knighted friend Sir Joseph Banks. It was his opinion that mattered most.

"You've been acquitted of all charges, so who am I to say otherwise?" he responded. "You did your best and no man can do more."

"Cook would have done better, I think," Bligh persisted, needing more vindication than just this well-worn platitude.

"Cook ended up with a *spear* in his back!" Banks answered, and with a shrug added: "But at least it saved him from your fate."

Bligh looked puzzled.

"Cook's men had no desire to stay on the islands after his murder," Banks explained, "whereas *your* crew's desire was your downfall. You were dealt a bad hand from the start with no marines on board the Bounty for discipline. And with the initial delay in setting off, your men were fed up before the mission even got underway. Your biggest problem was having to stay so long in Tahiti with all its temptation. It gave your men time to establish relationships and become responsible for them."

"Exactly!" Bligh sat forward eagerly in his seat to say. It was such a relief to finally have someone understand.

Banks, however, had an agenda of his own.

"You've no need to question my support, William. You've got it and always will. But now, I'm going to ask you a favour in return."

"Anything," Bligh replied, relaxing back in his chair.

"I don't want you to think too harshly of Christian."

At the mention of that name, Bligh's blood ran cold. The man betrayed him twice over. Even if he *could* forgive him for leading the mutiny and sending his fellow seamen to what should have been their death, he could never get over the fact that Christian rejected his initial hand of friendship.

"You can't ask that of me."

It was a flat refusal, but Banks was firm:

"I can and do, because I feel sorrier for him than you. You've been unfairly criticised, but he's been damned."

Bligh winced at these words. With love and hate so closely akin, the intensity of one impacted on the other. He had cared for Christian above all men and the acute hurt of his defection struck hard at his pride. Yet, much as he wanted to wring the man's neck, he baulked at the thought of his punishment being eternal.

"I am in hell … I am in *hell*." Christian's words came back to him as clear as day.

Knowing himself to be partly to blame, Bligh felt no pleasure at the prospect of him suffering damnation forever. But still, he could never, *never* forgive.

"So you'll show no mercy?" Banks reiterated.

And Bligh straightened his shoulders to reply:

"Not in *this* lifetime."

SIXTEEN

Two ships set out as a direct result of the Bounty trial.

The first was the HMS Providence. Such was Admiralty's faith in Bligh, that he was promoted to captain and put in command.

"It's back to the South Seas for you to finish what you started," Banks informed him. "But this time you go better equipped with a full contingent of marines and a far more obliging crew."

With the backup of both, Bligh was to make a great success of his second breadfruit expedition. Despite a flare up of the malaria which nearly killed him in Coupang, he was to show no sign of faulty leadership, and when he left the ship two years later, he was destined to be cheered by the crew as a mark of respect. Enough of it, he would hope, to finally put the hex of the Bounty behind him. Yet still, there remained the unresolved question of what happened to Christian?

"He sailed to safety," Chief Tynah told him when The Providence stopped over in Tahiti.

"*But where?*" Bligh was left to wonder, half of him hoping the man was dead, while feeling lonesome at the thought.

It was a state of ambivalence which was to stay with him for the rest of his life.

The second ship to set sail in November 1790 was the HMS Pandora under the command of Captain Edward Edwards. He was commissioned to track down the mutineers and wreak revenge, a practice he had honed to a fine art. They called him "the Bounty Hunter", but never to his face, because his brutality put Bligh's in the shade.

Given their common ground, however, a certain confusion existed as to which captain did what and Bligh was incensed by the comparison.

"We have *nothing* whatsoever in common!" he raved at Banks. "Edwards is a sadist and I resent having his behavior mistaken for mine. He'll make the mutineers suffer alright, when he catches them, whereas I treated them very well under the circumstances."

"Both your names are now synonymous with the Bounty. For better or worse, parallels are bound to be drawn. It's out of your hands."

Banks' logic was frustrating and clenching one of those hands of his, Bligh slammed it hard against the wall.

"The *damned Bounty* … will it *curse* me forever?"

Much the same question was asked by the four loyalists who were forced to stay with the mutineers in Tahiti. They never counted themselves among their rebel ranks and were certain that they would be welcomed home as heroes.

When the Pandora sailed into Tahiti's Matavai Bay, tears of relief and heartfelt patriotism burned in their eyes.

At last … their lifeline to London!

"We must be the first on board," said Peter Heywood, whose loyalty had proved greater to the Crown than to his friend Christian.

At the eleventh hour, he chose not to follow his friend to Pitcairn and now, leaping into one of the native canoes, he, Coleman, McIntosh and Norman rowed fast towards the ship. It had been a dangerous gamble for the latter three, yelling down their support to Bligh when he was set adrift, but they were glad now that they did, for soon they would be rewarded for it.

"Bligh lives! Slap them in irons!" Captain Edwards said in greeting.

Shocked by the news of their commander's survival and the fact that their hands were being strapped behind their backs as if *they* were to blame for his attempted murder, Coleman struggled to explain.

"But Captain, we're on *your* side … *loyalists*, held against our will. We are completely innocent of the mutiny. *Tell* him, Lieutenant."

In his desperation, Coleman turned to ask help from the one man he recognised among Pandora's crew. It was the much maligned ex-Bounty midshipman Thomas Hayward who signed on to the Pandora as 3rd lieutenant with the express purpose of exacting revenge. Ironically, Coleman and Heywood were the only two men who had treated him well, but with no love lost, Hayward looked away and left them to their fate.

Edwards paused to consider it, his dark eyes set deep on his cruel face.

"It is not for me to decide," he ruled. "You'll be dealt with when we get back to England. In the meantime, throw them into The Box."

"Pandora's Box", as it was less than affectionately known, was the makeshift, 11 foot by 18 foot. timber cell built on the quarterdeck to house the mutineers. The 14 of them, who Edwards scoured the South Sea islands to find, were chained in it with irons clamped so tight that they could not lift their limbs, the efficiency of their fetters being checked on a daily basis.

"Lie still and shut up!" Pandora's able seaman, Larkin demanded, as he thumped his foot down hard on each of their chests in turn and yanked their cuffs over their hands, in the rough process, ripping chunks of flesh from wrists already raw to the bone.

"Just deserts ... just deserts," Edwards replied when the prisoners begged for mercy.

Far from shrinking from the brutality of their torture, he regretted only that his crusade stopped short of finding and inflicting the same on the main culprit, Fletcher Christian.

"He's dead!" mutineer Henry Hillbrandt suddenly volunteered, as Christian had instructed him to do.

The bulletin came out of the blue and Edwards swung round on him, fit to kill.

"Why didn't you tell me this before?"

Because it's a lie to get you off his scent, Hillbrandt thought before he said instead: "You didn't ask."

For this facetious piece of game play, his rations were cut in half.

Hillbrandt shrugged off this further deprivation as being of little account when he was already starving and sweating with the rest of the mutineers inside the wooden hell-hole. There, half dead from thirst and knee-deep in each other's excrement, they were exposed to every extreme of nature: the searing heat, torrential rain and the host of rats that came to feast on their shit and sun-blistered flesh.

So how, Hillbrandt thought, *could it possibly get worse?*

To dare the devil was asking for trouble and, in this case, resulted in a tempest of demonic fury that smashed their ship, en route to the Torres Strait, onto the outer Great Barrier Reef, leaving them only a few frantic minutes to swim for their lives.

"We can't just leave them in that box to drown," bosun's mate William Moulter screamed through the storm to his captain.

But intent on making his own escape, Edwards appeared unperturbed as he climbed into a lifeboat.

"One way or another they're going to die. What does it matter if it's here or hanged back home?" he replied as he looked back to see the Pandora list heavily to the left. Already the quarterdeck was half submerged, as were the men still shackled, hand and foot, inside the box.

At the sound of their blood curdling screams, it was Moulter who risked his life to help. Leaping from the safety of his lifeboat back on board, he ran to save them; unchaining nine before he was dragged underwater wrestling with key and lock to free his last. By then, his breath had run out and there was nothing he could do for the other four who remained manacled to the deck. They went down with the ship, their eyes and mouths gaping open in terror as they clawed the water for his help.

Thirty-one of Pandora's crew went down with them. The remaining 89 of the ship's company, along with the 10 prisoners who managed to get to the lifeboats, assembled on a small cay and after two nights spent on the sandy island, sailed for Timor in four open boats. They survived an arduous voyage across the Arafura Sea and arrived safely in Coupang, but on their way back to England on the next available frigate, 16 more of them died from disease contracted in Batavia. Only 78 of Pandora's 134 complement returned home.

Yet in Edwards' mind, the only tragedy was that he failed to round off his mission by hunting down Christian and the Bounty. When back in England, he apologised for as much, happy at least to know that the punishment for those he *did* bring back was swift and savage.

"Guilty! Death by hanging!" was the sentence handed down to able seamen Burkitt, Millward and Ellison, who were executed on the HMS Brunswick in October 1792.

The trial began before Bligh was even back from his breadfruit expedition, because Admiralty ruled it more humane to go ahead without him. The alleged mutineers, it was believed, had already suffered the enormous ordeal of the Pandora wreck and the deplorable hardships of making their way home. Now that they had reached friendly shores and their necks were on the line, it seemed unreasonable to make them wait.

For Peter Heywood who was wealthy enough to secure competent counsel, the verdict was less severe: *Guilty,* but given the King's pardon by right of his family connections.

When he was initially condemned to death, his uncle, Commodore Pasley, secured the services of his friend, Judge Aaron Graham, who had extensive naval court-martial experience.

Heywood's main stumbling block was the damning testimony of fellow midshipmen John Hallett and Thomas Hayward. Due to their jealousy of his close ties with Christian, it weighed heavily against him. Fortunately, the integrity of his own evidence and his determination not to speak ill of either Christian or Bligh made a very favourable impression on the judges.

The instant the court martial was over Admiral Lord Hood pulled him aside.

"Mr Heywood, I would like to offer you a berth on board my flagship Victory."

"No!" Commodore Pasley answered in his nephew's stead. "I want Peter on board my own ship Bellerophon."

Despite his link with Christian and perhaps *because* of his stoic support of same, Heywood was to be sought after throughout his distinguished naval career. Nothing in his past was to work against him and after rising honourably through the ranks, he was to die at 58, just two days before his promotion to admiral.

Acquittal was the finding for the rest: Morrison, Norman, Simpson, Coleman, McIntosh and Muspratt. And the verdict was the same for fiddler Michael Byrne, who miraculously saw his way clear of his blindness and being shackled in Pandora's Box, to not only survive the mutiny and his stint in Tahiti, but the sinking of his prison ship and the long trek home. He had good reason to be grateful to God.

As did Bligh, for justice had been done and come down in his favour. Christian was tried and found guilty *in absentia* and all would have been right with the world, but for the bloody-minded interference of Christian's older brother Edward.

For the second time, the renowned lawyer had been forced to suffer a slur on his family name and endured a humiliating few months believing his brother's exploits had taken it beyond redemption. But then he received an intriguing letter from Peter Heywood:

Sir,

I fear you may be inclined to judge too harshly of your unfortunate brother. As one who knew him to be of a most worthy disposition and character, I feel it is my duty to undeceive you as to the false reports of slander and base suspicion in regard to his behavior on the Bounty. Christian was not a vile wretch, void of all gratitude, but merely a victim of circumstance, ruined only by the misfortune of serving under Bligh, who knew and envied the fact that he was equipped with every virtue and beloved by all.

I am Sir, with esteem, your most obedient, humble servant.
P. HEYWOOD

Though he refused to belittle Bligh at the trial, Heywood still harboured a personal resentment over his often irrational behavior on the Bounty, but more so, his unwarranted treatment of Christian. Unable to fathom the depth of Bligh's psyche or his reasons for turning on a friend, it never occurred to Heywood that it had anything to do with him.

Heywood's naive prejudice was hot enough to rekindle Edward Christian's pride, which was a powerful weapon now that he was a man with a host of legal credentials and the backing of high society. Using both, he struck out to ruin Bligh with a burning dedication to set the record straight.

He had a way with words and after privately interviewing the men from the Bounty, he selected the best of them to put in print and distribute throughout England. His pamphlet titled: *An Appendix to the Trial*, put a whole new slant on the case.

> *We all admired and obeyed Mr. Christian without him once having to utter a harsh word. Every one of us would work up to our armpits in blood to serve him and would gladly lay down our lives if he asked.* Joseph Coleman was quoted as saying.

As was Muspratt:
> *Mr. Christian was sorrowful and dejected after the mutiny; so hugely altered in mood and looks that it seemed he would not survive the dreadful catastrophe. Although he kept up discipline on the ship, he was generally below with head in hands and told me that he would readily sacrifice his life if the persons in the launch were all safe on the Bounty again.*

After several pages of the like, Edward Christian concluded:

Public justice can allow no vindication of any species of mutiny, yet reason and humanity must distinguish between the sudden, unpremeditated act of desperation and the foul, deliberate contempt of every religious duty and honourable sentiment when they judge a young man, who if he had served on board any other ship under any other captain, might still have been an honour to his country and a glory and comfort to his friends.

This blatant absolution of his brother's name at the expense of Bligh's caused a stir in British society. Bligh did not mind so much about its predictable impact on gossip mongers who fed on the like, but he cared very much indeed when Admiralty embraced the argument; doing so, with such enthusiasm, that its First Lord, the Earl of Chatham, declined to formally receive him at his triumphant return on the Providence. Instead, all praise for the mission's success was lavished on his second-in-command, Lieutenant Nathaniel Portlock.

Portlock was a good man and Bligh begrudged him nothing, but he was hurt to the quick by the shabby way *he* was treated. Immediately, he wrote a formal document of rebuttal:

One of the hardest cases that can befall a man is to be reduced to the necessity of defending his character by his own assertions only.

He was greatly offended by the unfair criticism and felt himself to be all alone. It was a state of self-pity which was soon remedied by a letter sent to the editor of *The Times*:

The shafts of envy are ever leveled against conspicuous merit. Captain Bligh's general conduct during his last expedition, which was crowned with the most ample success, his affability to his officers and humane attention to his men, gained him their high esteem and admiration and must eventually dissipate any unfavourable opinion hastily adopted in his absence. I trust that this imbecile and highly illiberal attack made by the brother of the Arch-mutineer will be received by the world with that indignation and contempt it so justly deserves.

Dr Edward Harwood,
Surgeon to His Majesty's ship *Providence*.

Admiralty was suitably contrite, having condemned one of its finest on hearsay. It was not ashamed enough, however, to take Bligh off half-pay or put him immediately back into service. Despite the fact that England and France were at war and its country was in need of every seaman available, he was left land-bound, a captain without a ship.

SEVENTEEN

Officially, Fletcher Christian was guilty, presumed dead.

In reality, he was sitting on Pitcairn beach with his wife and twin babes at his side and their two-year-old toddler playing at the water's edge.

"You not happy," Maimiti said, as she had done many times before.

Since leaving Tahiti, he had not been himself, with his mood remote and eyes ever fixed on the horizon.

"You want to go home?" she asked, her heart aching with the knowledge that he dreamed of nothing else.

Christian stood up, brushed the sand from his legs and put a swift end to the subject.

"What point is there in dwelling on the impossible? There's nothing left for me there," he said, as he scooped up his small dark-haired son and walked back to his hut.

Closing its thatched door, he leant heavily against it and fought back tears. His past was a travesty, his present barely tolerable and his future was lost to him forever. The instant he set foot on Pitcairn he knew he had made a terrible mistake. The security of its warm sand and sweet scent of foreign flowers belied the desolation it would inflict and every day he wished he had the guts to go home to face the hangman's noose.

"Speak for yourself," Quintal threw back when Christian suggested as much to his fellow mutineers.

It was an option they rejected out of hand, and fearful of any second thoughts on the matter, Quintal decided to remove all temptation: firing up a torch of bamboo and hot tar, he hurled it onto Bounty's deck.

"What in the hell are you doing?" Christian screamed out as two of the mutineers restrained him and the others followed Quintal's example.

The fire took hold in seconds, devouring the deck and reducing the mast to cinders, while white-hot fingers of flame licked up the rigging and set the sails ablaze.

"They'll never find us now," Quintal said proudly with his arms akimbo and eyes all the madder as they reflected the inferno.

Its crackling hissed to a smoldering stop as the Bounty sank into the sea. With it went all the supplies they needed and the last semblance of Christian's hope. Gone was his only link with civilisation and his last chance of ever rejoining it.

But then what would be the point in that? he asked

himself, when there would be no forgiveness for a man guilty of mutiny and murder.

Existing at the edge of the world meant that there was no news of it. He had no idea that Bligh had survived. In fact, he was sure he was dead, for his spirit seemed always to haunt him. Far from being afraid, Christian welcomed its company; many times wondering whether Bligh's wandering soul was as lonely as his. Come heaven or hell, he prayed only that his own eternal punishment would be sooner than later so that he and Bligh could meet again and finally share the blame for what went wrong.

EIGHTEEN

Nature abhors a vacuum and Bligh, having rid himself of one nemesis in Christian, now had room for another.

John Macarthur was on his way into Bligh's life via the HMS Neptune, which was part of the Second Fleet bound for Sydney Cove. Its six ships, carrying new settlers, convicts and supplies, set out from England at much the same time Christian left Tahiti for Pitcairn Island, both with the intention of exploring new territory and making it their home.

As a young lieutenant in the New South Wales Corps, Macarthur was a man on the move who had a lot in common with Christian. Both were charismatic and handsome; born leaders on a collision course with Bligh. But Christian, with his all-encompassing charm was a victim of fate, whereas Macarthur was a master of manipulating it. He was an exceptional man, who had to make his own way in the world and did so with cold-blooded brilliance and the bare minimum of scruples.

If Bligh thought he had his hands full with Christian, he was to meet his match in Macarthur, who had a temper, tenacity and a slight streak of madness that rivalled Bligh's own; neither of them knowing how or when to give up and both happy to go to their graves to keep their argument alive.

To start, 24-year-old Macarthur, along with his lovely wife Elizabeth and baby son Edward, were booked on the convict transport Lady Juliana to travel to New South Wales, but its captain, Tom Edgar, refused to let him board.

"I will not have that man on my ship! The upstart *enjoys* making enemies," he complained, having sustained a flesh wound in a duel to which the corps lieutenant challenged him over an issue of pride.

Macarthur had an excess of it and resplendent in his army uniform, saw red when the captain called him "Jack Bodice". It was a slap in the face, alluding to his prior profession as a mercer. Not that Macarthur was ashamed of his family's trade, but it wasn't the picture he wanted painted of himself. The whole point of him sailing to the other side of the world was to leave his less-than-dashing past behind to become a man of consequence.

"Pistols at 10 paces!" he demanded to counter the captain's insult.

The result was a wound to the captain's leg, and at the sudden, painful twinge of it, Edgar continued: "If he wants to travel with our Second Fleet, he can do so on the Scarborough."

Macarthur did, but within only two weeks of the trans-global voyage, he made himself so obnoxious that its commander *heaved to*, mid-ocean, to transfer him to ship number three: HMS Neptune.

"I apologise for this inconvenience," Scarborough's captain, John Marshall, said as he helped Macarthur's wife and ailing infant son into the rowboat."

It gave him no pleasure to treat such a fine woman in this way, but he could tolerate her husband no longer.

"You are doing what you must," she replied with a courtesy clipped only because of her chronic seasickness and mourning for her recently still-born daughter.

To be dragged, vomiting, from her bed and transferred to another ship through rough water was a nightmare, but she refused to make a scene. *That,* she left up to her husband who was accomplished at it. It was not the first time that his temper had put them in an awkward situation and she was sure it would not be the last. She had married him, however, for better or worse. This was *the worse,* but she was so very proud of what, in him, was *the better.*

On this occasion, it was the fact that he was battling on moral grounds, bombarding Captain Marshall with complaints about the appalling quarters he and his wife were given and the draconian conditions inflicted on the convicts shackled below deck. The stench of their suffering was intolerable and the frequency of their deaths, alarming.

"Those people are dying down there while you hoard their food for your own profit," he accused the captain.

It was true and certainly something Marshall did not want broadcast. He had to shut Macarthur up fast and did so by passing the problem to the Neptune.

Its captain, Donald Traill, was not as thin-skinned as his Scarborough counterpart. Although they shared an agenda of self interest, Traill was not ashamed of it and was even more serious about culling his convict cargo, because it equated to money in his pocket.

The more scurvy-ridden prisoners who died meant fewer mouths to feed and more food left over to sell in the South Seas; while, less bodies on board lightened the load and sped them on their way to their market. For a man without conscience, his reasoning was sound and no one dared object; no one except Macarthur.

"I'll see you hang for what you're doing when we reach Port Jackson," he threatened.

"Presuming you *get* there in one piece."

Traill's snide remark inferred otherwise and Macarthur met the challenge head on.

"I'm not scared of you," he threw back. He'd never been afraid of anything or anyone and didn't intend to start now. "If you don't want me on board, there are three other ships in the fleet that can take me."

"Not anymore! We lost sight of them in last night's storm. So you're stuck with my Neptune or nothing. And if you choose the latter, I'd be happy to personally throw you overboard."

For 10 long weeks at close quarters, they continued to do battle, many times coming close to killing each other. With nothing but the tedium of travel to intervene, they were in desperate need of a diversion and found it at the Cape of Good Hope.

"The Guardian's been wrecked," was the news that greeted them at Cape Town.

It was one of the Second Fleet's three ships that had gone astray in the storm. The other two, HMS Surprise and the Justinian made it through and continued on their way to Port Jackson, but in trying to steer clear of the treacherous Roaring Forties winds, Guardian swept too wide south of The Cape and hit an iceberg.

"All hands on deck!" its commander, Lieutenant Edward Riou, shouted through the chaos.

His ship was critically damaged and in immediate danger of sinking. Frantic attempts were made to repair her, but with the freezing sea seeping in her sides and the hold waist-high in water, Riou ordered his crew to abandon ship and row to safety.

"But aren't you coming, sir?" his master-at-arms asked.

The absence of Riou's reply said that he was going down with his ship.

But miraculously, the old girl, built sturdy to fight in the American War of Independence, stayed afloat. For an unparalleled nine weeks of backbreaking, round-the-clock work, Riou and his few remaining men managed to sail the crippled ship back to The Cape.

By then it was reduced to little more than a raft, the most commendable of those who had participated in its salvage operation being the convicts on board. Among them were men of exemplary courage and education who had fallen foul of the law for nothing more than the crime of poverty. To keep their families alive, they dared steal a slice of bread and were condemned for the term of their natural lives. Prolonging them held little appeal, but to stand by their Captain Riou, who they knew was a thoroughly decent human being, was well worth their effort.

With a battalion of the like, I could conquer the world! Riou wrote in the ships log in regard to them.

He closed its hard leather cover, determined to secure them a royal pardon as soon as they arrived in New South Wales.

In the meantime, having reached South African shores, he roared out the order:

"Run her aground! I don't want what's left of her to sink."

Guardian's iron and shingle ballast had been washed through the gaping hole in her water-logged hull and there were enormous breaches in her bow and stern. But because the lower deck held the strain, a large number of casks in the hold had floated up to keep her buoyant.

They took one last look at her in disbelief and then dragged themselves up the beach, soaked to the skin, with their clothes in rags.

"Well that was a pleasant little sea voyage," Second Lieutenant Michael Johnson quipped as he and Riou turned to salute the remnants of their sea-weary ship.

"God bless her wooden walls," Riou said. "How she held together and got us safely here I'll never know."

He put it down to a miracle, one which was confirmed the very next day when a hurricane struck the coast and shattered the beach-bound ship to pieces.

– oOo –

Two hundred and fifty-eight dead was the body count given to Governor Arthur Phillip when the other five ships of the Second Fleet docked at Sydney Cove.

"But this is an outrage!" he exclaimed when confronted with the statistics and the sickening sight of the convicts' condition.

Near naked, they lay locked in their chains below deck, half of them emaciated and the other half dead. Those who survived scurvy and the months of unremitting brutality were unable to speak or even get to their feet. Their bodies were caked in their own excrement, infested with lice and slashed with welts of blood and puss from the savage cat-o-nine-tail floggings they had endured.

Incensed, Phillip swung round on Traill.

"I shall see you suffer for this atrocity," he vowed.

It was a promise he could not keep, for although Traill was later to be tried at the Old Bailey for murder, his case was to last only three short hours before the jury set him free, none of the 12 wanting to trouble the judge to sum up the evidence.

But that shabby outcome was beyond Phillip's control and for now his tone changed when he welcomed Elizabeth Macarthur. She was the first woman of quality to set foot on the new colony's soil and he was relieved at the prospect of her charming company. It was an open admiration, which along with his many offers of hospitality to come, was Macarthur's ticket to Sydney's society. From there, it was only a short climb to the top of it.

Right now, standing at the dock, he cast a shrewd eye over the potential which lay before him. Here, in Sydney Cove, all was raw and ripe for the taking, the optimistic smell of fresh timber being hammered into homes and the sound of masons chiselling sandstone into building blocks reeked of prosperity for any man with the guts to take it.

Macarthur grabbed it with both hands. By 1793, through astute investment and the cutting of a few legal corners, he accumulated enough wealth and grants of land to build an estate 12 miles inland from the harbour. Sitting on a hill to celebrate his elevated status in the colony, his brick and stone homestead overlooked the rest of its people, affording panoramic views of Parramatta River, the region's lifeblood.

He called the property Elizabeth Farm as a compliment to his wife. She, having to turn a blind eye to the fact that its foundations had to be hacked from the hard earth by the same convicts whose cause he so nobly championed at sea.

NINETEEN

"They're dead!" the doctor said.

Bligh was devastated and Betsy, still bleeding profusely from prolonged childbirth, was beside herself with grief. Having provided her husband with a brood of daughters, she thought it a gift from God when she delivered twin sons and could not comprehend His cruelty in immediately ripping them away.

It was the latest in the long list of events blighting his life. Bligh had been land-bound for 18 months, but twiddling his thumbs in excruciating boredom was the least of his worries. Since the Bounty trial and the devastating effect of Edward Christian's smear campaign, he and his family had faced one insult after the other. Their friends had dropped them and although Admiralty was shamed out of its snub of him, it still believed that the stigma attached to his name prohibited it putting him back into service until the air cleared of controversy.

That day came on April 16, 1795.

"Saints be praised!" Bligh said when Admiralty's dispatch finally arrived and he went to show Betsy. "I've been given a ship at last. Not a particularly interesting one, but I'll take anything I can get."

Since the French Revolutionary War began, there had been a series of land and sea skirmishes, the latest of which saw the French invade Holland and expel its British ally.

We don't like being pushed around, England decreed.

And when Holland then broke what had always been a flimsy alliance, Britain started seizing its ships and colonies and ordered the commander of its own North Sea fleet, Admiral Adam Duncan, to blockade all Dutch ships anchored at the Frisian island of Texel.

It was a time of crisis which, at last, gave Admiralty a good reason to delegate command of the 24-gun armed transport Calcutta to Bligh as part of Duncan's convoy.

That band of British battleships dug in for the duration, just daring any Dutch vessel to make a move.

None of them did, which made it a very boring two-and-a-half-year business, its tedium relieved only by the regular gales that blew their British ships off their moorings and the time they killed by doggedly beating their way back to them.

Ho, hum … Bligh wrote in a letter to Betsy.
Almost makes one hanker to be back on the Bounty.

He did not mean it, of course and was all forgiving of Admiralty when it transferred his command to the HMS Director, a 64-gun, 500-man ship of the line. At the sight of the flag flying from its majestic mast, Bligh saw his door to glory fling wide open. Nothing was going to stop him now.

Nothing, that was, except his reputation.

"It's that Bounty bastard," he overheard one of the crew mumble when he first set foot on board.

He stopped dead in his tracks. It was first time he heard his epithet and it took him aback. So far back to his notorious past that he thought he was imagining it when the very familiar rumblings of insubordination began again on board the Director. Having kept a strict check on his temper and gone out of his way to accommodate his crew, he was perplexed.

"I don't understand why such a happy ship suddenly isn't," he confided to his 2nd lieutenant, John Addlington

"Surely sir," he replied, "you of *all* people should recognise the symptoms. It's the whiff of rebellion in the air."

Bligh turned on him, furious at the inference.

"Oh not against *you,* sir … I do beg your pardon," Addlington quickly recanted. "It's all these new ideas of equality blowing in from the French and American revolutions. Nothing any longer seems sacred, none of us are safe."

For England, this new idea of "liberty for all", manifested at The Spithead where Bligh's North Sea fleet was stationed.

> *I can't believe it's happening again,* he wrote to his wife. *That through no fault of my own, I am involved in another mutiny!*

Slightly sympathetic with his plight, his crew offered him a brusque apology.

"It's a point of principle, sir, that's got nothing to do with you. We blame the government from whom we're demanding better pay, along with the abolition of brutality and involuntary service. We involve you with regret, but it's our only chance of getting what should be our right."

For two weeks the mutiny proceeded in this civilised way with the sailors on strike and their ships at a standstill. However, true to their word and trusting Admiralty's promise that it would seriously consider their case, the crews continued to carry out their basic duties, with the assurance that they would take action if enemy ships were sighted.

But with Admiralty fretting over the French taking advantage of the situation, it was a dangerous gamble. To even the odds, Admiral Lord Howe finally intervened and put an end to the stalemate by granting a few of the mutineers' terms and negotiating their royal pardon. It meant compromise on both sides, but at least the mutiny was over and some maritime abuses amended.

Now free to distance himself from the trouble zone, Bligh sailed to the navy's anchorage at The Nore – a sandbank at the mouth of the Thames Estuary. There, he was seeking a haven, but instead found himself embroiled in a mutiny much worse, which upped his tally to three.

"Will I *ever* get this monkey off my back," he complained to Addlington.

"Not for the time being, it appears," his lieutenant replied, looking out the porthole at the red flag of rebellion being raised on the HMS Sandwich moored close by.

On board the 90-gunner, ex-officer Richard Parker

had been dubbed "President of the Floating Republic". Well educated and ever outspoken on behalf of the oppressed, he was a gentleman and persuasive orator, clever enough to match words with the best of them. He was using his skill to campaign for improved conditions for the lower naval ranks. His agenda was to put an end to press gangs, unequal pay and poor quality rations, while demanding the removal – permanently from service – of all officers who derived pleasure from inflicting excessive punishments on their crews.

In his zeal to put right what was wrong, he was taking his Nore Rebellion to a new level by blockading the Thames. It was a drastic move, which at this critical time for his country deprived it of supplies and the upper hand in the Napoleonic War.

"You go too far," warned Edward Riou, who after his heroic odyssey on the wrecked Guardian was now captain of the HMS Bulldog.

Although sympathetic to the crusader's cause, Riou was more concerned about Britain's welfare and the catastrophic impact Parker's tactics would have on it.

But at this point, Parker was beyond backing down and could not afford to have anyone contradict him.

"That's a coward's opinion and I challenge you, *coward*, to a duel!"

It was laughable to accuse Riou of as much when he was renowned for his courage and was held in the highest esteem by both sides. He was also a decent enough man to realise that Parker was well-intentioned, but speaking in the heat of the moment. For the sake of all, Riou thought it better to risk his own reputation by backing graciously away from the dare.

"Yours is a noble cause, Parker. Don't ruin it."

Bligh wanted no part in the whole affair, but that decision was taken out of his hands. All officers who were deemed unpopular or guilty of cruelty were sent ashore by the mutineers, and whereas Bligh was not among them at first, his refusal to give the rebels access to his ship's small arms left them no option but to send him, with the rest, to the banks of the Thames.

As part of his reluctant escort there, ship's gunner Ian Nesbitt stood nervously before him.

"Could I ask you, sir," he said with cap in hand, "that you present our list of demands to your superiors?"

Bligh had every right to refuse, but thought better of it. He knew his country's cause was greater, but he did not want to deny his men his support. Quickly, he scanned the written demands and seeing them as succinct and fair, nodded his consent.

Admiralty was not as broadminded, but was impressed with Bligh's performance. Not only had he kept his crew's respect, but also that of Admiralty. Far from being a man who inspired insurrection, it was beginning to think very highly of his opinion and pegged him as the perfect intermediary.

"We want you to go back to Yarmouth to rally our ships there," they ordered.

And flattered, Bligh complied.

"We need your help with the situation at The Nore," he said to all the ships' captains there, but their ambivalent attitude had him return empty-handed.

"It would be unwise, I think, to expect sailors in one British fleet to go against another," was his advice to Admiralty.

It accepted Bligh's assessment, which proved correct when three ships from Yarmouth *did* sail to The Nore, but threw in their lot with the rebels.

Here, Admiralty drew the line:

"We refuse all your demands and will negotiate no further," it stated with the same unbending British determination that had driven back centuries of foreign invaders.

The mutiny collapsed in the face of the ultimatum. Its leaders were offered up for court martial and it was generally felt that their punishment was lenient, considering the danger they imposed on the nation.

Only Parker and 35 of his fellow ringleaders were hanged from a yardarm. They went to their deaths failing to achieve their full objective, but having broken the back of Britain's inhuman system.

Much was made of their execution day. With macabre, fair-like excitement, flags flew from every ship. They were anchored side by side and bow to stern, some close to sinking from the weight of the sightseers who were invited to share the show.

For Bligh, it was no spectator sport. He was in no mood to celebrate a brave man's death. At Admiralty's command, he ordered his crew into line to watch the proceedings, while he turned his back on them.

Standing before the hangman's noose on the deck of HMS Sandwich, Parker asked the chaplain for a glass of water. He lifted it and said:

I drink first for the salvation of my soul and next for the forgiveness of all my enemies.

Shaking hands with the ship's commander, he walked alone to the platform specially built on the cat-head to afford the thousands of onlookers a better view of his suffering.

"May I have a moment to collect myself?" he asked.

He knelt, prayed and then stood to say: "I am ready."

The rope was placed around his neck, but before the cannon could be fired to signal his lynching, he leapt from the cat-head to bring a swift end to proceedings. He was dead before his audience got the chance to relish them, his neck snapped clean and the rope swinging wide with his body rotating at the end of it. The sound of its taut creaking echoed through the awestruck silence and a disappointed crowd turned away.

"Resume duties," Bligh ordered, his voice dulled with depression.

And in the same frame of mind, his crew broke ranks to obey, one of them pausing to say: "I would like to thank you, sir, for the fair way that you handled this difficult situation. We are all in your debt."

Still mourning Parker's death, Bligh could not dredge up a smile, but was immensely proud of this compliment from his crew.

"I wonder what Fletcher Christian would think of me now?" was his first thought.

And his second:

"Why in the hell should it still matter?"

TWENTY

All that mattered to Christian was to get out alive. When the killing spree on Pitcairn Island began, he was going about his morning duties and taken by surprise.

His assailant leapt on him from behind and smashing a rock down hard on his head, knocked him out cold. He was left for dead on the banks of the lagoon, just one of the mutineers to be murdered on this bloodthirsty day of native reprisal.

As the leader of their small community, Christian had done his level best to keep the peace, striving for moderation in all things.

"Our Tahitian friends must have equal say in all affairs," he had insisted.

It was a fair system which worked well until one mutineer's wife died and he demanded another.

"I'll take that one," armourer's mate John Williams said, pointing to the bare-breasted consort of one of the natives.

Given that the Tahitians were always so obliging in sharing their females' favours, he thought nothing of it; least of all, that his cavalier taking of another man's wife would trigger a massacre.

It did, and so it was only fitting that he was the first to be hacked to pieces when the natives went on their blood-crazed rampage. When they found out how satisfying it was to kill a white man, they went on to murder more, inflicting their crude weapons on able seamen Martin and Mills and botanist's assistant William Brown.

The three men saw their assassins coming, but in their stark terror, they could not flee fast enough through the sand to escape. The blunt base of the natives' stone axes hammered holes in their skulls; while their sharp, reverse edge severed their heads.

An all-out war erupted and within a few hours almost all the men on the island were dead. Running short of Englishmen to kill, the Tahitians then turned on each other, as the mutineers' grieving widows picked up their dead husbands' muskets and fired them point blank at their own kind.

"I'm getting the hell out of here!" Quintal said as he headed for the safety of the hills.

He was followed by William McCoy, both staying hidden until the carnage was over and it seemed safe to return to the village to see who had survived. When Quintal emerged unscathed from the jungle, his consort rushed at him with bloodied club in hand.

"Why you not dead?" she screamed, having suffered for so long at his brutal hand.

She could not hear his answer because she had no ears. He had bitten them off in a drunken rage two years before when she failed to catch a fish for his supper. Normally he would have slapped her into submission for daring to talk at all, but under the present circumstances of wholesale slaughter and the fact that he was one of only four mutineers left alive, he thought he'd better hold his tongue and forgo the use of fist and teeth.

"Get out of my way!" he snarled instead, shoving her aside and heading with McCoy back to their stash of *ti-root*, which they had learnt to distill into toxic liquor.

With the massacre now over, it was their best means of healing wounds and dispelling fear. So in the weeks that followed, they drank it in copious quantities. Its poison drove them madder by the day, until on one of them McCoy tied a rock around his neck and delirious, hurled himself off a precipice. And on another, when Quintal's threat to kill everyone left on the island had them beat *him* to death instead.

But no one had seen or heard anything of Christian since Massacre Day.

"He dead," Maimiti assured all those who asked, covering the ears of their children as she spoke.

It was a lie, but either way she knew she would never see him again.

That was the immediate decision she made when she found him lying unconscious at the lagoon. Blood was flowing from his forehead and assuming him dead, she ran screaming to his side. When he groaned and rolled over, she looked urgently around for help, but with her fellow Tahitians at the peak of their killing frenzy, there was none to be had and no point in trying to nurse him back to health. If she loved him, she had to let him go.

The only way to do it was to get him into the old canoe resting on its side in the sand. It was barely seaworthy, but was his only chance of escape. Painstakingly, she dragged him there and in one moment of moaning consciousness, he lifted and dropped himself into it.

"Water," he gasped before passing out again.

She ran back to their hut to grab coconuts, water and yams and threw them into the boat. Then, with the astounding strength that only such an emergency could muster, she pushed the canoe out into the lagoon, swimming with it as far as could before she kissed its Koa-wood stern and set him adrift at sea.

It was 15 days before he was picked up.

"Boat ahoy!" came the call from the crow's nest of the American Trader en route to Port Jackson.

Its timing was perfect considering that Christian's supplies had run out three days before. He was on the brink of death, lying dehydrated under the blazing tropical sun, his skin scorched and mouth swollen from thirst. But at the sublime sound of another man's voice, he made the supreme effort to raise his head and focus his salt-encrusted eyes on the ship coming towards him at full sail. Its name was written bold on its prow: *Hope,* which gave him, at last, just that.

He waved it down with the slow sweep of his arm and watched with unmitigated relief as it heaved to alongside.

"Can you tell me your name, sir?" its captain, Alec Page asked in his thick American drawl.

The reply came from a man too sick to think straight: "Acting Lieutenant Fletcher Christian of the Bounty."

Through his parched lips, his words were little more

than a whisper, but were loud enough for the captain to register surprise and then lean forward with avid interest.

"What's that you say?"

Suddenly more coherent, Christian realised his mistake and the four-year lapse which facilitated the news of his ship's infamy to spread worldwide. He said no more and to avoid interrogation, slumped back on his stretcher in a dead faint.

He and his head wound slowly healed under the care of Hope's crew, He wanted to thank them for their help, but knew it was imperative to stay silent for the three weeks it took to reach Norfolk Island.

"Here's where you get off," the captain told him.

Having respected his castaway's privacy, he was keen now to hand over responsibility for him to the commandant of the Island's convict settlement.

"I don't know who he is. He refuses to speak," Page reported to English Lieutenant-Governor Philip Gidley-King. "Given where we picked him up and the state he was in, we guessed he'd escaped from here."

"He's not one of ours," Gidley-King replied, knowing that in his fledging penal colony, all settlers and prisoners were present and accounted for.

He walked over to take a closer look at Christian, his keen eye searching for any clue as to his identity. The clothes Page had provided him gave nothing away, but the tattoos on his arm and chest were consistent with the sort sported by those in the English navy.

"My name is Francis Chapman. I'm not a convict," Christian suddenly volunteered, his well-spoken English putting an end to conjecture.

"Of what ship?" Gidley-King asked.

"That, I prefer not to say, but will tell you that it sank."

The more he said, the more of a mystery he became and the Governor pressed for clarification.

"I can only presume then, sir, that you are a deserter, for a sole survivor would mourn the loss of his ship and take pride in its memory."

To this he received no reply and so he continued:

"A deserter, sir, is the worst of criminals and warrants a sentence served here. At least until information is provided to the contrary."

Page eyed Christian shrewdly, not in the least convinced by his abrupt account of himself. He was sure that the name he'd given to the Governor was false and that the one he rambled off at his rescue was the truth. However, having grown to like the man, he didn't want to expose him to the hangman's noose and the vilification of the world.

"Keep up your charade if you must, Mr Christian," he said quietly in farewell. "Your secret is safe with me."

TWENTY-ONE

It was closing in on the end of the French Revolutionary Wars and Napoleon Bonaparte was marching from triumph to triumph across Europe. His enemies feared his military genius and his troops were so enamoured of his willingness to share their swordplay and suffering, that they referred to him fondly as their Little Corporal, despite the fact that he was their General and Commander of the Interior.

"The time is ripe to invade Britain," the French agreed.

But Bonaparte had second thoughts on the strategy.

"Not by sea!" he insisted. "Our navy is still not strong enough to compete with theirs. Better that we do it through Egypt and undermine England's access to its trade interests in India."

He had a head for lateral thinking and a dream to erode the English Empire from inside by destabilising its economic foundations. Already those foundations were precarious, having been hit hard at the Battle of Santa Cruz.

There, in the Canary Islands, British Rear-Admiral Horatio Nelson had not only lost the fight, but the lives of nearly 400 of his men, along with his own right arm.

"You'll have to have it amputated," his doctor had told him, which all seemed a little one-sided when he had already forfeited the sight in his right eye during the Corsican campaign. Yet the pain of losing both was nowhere near as sore as his defeat in war.

"For the rest of my life, this stump of flesh will remind me of it." he said with contempt. "I tell you now … I will never lose another."

It was in this frame of mind that he set out to engage Napoleon's fleet at the Battle of the Nile and Bligh only wished he could go with him. As it was, he, his ship Director and the entire North Sea Fleet were stationed far from the action, having just fought the Battle of Camperdown off the North Holland coast. It was their most significant clash with the Dutch. The result: a resounding British victory and Bligh being hailed a hero.

"*Shorten sail!*" he ordered en route to the encounter.

A strong, north-easterly wind had picked up and pushed his Director too far ahead of its escorts. The dissipating fog was depriving the Dutch ships of cover and Bligh could see their shadowed outline emerge from the mist. His advance towards them from his fleet's rear ranks, however, was coming close to outdistancing its leaders.

A flurry of signals from Admiral Duncan's flagship Venerable were fluttering up and down, half of them indecipherable in the haze and the rapidity of those visible, throwing the crews into confusion.

But with sudden clarity Bligh was thrust into the fray. First came the thunder of distant guns and next two spurting jets of water off Director's bow. The enemy had opened fire and targeted his ship. With no time left to make sense of Venerable's mixed signals, Bligh took the battle initiative and headed for the narrow gap between the 64-gun Dutch Haarlem and Alkmaar. When coming abreast of the latter's stern, he braced himself for impact and bellowed the order: *"Fire!"*

Flames ripped down the length of Director's sides as its guns spewed round-shot and grape. Haarlem was taken off guard and could reply with only a ragged broadside from its starboard batteries. Bligh's first blow was a success, but it was countered by close calamity. The speed of his aggressive action had him near rear-end his ally HMS Monarch as it traded shots with the Jupiter.

"Larboard helm. Let her fall away!" he roared urgently through the chaos of cannon fire and belched gunpowder fumes.

His quick thinking saved them from collision. There was a sickening thump and splintering of timbers as Director grazed Monarch's port side, but minimum damage was sustained.

Yet bedlam still reigned and with all battle formation lost, Bligh climbed the mizzen shrouds to see for himself what was going on. He was met with an explosive red cloud of chaos.

The only thing making itself clear through the smoke was that England's windward division was seeing the worst of the action. Dutch Admiral de Vries' flagship Vrigheid was pounding Venerable into submission. Filled with a volcanic surge of vengeance at the sight, Bligh made the rash decision to abandon his unwieldy battle in the rear and speed towards its rescue.

En route, he exchanged sporadic shots with the Leyden and Brutus, but did not linger to engage them because his eyes were set on the main prize: the 74-gun Vrigheid.

"I'll get that Dutch bastard," he vowed and when 20 yards from it, opened fire.

It was a brief moment of victory for Bligh's much smaller ship, but although the Vrigheid was weary from action against Venerable, Ardent and Powerful, it was still in fine fighting form. Slowly, like a bull goaded to the charge, it turned its impressive guns on Director.

Heaving to the continuous recoil of her own cannon, Director was undeterred. Its iron hail crashed into Vrigheid's bows, destroying her decks and rigging, as thuds below and the clang of iron striking iron told Bligh that his ship was wounded in return.

But then came his master shot that hit the Dutch foremast. Seconds after registering the blow, it creaked forward, teetered, and then collapsed in a wild web of rigging, shrouds and spars. Down came the main and mizenmasts, followed by their flag in tattered defeat.

"Cease fire!" Bligh called through the chorus of his crew's hat-waving and cheers.

Like them, it was impossible to hide his elation. Not only had he successfully engaged three enemy vessels, but he had just captured the Dutch flagship and its commander-in-chief, Vice-Admiral Jan de Winter.

It is with the greatest pleasure and pride, Admiral Duncan wrote in his report to Admiralty, *that I make known the gallant behaviour of my captains and their crews.*

Bligh stood out among them and Duncan personally commended him for his valour, before formally having to accuse Captain John Williamson of the opposite.

"Are you going to testify against him?" Captain Mitchell of the Isis asked Bligh.

"I've be summoned to do so," he replied.

"Williamson will suffer twice over at your account, no doubt. It won't be the first time you called him a coward."

Bligh jarred at this reference to Cook's last expedition. Yes, he accused Williamson of the same back then, but he had since done a lot of living. He'd learned what it was to be afraid and had a keener understanding of human frailty. Knowing that he had a few weaknesses of his own, he was no longer so eager to call another man out on them.

It was for this reason that he kept his answers in court short and noncommittal.

"To your knowledge, Captain Bligh," the naval prosecutor asked, "did Captain Williamson actively hold his ship back from battle and refrain from going to the aid of His Majesty's ships, as was his duty?"

It was true, as was the fact that Williamson had run away and left Cook's body to be mutilated on Tahiti's beach. Bligh always craved retribution for that, but when he cast his eye in Williamson's direction, he saw a man standing stiff with tension and loathing for himself. It was clear he had been punished enough.

"I am quite unable to say where and what Captain Williamson's Agincourt was doing during the battle," Bligh replied. "I was pre-occupied elsewhere."

"You let the coward off the hook," Adamant's Captain William Hotham said at their victory celebrations.

"It's of no consequence," Bligh replied with a shrug. "He was condemned by others' testimony. There was no need to add my own."

Hotham raised his glass in salute.

"Careful Bligh. You run the risk of exposing yourself as a kind man."

His reputation, in fact, had increased ten-fold as a hard-shelled disciplinarian with a hot temper and sometimes soft underbelly. But right at the moment, along with the rest of the North Sea Fleet, he was simply worried about Admiral Nelson.

Bonaparte had all before him. His ships were assembled for action and the news that they were ready to invade England was chilling.

For some time, Nelson's Mediterranean Fleet had them blockaded at port, but when a gale blew his English ships from their station, the French flotilla slipped away over the horizon, leaving no clue as to their destination or which way Nelson should sail in pursuit.

The answer to the difficult question was global. The French could have just as easily fled to India as the Americas. To chase them at random around the world would expose England to attack, while to do nothing would make it a subject of ridicule. Either way, the monumental decision was Nelson's to make.

"Better his than mine," was the opinion of every captain of the North Sea Fleet. Too far away to render assistance, they could only sympathise and mentally share his anguish.

It was not clear how Nelson made up his mind, but whether guided by the North Star or a power higher in the heavens, he suddenly struck out for Egypt and found the French Fleet at Aboukir Bay. That was a miracle in itself, but his ensuing victory over it electrified Europe and marked the first reverse in France's fortunes.

For Napoleon, the bad omens were clear when, like Alexander before him, he ventured into the Great Pyramid for divine inspiration. He staggered from it, shaken and gasping for air for having trespassed on holy ground and putting himself on a plateau with the gods. His punishment was defeat and his humiliation almost worse than the appalling loss of French lives.

One of whom was French Vice-Admiral Francois-Paul Brueys of L'Orient, who having let his ship remain at anchor until it was too late, was struck in the stomach by a cannonball. He writhed in excruciating agony on deck for 15 minutes before he died.

"It was his own fault for not moving fast enough and losing me my battle," was Napoleon's disgruntled assessment.

Yet his attitude softened at the news that the same ship's captain, Louis de Casablanca, had his face blown away by flying debris, while his 12-year-old son's leg was torn off by cannon fire as he stood at his dying father's side.

That France should be forced to tolerate such stark tragedy made Napoleon more nobly remark: "If, in this disastrous event, mistakes were made, they were expiated by those men's glorious end."

There was nothing more he could say now that his troops were isolated in Egypt and his dreams of marching on India were dashed.

"They say Napoleon shot the nose off the Sphinx in rage," was the rumour doing the rounds in London.

"That's ridiculous!" Nelson said in angry defense of his enemy. "Bonaparte may be many things, but a vandal is not one of them. Why would he desecrate the very thing he's taken such care to excavate?"

Nelson's word being "gold" put an end to the gossip. And as the bells rang out in triumph throughout England, the Head of Admiralty fainted flat to the floor, overwhelmed by the enormity of the good news and his blissful release from anxiety.

TWENTY-TWO

It was little wonder that Bligh was proud to fight under Nelson's banner at the next Battle of Copenhagen. He went in command of the 56-gun Glatton, setting sail in a fleet of two columns, each ship setting its course by the one ahead; by day, following the leader's billowing, white sails and by night, guided by its bobbing stern lanterns.

Although Admiral Sir Hyde Parker was in overall command, it was the nation's hero, Vice-Admiral Nelson, who was expected to lead the main attack on the Danish-Norwegian Fleet.

It did not start well when three of Hyde Parker's ships ran aground and the Danes opened fire. The British line was in place, but with little room to manoeuvre they were coming under heavy bombardment, fighting to the thunder of two thousand guns and the constant rattle of small arms. Through the sound of dying men's screams and splintering timbers, they battled on with the English out for blood and the Danes determined to sink their own ships rather than surrender them to Nelson.

That seemed unlikely when, at midday, the conflict was still in full swing with the British seeing the worst of it. HMS Isis was close to destruction and Monarch was near crippled from the combined fire of Holsteen and Sjcelland. English ships Bellona, Russell and Agamemnon were flying signals of distress, and fearing that Nelson might fight himself into a corner and be unable to retreat, Admiral Parker issued the command:

"Fly the signal of recall and give Nelson instruction to withdraw at his discretion."

"The *hell* I will!" Nelson said on seeing it.

He'd fought too long and hard to turn back now, but it was treason to disobey an order.

Perhaps excusable, though, he reasoned, *if one were unaware of it.*

He turned to say as much to his flag captain.

"You know, Foley, I only have one eye. I have the right to be blind sometimes."

He lifted his telescope to that blind eye and with his mouth twisted in concentration, tried to focus through it.

"In all honesty," he followed through, "I *see* no signal. I'll have to fly my own."

His was a command to do the exact opposite: to hold their ground and continue at "close action".

His flag signal was hoisted to prime position on his flagship Elephant's masthead, causing a moment of total confusion for the other English captains. None of them knew which order to follow or which way to turn.

Of Nelson's men, it was only ex-Guardian's Edward

Riou, now captain of the Amazon, who could not see Nelson's signal through the battle smoke. To his detriment, he obeyed Parker's instead. In doing so, he withdrew his force from its attack on the Tre Kroner fortress and unwittingly exposed his ship to heavy enemy fire.

Bligh was only glad that he didn't see it happen, for they had become the closest of friends. Their similar experiences and missions often had their paths cross at sea, while when in London, Riou never failed to drop in to Bligh's house for tea.

"Good luck," Riou had said to him before the battle began.

And shaking his friend's hand, Bligh wished him the same, not realising he would never see him again.

"*Cease fire!*" Riou ordered at the peak of combat to clear the dense smoke that surrounded him.

He could not see through it and fearing that he might ram an ally's ship, he wanted to clarify his position.

It was a fatal mistake, for it also gave the Danes a clear view of him.

Already wounded with a bloodied bandage wrapped round his head, Riou was leaning heavily on a gun when his ship swung into mid-channel and showed its stern to the Danish guns. They opened fire and as Amazon pitched and hurled its crew across its deck, Riou knew it was the end and ran to help haul on the main-brace.

"Come on then my boys, let us all die together," he called out, as he quickly scanned the seascape for Bligh's ship to signal farewell.

Those were his last words before a piece of chain-shot spun in his direction, the two cannonballs, strung together with chain, whipping round his waist and cutting him in two.

When Bligh heard the news, he gagged in bereaved revulsion.

"A brave man," he said, restraining his vomit and tears.

It was a sentiment Nelson shared.

"We all loved him," he said when truce negotiations were underway and he invited Bligh on board the Elephant to congratulate him on his initiative.

Not only had Bligh navigated Glatton safely between the banks where lesser captains had run their ships aground, but at a pivotal point in the conflict he had made the controversial choice to follow Nelson's lead in preference to Parker's. It ensured that all ships behind him kept fighting and secured England's victory.

Nelson would be forever grateful. And that gratitude carried enough weight to have Bligh promoted to a position of power.

TWENTY-THREE

News arrived that the next Governor of New South Wales was on his way.

"So they're sending us the old Bounty bastard are they?" John Macarthur said to his wife, Elizabeth, over breakfast. "Well, let's hope he's an improvement on the last three."

With practised calm, she poured him a cup of tea and replied:

"I'm sure he will be, if you give him a chance and don't fight him every inch of the way as you did with the others."

He put down his newspaper and looked at her.

"And I'll continue to do so until one of them has the sense to see things my way."

His way had proved fruitful since their arrival in Sydney. In those nine years, he had become a father of four sons and a very wealthy man, well able to afford the luxuries in life, like the Worcester bone china cup she handed him.

He'd had it specially imported from England, along with their grand piano and library full of fine books.

It had been a surprisingly easy road to the top down south, one which he owed to the fledgling colony's dependence on men of his kind. Those who were not afraid to break new ground and were determined to conquer at all costs.

"Much like Napoleon," he once said in arrogant comparison, which wasn't so far from the truth.

While the famed Frenchman ruled abroad, Macarthur had made for himself a nice little kingdom in New South Wales where he would have ruled supreme were it not for the niggling interference of England's colonial governors.

Each in turn was initially won over by his charm, but within weeks loathed him more than any man alive.

"I pity his poor wife," Governor Phillip had said having formed a fond attachment to Elizabeth.

He admired her beauty and exemplary courage in being the first lady to venture to the southern unknown. But more so, he respected her forbearance in regard to her husband. That firebrand whose obnoxious conceit and obsession to clash with all who crossed his path never once made her complain or compromise her dignity.

When Phillip left for London, he was glad to see the back of him and could only sympathise with his own successor, Governor John Hunter, who as a naval veteran of the American War of Independence, believed his war years were over and had no idea that the battle had just begun.

His was worse than his predecessor's because Phillip retained some modicum of power. By the time Hunter arrived, Macarthur was firmly ensconced in the colony's hierarchy. His rise to power having been accommodated by fellow army officer Major Francis Grose, who was Acting Governor for the two years it took to organise the swap.

It was a wild time of plenty for the military, with the unsupervised New South Wales Corps running amok, indulging in atrocious exploitation of convicts and rampant rum trafficking. Both made Macarthur a fortune, as hand in glove, he and Grose took control of the courts, all public lands and stores.

"I'm promoting you to captain, paymaster of the regiment and superintendent of public works," Grose informed Macarthur at the onset of his command.

As a clever man, Macarthur did the three jobs well. So well, with the help of the massive land grants Grose gave him, that he was soon rich enough to concentrate almost exclusively on his commercial interests at the expense of his military.

The prior were flourishing when Governor Hunter arrived, and Macarthur, as a soldier of substance, was voted the man most suited to formally greet him. Impressed with the captain's style and stature within the community, Hunter did not realise that he was wining and dining his most formidable enemy: a would-be dictator who had the backing of the army and who shared its grievance over the fact that each governor was drawn from the ranks of the navy rather than their own.

From the start, as a victim of that age-old antagonism between the armed forces, Hunter was helpless. And later, when a little wiser, he wrote to his predecessor, Governor Phillip:

As for this chap, Macarthur ... he is the Devil Incarnate! A pretty bully and flagrant opportunist who forfeits fair play to work it all his own way. Why didn't you warn me?

By rights, Hunter could have had all officers of the New South Wales Corps arrested and sent home for trial.

But that would incite rebellion, he scribbled in the postscript. *And I'll not have that on my head.*

Come Round Three and the arrival from Norfolk Island of Governor Gidley-King, Macarthur was an impregnable fortress of power, whose finesse and financial success seemed insurmountable.

His constant quarrelling with his fellow settlers and false allegation that Hunter was ineffective and trafficked in rum, had led to *that* Governor being recalled to London to answer the charges and to spend the next four years of his life, fighting to restore his reputation.

It was for this reason that Governor King came well prepared. Unlike those before him, he was not beguiled by Macarthur for an instant and was more than ready to take him on.

"I'm overturning your court's ruling in regard to naval Lieutenant Marshall's one-year conviction," King decreed on his first day of business.

"But that navy lout assaulted me while I was investigating him for theft!"

Macarthur was incensed. Marshall had insulted him and he wasn't going to let him get away with it.

"Of that I'm aware," King replied, putting quill to paper to sign the order. "His case will be tried in London."

"On what grounds?" Macarthur demanded, having long since forgotten that he was of lesser rank and consequence than the Governor and should not address him with such contempt.

King remained unperturbed as he looked up and replied:

"On the grounds that you and your court, Captain Macarthur, refused to hear Marshall's objection to an officer of the NSW Corps hearing his case."

"But this is just navy versus army nonsense," Macarthur dismissed with the sweep of his hand.

"No," King rejected firmly. "It is because Marshall knows that *here* you have the military court in the palm of your hand."

"I object to your inference."

"It's no inference, sir, but a fact which I refuse to debate."

Macarthur strode from King's office and slammed the door.

He wasn't accustomed to being defied, even by a man who had the authority to do so.

"Well we'll see about that!" he hissed, before he set about arranging a petty boycott of King among the corps.

He knew that his fellow soldiers would comply because they always did; those among them who were not in awe of his popularity doing so in fear of him making their lives hell if they did not.

But one of the more senior among them suddenly broke ranks.

"I'll not involve myself in it," Colonel William Paterson said to Macarthur's surprise.

Despite Paterson's fine reputation as an administrator and explorer, Macarthur had always seen him as a weak sot incapable of strong opinion. The fact that he had just voiced it left Macarthur no option but to resort to blackmail by releasing personal information of a carnal kind that shamed him.

"For that, I challenge you to a duel!" Paterson had no choice but to say.

And as a master of the art, Macarthur smiled. Within hours he was turning at 10 paces to draw his pistol and shoot Paterson in the shoulder, inflicting a wound which had him hover at death's door for months.

"You're under arrest!" King said, delighted, at last, to have the hook he needed to put the captain in chains.

Macarthur's response came as an undisguised threat.

"As you wish, but I warn you … it won't go down well with the corps."

He was right and in an attempt to diffuse the explosive situation, King offered him an alternative.

"You can take over as commandant of Norfolk Island."

At this, Macarthur laughed out loud.

"*That* sir, I refuse to do, but I'm prepared to be court-martialed by my fellow officers."

"I will not permit such a travesty of justice," King ruled before sending Macarthur back to England for trial, along with a dispatch denouncing him to the Commander-in-Chief of the British Army.

It was a bulky document brim-full of his dubious deeds, which mysteriously went missing. There was no question as to who hurled it into the sea when Macarthur had every reason to destroy it and no one on board was brave enough to stop him.

Yet, the Duke of York's rebuke was not for him, but for King:

> *Captain Macarthur must go back to be tried in Sydney where all evidence and witnesses are on hand. And I must add, Governor King, that I am greatly disappointed in you for failing to deal with this issue yourself when we in England are weighed down with far greater worries of war. Your orders to transfer Macarthur to Norfolk Island, however, stand.*

Not if I'm not there, they don't, Macarthur decided before he resigned his commission and stayed for a further four years in England to avoid the posting.

It was a long time away from home and family, but he made every minute count.

Looking for a profitable niche in the worldwide marketplace, he concentrated on breeding sheep. With so much fertile grazing land in New South Wales at his disposal, it was an opportunity not to be missed.

"But what *I* offer must be better than the rest," he insisted, having already experimented with cross breeding to produce a superior fleece.

Two years before, he had asked a naval friend setting out for Cape Town to acquire for him any good class of sheep available. He was in luck, for the King of Spain had just presented to the Dutch government there a flock of their finest, pure merinos.

Fortune favours you, that friend reported back to Macarthur, *for the man entrusted to transport them to South Africa died on arrival and left them in the care of his dithering widow. She practically begged me to relieve her of them.*

They served Macarthur's existing New South Wales flocks well and he took advantage of his time in London to submit specimens of his new strain of wool to a Committee of Manufacturers.

"Well what do you think?" he asked. "I'll wager they surpass any Spanish wool available and are of significantly more value."

The committee agreed and while he had it wrapped around his little finger, Macarthur could not resist adding the conceit:

"Give me a few years with the promise of your trade and I'll have New South Wales thriving and riding almost entirely on the sheep's back."

Much impressed by his initiative, Colonial Secretary Lord Camden backed Macarthur with a further land grant of 10,000 acres of his choosing in the colony.

"Good God!" Sir Joseph Banks said in response. "You have to hand it to the man. He comes here to be tried for corruption and is sent home with a slap on the back and what amounts to the rights to near all of New South Wales!"

He was one of the few men in power who was not besotted by Macarthur. From their first meeting, they took an instant dislike to each other and when Macarthur made no bones about the fact, Banks became a strong opponent of his plan and had his grant halved.

But what Macarthur lost in England was soon recouped when he arrived back in Sydney.

"I'll have those 5000 acres there," he said, antagonising Governor King even further, for it was prime grazing land reserved exclusively for the government's cattle herds.

Already King had sent his objection to England:

> *If Macarthur ever returns here in any official capacity,* he scribbled down bitterly, *it should be that of Governor, as one half the colony already belongs to him, and it will not be long before he gets his hands on the other.*

To this piece of sarcasm, he received no reply, but to his second petition to have Macarthur's grant moved, Colonial Secretary Camden's answer came fast and clear. He rejected it outright and reaffirmed Macarthur's right to the land.

"I think I'll call it Camden Park," Macarthur said smugly.

And at this point, King gave up.

"I can only hope," he said, "that the next governor is a better man than I and has the guts to give Macarthur a run for his money."

Bligh was tailor-made for the job.

He was flattered when Banks offered him the tenure, but was suspicious of the disproportionately large wage on offer: *twice* that of King's.

"That's generous," he said guardedly.

"It needs to be," Banks confirmed. "There's trouble in the colony and we need to entice a strong man to go there and take control."

"What sort of trouble?"

"That which comes from lack of supervision: general disorder, rumblings of rebellion and the like."

Bligh jarred at the word, angry that his name was once again being linked with it.

"So that's why you think I'm your man," he snapped, his cheeks burning red with indignation.

Banks realised his mistake and fixed firm eyes on his friend.

"You're our man," he explained, "because, like General Cornwallis and our beloved Lord Nelson, we all believe that you're the best at everything you do."

Bligh had seen action with both and at the mention of Nelson's name, backed down.

"You don't play fair," he replied, having been reassured by the compliment, but still mourning the recent death of the nation's favourite son; their celebrations for Nelson's golden victory at Trafalgar, tainted black because it cost him his life.

As their most glorious of heroes, Nelson's name would go down in history and frankly, Banks was unabashed about using it once more for the sake of the empire. Its southern extremities were in dire need of a good man and Bligh's credentials were unbeatable. His knowledge of the South Seas was second to none, his loyalty to the Crown immovable, and his renown for never backing away from a fight was now legend worldwide. The errant New South Wales Corps wouldn't know what hit them.

"You'll be the appointed Commander of His Majesty's Naval Forces in the South Pacific," Banks continued without waiting for Bligh's consent.

He knew he would get it; if not because of Bligh's strong sense of duty, then for the flattery of being offered such a prestigious post.

"Your mandate is to stop the rum trafficking and establish a more equitable economy so that the colony can become self-sufficient in its agriculture. The free settlers there are being thwarted in their attempts to do so, complaining of corruption and the commercial monopoly run by that rogue Macarthur. Don't ever let him get the better of you."

- BAD HAND -

TWENTY-FOUR

Predisposed to dislike the man, Bligh was pleasantly surprised when he met him in person. On his arrival at Sydney Cove, Macarthur was there to greet him and nothing was too much trouble. His handshake was firm, his manner congenial and when he extended his hand to help Bligh's 23-year-old daughter Mary down the gangplank, she blushed in response; touched less by the summer heat, than the attention of such an attractive man.

The flash of flirtation did not go unnoticed and Bligh quickly set the record straight.

"May I introduce, my daughter's husband, Lieutenant John Putland."

A pleasant, young man in blue uniform extended his hand to Macarthur, but then withdrew it fast to cough up a mouthful of blood into his handkerchief. It had been a long, seven-month voyage for a man wracked with tuberculosis, and throughout, Bligh feared that his much loved son-in-law would not last the distance.

"And your wife?" Macarthur asked, politely ignoring Putland's infirmity.

"Unfortunately, she couldn't come," Bligh replied.

"Well that's a shame. My wife Elizabeth was looking forward to her company."

"As was I," Bligh admitted, climbing into the carriage Macarthur provided. "But she suffers from a morbid terror of the sea."

Macarthur raised an amused eyebrow.

"Forgive me for saying then, that she made an odd choice in her husband."

That was the family joke and quietly smiling at the thought, Bligh settled himself on the leather seat and cast his mind back to the day he brought Betsy the good news of his governorship.

"And it's for you, my dearest," he said, "to come with me as the colony's first lady."

She drew back in horror.

"Oh my dear … I couldn't possibly," she answered, waving her fan furiously in front of her face. "Just couldn't *possibly!*"

He took her hand in his.

"You'll be perfectly safe. I promise. I'll be with you all the way. It's only for a few years and I need you at my side."

Betsy's voice grew firm with fear.

"How can you *say* that, when ships sink every day? You know that I'm in mortal fear of even setting *foot* on a boat, let alone gambling my life on one for six months! I swear that in a past life I *must* have drowned at sea."

She shuddered at the thought and took another steadying sip of her tea. "No, I simply can't go. I will *not* go."

Bligh was at a loss, but then Mary, came to his rescue.

"I'll go with you father, if Mama agrees."

A look of foreboding flashed over Betsy's face, followed by one of unmitigated relief. Her beautiful second girl had always been capable and brave like her father and with her matching fair hair and blue eyes, was undoubtedly his favourite.

"But you, too, suffer so terribly from seasickness," Betsy reminded her.

"I'll deal with it," Mary answered in her dainty, indomitable way. "Certainly better than I would the thought of father going alone."

Mary knew him well and understood that he loathed solitude. He was a family man, through and through and needed the people he loved around him. She suspected that the mutiny on the Bounty would never have happened had Fletcher Christian not forfeited their friendship in favour of Peter Heywood's. Whereas the world would ever wonder what went wrong on that fated ship, Mary knew the way her father worked and would never let anything of the like happen to him again.

"Besides," she continued, "the sea air will be good for my husband's health."

And so it was settled. She would stay at her father's side come hell or high water.

– oOo –

The first instance came as soon as they set out from England on the Lady Madeleine Sinclair, a *transport* which, along with three convict ships, was under the convoy of HMS Porpoise, commanded by Captain Joseph Short. It was early days in their adventure, but almost immediately Bligh's temper snapped. Like Macarthur, he was incapable of avoiding confrontation.

Mixed signals were to blame when Admiralty issued ambiguous instructions giving Short the command of the store ship Porpoise and Bligh the command of the transport. As the most senior officer of the convoy, Bligh did not think twice about flying his commodore's broad pennant from the Sinclair.

"*I* am in command!" Short insisted from HMS Porpoise.

His reputation as a heavy drinker and harsh taskmaster added weight to his argument. As a man after Bligh's own heart, there followed many nautical miles of furious arguments between them, before Bligh suddenly changed his ship's course without conferring.

"*Fire shots fore and aft of her!*" Short ordered from the Porpoise, deliberately directing that order to Lieutenant Putland who was stationed on board.

"But sir ... you're asking me to fire on my own wife and father-in-law."

Short turned on him in an unholy rage.

"I don't ask. *I command.* Now do what you're told."

Putland had no choice but to obey, praying that his poor record as a marksman held.

"And the next will be amidships!" Short scaled his ship's ropes to roar across the waves at Bligh.

The latter's reply was a little less loud, but spoke volumes:

To fire on a ship carrying your superior officer is a court-martial offence which I will see to when we reach New South Wales.

Short was never one to think before he spoke and now was very worried. He *would* be at Bligh's mercy when they arrived in Sydney and his 600-acre grant of land was under threat. That would be hard to explain to his wife and children who had come with him. Already railing against having to up sticks and start a new life on the other side of the world, they wouldn't be too pleased at the prospect of facing another voyage straight back to Plymouth.

It nearly killed him to do it, but when they reached the Cape of Good Hope, Short apologised.

"I'm not of a mind to excuse you," Bligh replied.

His head was thumping with another of his migraines which robbed him of all sense of forgiveness and good humour.

"But *surely*, sir," Short continued, working hard on his humility, "you must realise that it was just drunken bluster on my part and not to be taken seriously."

"I take having cannonballs fired in my direction very seriously indeed, Captain."

Seriously enough for him to strip Short of his captaincy as soon as they reached Sydney and to cancel the 600-acre grant promised him as payment for the voyage. With Short's head spinning from this about-face in his fortune, he was sent straight back to England for court-martial.

We feel that this was a little harsh, wrote Sir Isaac Coffin to Admiralty. *And allege that Governor Bligh exercised abuse of power in influencing other officers to testify against Short.*

It was a grave accusation that threatened to have Bligh recalled as Governor.

"But it's not true," Banks and other supporters of his in England argued.

A fact which his wife, Betsy, proved when she personally interviewed the officers involved, all of whom flatly denied implicating her husband. So the case came down in Bligh's favour, stamping his authority on the colony and making Macarthur eye him more shrewdly.

He may be harder to break than the others, he thought. But never once did he doubt his ability to do so.

TWENTY-FIVE

The last person who posed problems of the like for Macarthur was Joseph Foveaux. A newly promoted captain of the corps who came to the colony when it was under the governorship of Gidley-King, equipped with a shrewd business sense which rivalled Macarthur's own.

As men of similar age, intellect and hankering for greatness, they instantly became friends; the only difference between them being that Foveaux was a master of disguising his agenda while keeping the regard of the people he manipulated to achieve it. That talent completely eluded Macarthur and he was most admiring of Foveaux's panache until it began to eclipse his own.

By rights, Macarthur had the edge having arrived in the colony two years prior, but it was Foveaux who was suddenly promoted to major.

For the first time sensing real competition, Macarthur said scathingly:

"It seems a might premature for an untried, young man stationed at the bottom of the world. Obviously, someone back home has his best interests at heart."

That help from home positioned Foveaux as foremost among the corps officers right when they were abusing the system and making money hand over fist. While Lieutenant-Colonel Paterson was absent from command, Foveaux called the shots and in a remarkably short space of time, catapulted his status up to that of the largest landholder and stockowner in New South Wales.

"Not for long," Macarthur swore, peeved that Foveaux had got there before him.

So he wasn't sorry to see him go, his smooth smile of friendship becoming more genuine when he found out that Foveaux's *true* goal in life was to advance his career in the military.

To that end, Foveaux suddenly gave up all business interests and volunteered to take over from Captain Rowley as acting Lieutenant-Governor of Norfolk Island. It was not a plum posting and incentives had to be offered for him to take it on. For Foveaux, they amounted to a huge leap up military ranks, which left the way open for Macarthur's easy ride to the top of a commercial empire.

"I'll buy them," he said to Foveaux, who to facilitate his meteoric promotion had to dispose of all his livestock in New South Wales.

It was an exchange of money for fleece which overnight saw Macarthur usurp Foveaux's title as landowner and sheep breeder supreme.

"Well there goes an excellent administrator and exceptionally fine man," Governor King said to Macarthur as they waved farewell to Foveaux at the wharf.

For King, there was great satisfaction in playing one man against the other and he smiled when no longer inclined to sing his friend's praises, Macarthur kept his mouth shut.

What does it matter anyway, Macarthur reasoned, *now that Foveaux is someone else's problem?*

– oOo –

The problem now rested with the residents of Norfolk Island, Fletcher Christian, alias Francis Chapman, among them.

It had been eight, long years since the American Captain Page had left him on the island, and considering its fearful reputation as the penal colony reserved for the worst of convicts, it hadn't been so bad. Its slapdash administration by a succession of unenthusiastic commandants, however, had left the isle in a deplorable state. Its facilitates were unpardonable, but at least its prisoners were not bolted to ball and chain and were permitted, in between their hard labour, to wander at will.

All that stopped when Foveaux arrived. As a fiend for detail and administrative excellence, he whipped the island into shape and the backs of its convicts to shreds; his sadistic streak manifesting itself as soon as he was beyond the view of his equals on the mainland.

"Twenty-four lashes!" he ordered for an emaciated prisoner who dared plead for an extra piece of bread.

"*Please* sir," the man fell to his knees to beg once more.

And Foveaux stopped to say: "And another 10 for answering me back."

It was a cruel world and such was to be expected, but with power going to his head, Foveaux took corporal punishment to new extremes.

"But she's a woman, sir," the guard protested when Foveaux ordered him to strip the female convict bare and inflict 12 lashes.

Foveaux had already made a name for himself as a harsh disciplinarian and now had added the rare distinction of sanctioning the flogging of women and the sale of those more desirable to the free settlers. He was a man on a savage mission and since he had taken over the Island, Christian had kept a low profile to avoid drawing attention to himself. By keeping his head down and sticking to the rules, he had so far ensured that Foveaux's gaze never strayed in his direction.

But this day, he and the rest of Norfolk's convict population were assembled to witness the whipping of the condemned woman. Under the stinging lash of the cat-o'-nine-tails, her back was butchered and she had already passed out twice. It marked the point when a decent man had to speak up.

"That's enough!" Christian suddenly said with authority.

Foveaux looked up in surprise, astonished that someone dared speak out, but more, because they did so with an educated English accent. As he walked towards the offender, the crowd of convicts parted to make way, each in mortal fear of their lives and dread of affiliation.

Christian, however, stood his ground, knowing there was nowhere to run and that he had effectively signed his own death warrant.

Expecting the brutal slash of Foveaux's riding crop across his face, he was surprised when the Lieutenant-Governor simply stopped before him to look more closely.

"Don't I know you from somewhere?" he asked in a civil tone reserved for his peers.

For despite Christian's ragged appearance, it was obvious that he was a man of quality and Foveaux was intrigued.

"What's your name?"

"Francis Chapman, sir."

That meant nothing to Foveaux, but he'd always been good with faces and was convinced he recognised the one in front of him. The name for which he was searching was on the tip of his tongue, its recollection connected somehow with prosperity and home. Some sort of public speaking came to mind and the vague recall of an eminent man standing on stage.

He hesitated, mentally sifting through his files for the answer, but then … no, it was gone … that flash of memory that brought him so close to putting his finger on the man's identity. Something told him, however, that it was important to remember, and lost in the process, he turned and walked away, astounding all for letting a convict go unpunished.

But that wouldn't be for long, Christian suspected, as he quietly melted back into the crowd. Soon he would feel the hangman's noose around his neck and he only hoped they'd make it quick and string him up from the closest tree rather than shame his family further by parading him through the streets of London. As for his children and wife in Tahiti, he had long lost hope of ever seeing them again, but for their sake, he was determined to die like a man.

He had never met Foveaux before, but the man was no fool and the penny was bound to drop. Who knew what likeness of the Bounty's head mutineer he might have seen when the trial was in full swing? There were many men who would have been happy to sketch it and Bligh had every right to immortalise the portrait in the corridors of crime.

But Foveaux had never laid eyes on anything of the like and had to rely on the written word. Fascinated by the mystery, he went straight back to his office and looked for the book he was after on the shelf.

"Ah, here it is," he said, dislodging the register of convict arrivals.

His own entries in it over the past four years were impeccable, but as he flicked back through the pages, their edges grew yellow and their contents scrawled. Finding the words hard to decipher, he asked his assistant:

"Can you remember when prisoner Francis Chapman was brought here?"

"Some time ago, sir," the sergeant replied, looking up from his work. "Dropped off by an American *trader* about seven years ago, if memory serves."

"The plot thickens," Foveaux mused as he turned back to the beginning of the book and traced his finger down the list of names to land, at last, on October 26, 1793.

There, in prior Lieutenant-Governor King's hand, was written what he was after:

Convict Name:	*Francis Chapman*
Conviction:	*Assumed Deserter from His Majesty's Service. Ship unknown. Found adrift at sea. Offender unwilling to reveal circumstance.*
Age:	*29*
Height:	*5'9"*
Description:	*Dark hair and complexion, blue eyes.*

Identifying
Marks: *Tattoos. Right Arm - Anchor;*
                  Left Chest - "Isabella"

Foveaux's eyes narrowed in thought.

Why would a man choose to submit to penal punishment rather than explain himself?

The answer hit hard: *To escape what was worse … a death sentence!*

Suddenly, the dam burst and in a gush of clarity, Foveaux's fragments of memory tumbled into place. All at once he could put a name to that face he once knew and track it back to an exact time and place.

The time was just after the Bounty trial, and the place: a mid-city auditorium where he and his friends, as army cadets, had gone to hear the renowned lawyer Edward Christian speak in defence of his condemned brother. The audacity of his attack set London back on its heels and for a while his cleverly spun web of half truths relegated Captain Bligh's reputation to the mud.

The similarity in facial features between that erudite orator on stage and the dishevelled prisoner Francis Chapman was not exact but close enough.

It couldn't be, Foveaux thought. *It's been years and the man was declared dead.*

But there was enough doubt and thrill of discovery to test his theory the next day.

"Fletcher!" he called out on the spur of the moment as Chapman's chain gang trudged by.

And in answer to his name, Christian looked back.

- BAD HAND -

TWENTY-SIX

Fully expecting to be hauled before the Lieutenant-Governor and hanged, Christian was perplexed by the strange silence which settled over their prison compound and Foveaux's sudden absence from it.

"He's sick," was the formal explanation from the sergeant-at-arms.

Within days, the convicts watched their stretcher-bound nemesis being carried to the wharf where a ship was waiting to take him back to England.

Christian stood at the gangplank, the last in the line to see him go.

"Stop here!" Foveaux ordered when, for a tense moment, their eyes met in acknowledgment of their secret.

Foveaux's pale lips parted.

"Saved by a bout of chronic asthma," he said in between short breaths before he was taken on board, leaving Christian none the wiser as to his intentions.

His replacement, Captain John Piper, came within weeks bringing the news that Norfolk's prisoners were to be transferred to the wilderness of Van Diemen's Land. There, at the command of King George, Colonel Paterson had been made Governor and charged with the duty of establishing penal colonies at Port Dalrymple and York Town.

Paterson's health was failing and he was not keen to play pioneer in this raw, southern outpost. Embittered and still nursing the shoulder wound inflicted by Macarthur, he winced when he picked up his quill.

We are experiencing many difficulties in lack of supplies, he reported to England.

But I have a keen eye for natural resources and have noted a huge outcrop of iron ore near Port Dalrymple. If I had carts and quarrying tools, I could equip the munitions of the entire Royal Navy! To that end, I have high hopes of this colony becoming a special punishment centre for the worst of criminals in ball and chain from whom I can exact the optimum effort in mining this rich resource.

Such was Christian's prospect when his convict ship anchored offshore.

Back on the New South Wales mainland at that time, Bligh's prospects looked much brighter. He'd been welcomed with open arms by Major George Johnston on behalf of the military, by judge-advocate Richard Atkins, representing the civil, and before leaving for London, Governor King had gifted him with three large tracts of land. Bligh called them Camperdown and Copenhagen in honour of his battles and Mount Betham out of respect for his wife's family.

It was Macarthur, speaking for the free settlers, however, who was the most forthcoming; ever at his best to impress and ingratiate himself.

Bligh and daughter Mary were regular guests at his Elizabeth Farm estate and the hospitality was happily reciprocated at Government House. Elizabeth was glad of intellectual company at last and her husband was using it for all it was worth.

"We're lucky to have the worst behind us," he said, pausing to pour gravy over his roast beef. "Poor old King had to contend with the Vinegar Hill uprising, but fortunately all that's done and dusted."

Before leaving London, Bligh was briefed on the bloody clash between convicts and the colonial guard which happened a year before. It resulted in the execution of nine of its Irish ringleaders and the brutal punishment of a hundred of their followers, many of whom did not survive the multiple lashes and subsequent deprivation of rations. Retribution had been swift and savage and baulking at its barbarity, Bligh was only glad that King bore the brunt.

"We won't see the likes of that again," Macarthur reassured as he topped up their brandy.

Bligh settled back comfortably in his seat, warmed by the drink and his good fortune in finding such a friend so far afield. From the start, they shared a rapport, just as he had with Fletcher Christian. They talked of him briefly, but soon dropped the subject when Macarthur saw that it was making Bligh uncomfortable. But he was intrigued, because behind the Governor's rage, there still seemed to lurk an affection for the man who betrayed him.

He made a mental note of it, knowing that it could be used against Bligh someday, if necessary. Arming himself with information such as this had served him well in the past and was sure to do the same in the future.

Bligh was just sorry the subject was brought up at all. At the sharp recall of Christian's name, he found himself clenching his glass.

Blast the man's eyes! he thought. *What he did was unforgivable ... but I miss him.*

Here lay the danger, for Macarthur and Christian were much alike in their appeal and Bligh could not risk history repeating itself. He had a bad track record in choosing friends, drawn as he always was to vibrant people prone to grow too big for their boots.

Instinctively, he glanced down at Macarthur's as he went to fetch his box of cigars. They were of the finest leather and fitted him to perfection; proof positive that this man of power had nothing left to prove. All, it appeared, was already within his stride and Bligh foolishly put his fears aside; a mistake when Macarthur was a man of *"more"* for whom nothing was enough and who always took what he wanted, ever ready, in those fine-fitting boots of his to trample over anyone who tried to stop him.

Bligh had no idea that that onus was about to fall on him.

"Something has to be done about it," he confided to Macarthur on his return from his inspection tour of the colony.

There, he saw for himself the NSW Corps' outrageous

abuse of the system and it shocked him. Assuming that Macarthur, in his prosperity, was well beyond his allegiance to it, he spoke freely.

"Things are going to change and fast."

He was acting on England's orders to break the corps' monopoly over the settlement's imported goods, namely rum. At the exclusion of all other forms of barter, the officers had made it the country's currency, upping their liquid assets at the expense of soldiering, while exploiting free convict labour to rear livestock in favour of agriculture. The colony was in crisis for lack of crops, but the all-powerful army clique made short work of the settlers' complaints. It was a recipe for disaster.

Governors Hunter and King ran up against the problem and were forced to compromise, but Bligh didn't know the meaning of the word and wasn't about to bargain. The problem was that naval officers were used to strict discipline, but army personnel resented another branch of the service exerting it over them. In retaliation, they blackballed Bligh's efforts by rallying round their leader, Major George Johnston, who was an old military comrade and strategic business partner of Macarthur's.

Bligh did not realise that they went hand-in-glove, and frankly, didn't care. His sole purpose was to establish the law and strip the corps of its scandalous, free rein.

The second he returned to town, he issued a general order:

> *All bartering of rum in lieu of coin is hereby prohibited. Severe fines and imprisonment will be imposed on anyone flouting the law.*

"So, you've declared war," Macarthur said, for the first time in a cool tone that took Bligh aback.

"I have indeed, but only against those who deserve it."

"And who might they be?"

"Those army officers paid to implement and protect English law, who are, instead, the culprits of its abuse."

"Then you take up arms against me."

"Not at all," Bligh replied, stung by Macarthur's suddenly aggressive manner, but still willing to explain. "You're no longer an officer, but a man of property and consequence."

Macarthur smiled smugly.

"I may no longer sleep in the same barracks, but my fellow officers can always rely on my support."

"Are you saying that I can't?"

"Not in so many words, but as a man of honour I will never betray my brothers in the military."

A dynamic silence passed between them as they mentally drew swords, but having second thoughts, Macarthur put his back in its scabbard.

"Listen Bligh," he said more sensibly. "There's money to be made by all, particularly England, if they support our sheep and cattle program. Our rum profits are merely used to facilitate it. If you're smart enough, you can take advantage of it yourself."

Bligh didn't like being bribed and seeing Macarthur's true colours, began to burn with rage. Like lava, the boiling heat surged through his body and exploded in a verbal attack.

"Don't bleat on to me about your wretched sheep," he bellowed. "You own 5000 acres of land in the country's' finest situation. When is enough, enough?"

"When I *say so!*" Macarthur fired back with matching temper and volume. "And may I remind you, *sir,* that the land was given to me on the recommendation of the Privy Council and the Secretary of State. Who are *you* to question my aspirations and credulity?"

His words hurtled Bligh into a state of star-studded fury. He was the *Governor,* for God's sake and could question what and who he bloody-well liked!

"While you were fighting for your flocks, *damn you,* I was fighting for Nelson! Don't even *presume* to challenge my power. Just remember that it's greater than yours."

The battle line was drawn and having long lost sight of playing second fiddle to any man, Macarthur stormed from his office, never to return on friendly terms. From here on in he and Bligh would work at cross purposes, forever locking horns in their respective quest for profit and popularity.

"We should work together," Bligh, in a weak moment, once proposed.

But Macarthur laughed in his face.

TWENTY-SEVEN

With the honeymoon over, it was all-out war.

Macarthur was a formidable enemy with his fierce reputation for winning at all costs. He had fought and won three duels, killing one man and winging two others, while having besieged Bligh's predecessors with his incessant arguments until they waved the white flag.

That was something Bligh would never do. Instead, taking the offensive, he promptly prohibited Macarthur's cheap distribution of rum among the corps, along with his importation of stills. Flush with power and the impact it was having, he then plunged the knife deeper:

And there's a problem in regard to the land Macarthur was granted by Governor King, he noted on his 'To Do' list. *It conflicts with my town planning interests and will need to be reallocated."*

That would be a devil's own job to enforce because Bligh's triumph was only on paper and far from the disciplinary hand of the Mother Country, it was Macarthur who really ruled the roost.

The reality was that Bligh was alone, just as he had been on the Bounty. He wasn't afraid of fighting his own battles, but doing so hadn't proved so successful on his ship and there was always the threat of a repeat performance on land.

For a time, however, their one-on-one war had to be put aside for problems more pressing. At the top of Bligh's agenda was the care of the free settlers who were suffering from the force of nature and that of the corps.

He dealt with it directly.

"I'm dividing the colony's supplies between those most in need," he decreed to provide relief for the farmers affected by severe flooding in the Hawkesbury River area. "And the amount of their loans from the colony stores will be based on no more than their capacity to repay."

The farmers were jubilant at his intervention.

At last, they thought, *a strong man to champion our cause and put Macarthur and his corps in their place.*

The floods had nearly destroyed them and the corps was forcing the cash-poor emancipists among them to borrow money at extortionate rates. Being of uneducated English stock and with little knowledge of farming, all hope seemed lost for the planters and their only option was to drown their sorrows in drink – a solution facilitated by the corp traders who paid them in nothing but rum for their goods before demanding from the farmers, in return, outrageous prices for their essential supplies.

"They need a competitive market to buy and sell their produce," Bligh announced, taking the situation in hand.

First, he provided a *line of credit* for farmers who delivered their crops to the colony stores after harvest. And second, the opening of those "stores" for sale to compete with the monopolists.

Macarthur was not pleased.

And unfortunately, the depth of the farmers' devotion to Bligh was outdone by the enmity his ruling stirred among the corps traders who were capitalising on the farmers' dire straits. What was fair and humane represented an alarming plummet in their profits and they were not going to let Bligh get away with it.

"He's not like the other governors," Major Johnston remarked as he watched Macarthur pace the floor.

Deep in thought, he answered:

"No, he's not."

Macarthur had not reckoned on Bligh being such a stumbling block. Unlike the rest, he refused to be bullied and as a supremely efficient man with a social conscience, he was operating at optimum capacity to put everything right.

"He has phenomenal energy for a man of 50. By rights the old Bounty bastard should be put out to pasture," Macarthur said scathingly as he flicked through the papers on his desk as if to find a solution among them.

There wasn't one and to top it off, Bligh now compounded his two initial pieces of interference by taking over the allocation of convict labour to stop the military helping itself.

"The corps is up in arms!" Major Johnston exclaimed in the hope of stirring Macarthur into action.

But instead, his friend gave a derisive snort at the irony -- his old band of brothers having long since forsaken muskets to muster cattle. Johnston and his troops, however, had every reason to be annoyed when every initiative of Bligh's to better the colony's economy was wreaking havoc on their takings.

"Are you going to step in?" Johnston asked, unwilling to do so himself, but always ready to second any of Macarthur's moves.

Playing lickspittle had earned him the title of *"Jack Bodice's tool"*, which was not entirely fair when he proved himself to be an unyielding commanding officer at the Battle of Vinegar Hill. Macarthur, however, was far more daunting than any Irish rebel and Johnston was happy, if not compelled, to be used by him to get rid of Bligh.

"In my own good time," Macarthur replied. "Preferably when Bligh isn't so busy being noble."

Only a month before, their new Governor had added another leaf to his laurel by personally paying for some acres of land to use as demonstration farms. It was an act of generosity, way beyond the call of duty, to help train the emancipists. Those convicts who had been set free but were new to the ways of the land and were struggling to make ends meet. Full of enthusiasm for his project, Bligh wrote home for help:

> *I would like to request that a programme be put in place to promote the migration of yeoman farmers to New South Wales. We are greatly in need of their expertise and I feel that now is the time to lure them to our shores with some attractive incentives.*

This was a piece of forward thinking for which Bligh should have been commended, encouraging, as he was, the relocation of professionals to this rich land of resources, rather than filling it with convicts who were unable to take advantage of them. Much of what he proposed fell on deaf ears, but he was proud of having put the idea forward.

He was just as proud of his daughter for her help in civilising their new world.

As mistress of Government House, Mary headed Sydney's society. After a few days of shyness, she quickly adapted to her elevated position and now fully expected her visitors to bow in her presence, while entertaining them with her prowess on the piano and delightful dinner-table talk.

Around that table sat the most prominent of the colony, bar Macarthur whose chair, directly to Bligh's right, was taken by a man almost his match in power and decidedly his superior in principles.

Like Macarthur, Robert Campbell was a strong Scot, whose ties to Bligh were strengthened by his wife Betsy's same heritage. Even in her absence, that Scottish background stood Bligh in good stead and assured him of Campbell's support. He was a businessman of substance and flawless reputation who even Macarthur respected.

In part, that respect was returned.

"Macarthur's a man of outstanding initiatives," Campbell was first to admit. "But I don't always approve of his methods in implementing them."

When Bligh had first arrived in the colony with his courage and clout, Campbell's course was clear. He would stand at his side and like a true Scot stay faithful to his word. With dour expression in place, he passed the salt and pepper to the man sitting next to him.

Edmund Griffin, with his thin, white hair and sallow face had come out to New South Wales on the First Fleet and served as secretary to the Governor under Phillip, Hunter and King. That constituted more than 18 years of service and as a fixture in the position, he seemed set to stay in it forever.

Every bit as sanctimonious in her status, his wife was engaged in a solemn conversation across the table with Reverend Samuel Marsden, who came to the colony as a gangly, young Anglican cleric, but since being made magistrate, had accrued 300 acres of land, 1418 sheep and a remarkably prosperous paunch.

"The colony's most practical farmer," Governor King had called him to challenge Macarthur's sterling contribution as their wool industry's founding father.

"Yes, but mine's the superior fleece," Macarthur countered, confident in the knowledge that it was *his* sheep which were the colony's greatest money earner.

Both were valid claims which made Marsden and Macarthur despise each other.

Six days of the week, Macarthur held the upper hand, but on Sundays, Marsden took advantage behind the pulpit by making his rival the subject of his sermons. There, with the spirit of the Lord upon him, he denounced Macarthur for his lead role in rum trafficking and for embracing the evils of alcohol.

"Perhaps it would be best if you dropped it now," Bligh advised, as he and Marsden shook hands at the chapel door.

He was not comfortable with Marsden's Sabbath Day

witch-hunts. As Governor, they weakened his case and he didn't believe in backstabbing a man when he was not there to defend himself.

"My very point," Marsden replied. "Macarthur never comes to church and is not a God-fearing man."

That, Bligh believed was none of his business and well beyond his authority.

"It is not my place to question another man's faith," he replied, cutting their conversation short.

Bligh didn't indulge in vindictive gossip. If there was someone he disliked, he preferred to tell them to their face, without the whispered complicity of others. Certainly church was not the forum for it. The last thing he wanted was to stir the wrath of God when, since the Bounty, he wasn't so sure that he had Him on side.

But harking back to the dinner table and Marsden's threats of damnation, Mrs Griffin gave a tsk of disapproval for those who indulged in the dreaded drink as her eyes drifted in the direction of Henry Fulton, the former and far more liberal minister of the Church of Ireland sitting two seats away.

For his part in the Irish Rebellion of '98, Fulton was transported, but promptly pardoned by Governor Hunter who sent him to minister to the convicts on Norfolk Island. When Marsden made a brief trip back to Britain, Fulton was recalled to the mainland as acting colonial chaplain and became so popular that he was loathe to leave.

He, too, was a fan of Bligh's, not only for his interesting tales of the sea, but for the rollicking good times his rivalry with Macarthur provided. They made for the best entertainment Fulton had had since leaving Ireland.

In that spirit, he caught Mrs Griffin's scornful eye and unable to resist, swilled his glass of wine in one go.

"But surely in this rough and ready world of ours, a drop or two can't be condemned," he then said with a sigh of satisfaction and a wink which had her sit back shocked in her chair, disdainful of the man and his "bog Irish" background.

The only thing worse, to her way of thinking, was Mrs Palmer's strident voice resounding from the other end of the table. She was a fellow guest, who as an American, had married English naval officer John Palmer after the War of Independence and come with him to New South Wales when he was appointed commissary general of the colony. Always obnoxiously familiar, she was at this moment bending hostess Mary's ear and in between loud bouts of laughter, following Fulton's example by gulping down glass after glass of red wine.

Mary, however, was in control and did not mind. She enjoyed Mrs Palmer's forthright company because its contrast enhanced the educated refinement of her own. Ever sorry to leave it, this evening she had no choice.

"It you'll excuse me, ladies and gentlemen," she said, neatly folding her napkin when coffee was served. "I must see to my husband."

TWENTY-EIGHT

Tubercular John Putland was gravely ill. Death was at the door and knocking all the more persistently now that he had lingered beyond the doctor's three-week prognosis.

Mary nursed him constantly and her calm gave him comfort. So it was Bligh who suffered most. He loved his gentle son-in-law and thought of him as his own; compensation, he felt, for the twin boys he and Betsy had lost.

It was hard to say goodbye.

"Look after Mary," John whispered as he gasped his last.

And clinging tight to his son-in-law's dead hand, Bligh hung his head as tears rolled down his face.

In a far more sober mood than Mrs Griffin had witnessed at the dinner party, Henry Fulton officiated at the funeral.

"Ashes to ashes, dust to dust," he said as he handed Bligh John's sword to place on his coffin.

Bligh was in deep mourning and needed to wallow a while until he came to terms with his grief. Life, however, in the troublesome colony went on, while his mind swung erratically between outrage over the premature death of a man he loved and fury over the actions of another man he loathed.

– oOo –

Macarthur, it appeared, had no respect for the dead and was using his Governor's weak moment to further his own cause. While Bligh, battling his way through bereavement, lost all sense of perspective and control of his temper.

"I couldn't give a *tinker's cuss* about what they *want*. They'll do as I *say!*" he screamed at Macarthur who came to complain about Bligh's treatment of Major Johnston's troops.

"They are *his* to command, not yours," Macarthur shot back, fed up, as was Johnston, with Bligh's interference in their every sphere of activity.

"Governor or not," he continued, "It's not your place to give orders to the corps without first deferring to its commander."

About this, Macarthur was right, but Bligh wasn't about to give in.

"Well then tell him to order them to do their job or apply for another one himself."

Macarthur cocked a self-righteous eyebrow.

"I can't imagine what his men have done wrong to put you in such a state, sir."

"They were out of uniform," Bligh stated, suddenly aware of the banality of his argument. Too late to turn back, however, he plunged in deeper. "What's more, they left their rifles lying on the ground and had their shirt and tunic buttons undone while they guarded the chain gangs."

"Forgivable, one would think, in the extreme heat," Macarthur replied crisply. "But be that as it may, you humiliated them with your very public reprimand."

"Good! Just as I intended."

Bligh was wholly unrepentant and incensed that this jumped-up wool merchant was daring to question his authority. Whipped into a fury, he went on:

"But worse still … three of Johnston's men, *including* Lieutenant Minchin, to his shame, disgraced themselves by making a fool of my daughter in church."

At the last Sunday's service, Mary had urgently grabbed for her father's hand:

"Oh Papa," she said, "I think I'm going to faint."

In the stuffy confines of the chapel, she collapsed to the floor, alarming her fellow parishioners and setting the small group of soldiers at the service off into a bout of snide laughter.

With little he could say in their defence, it was Macarthur's turn to be contrite.

"Perhaps you made too much of it, Bligh," he said in a feeble attempt to brush aside the unchivalrous incident. "After all, they were just foolish young men having fun."

Grim faced, Bligh corrected him.

"It was *appalling* behaviour, sir, unbecoming of *any* man, let alone those in His Majesty's service. My daughter is a lady of quality who's never done them harm. They should have run to her rescue rather than make her the object of ridicule. You and Johnston should be ashamed."

Macarthur was, but refused to admit it; the silence

between them making for an emotionally charged moment which was soon to be followed by another.

"It's a pity Fletcher Christian didn't slit his throat when he had the chance," Major Johnston muttered to Macarthur over drinks in the officers' mess some hours later.

"Keep your voice down," Macarthur warned, calmly sipping at his tankard of ale. "Or one day you may be accused of as much, when Bligh goes too far."

He already had, to the officers' way of thinking, when he recently reclaimed the crown land Governor Phillip had zoned for public use behind Government House. Hunter and King granted short-term leases over it to men like Macarthur, Johnston and Governor Paterson and extended the courtesy to deserving non-commissioned officers of the corps.

"But we've just finished building our homestead on that land," Sergeant Tom Whittle protested.

"Well that was a stupid thing to do. You'll have to knock it down," Bligh ruled.

He made no bones about it. He was sick to death of the NSW Corps trampling over his authority and taking what it wanted in flagrant abuse of the law.

Whittle ran to tell Macarthur.

"He can't make me do that!"

"I'm afraid he can," Macarthur disagreed, disappointing the sergeant with his easy compliance. "To be fair, Whittle, you've only yourself to blame for having taken the gamble of erecting your homestead on land that, by rights, wasn't yours."

Whittle scowled and kicked at the dirt.

"I thought you'd be on my side."

"I can't risk defending anyone whose complaint isn't entirely justified. Bring me one that *is* and I'll fight to the death for it."

Whittle's eyes narrowed at the mention of the fatal word. The way he was feeling at the moment, he would be happy to strike the first blow.

The same sentiment was shared by the entire corps and Bligh suddenly saw the warning signs. It was easy enough to do when *"Death to the Tyrant"* was slapped in red paint all over a mid-town brick wall and the word "assassination" was being bandied about the colony.

Thanks to the Bounty, Bligh had experienced the like and thought it wise to employ an armed escort whenever he went on his rounds. It was the sensible thing to do, but the pretence alienated him even further.

"Who does he think he is?" his enemies sneered as they watched his carriage roll by.

And in response, he doffed his hat.

When one soldier spat in open contempt as he passed, however, Bligh knew that he was sailing too close to the wind. What he needed was more protection, both physical and legal.

He certainly wasn't getting the latter from the colony's judge-advocate, Richard Atkins, who was appointed to the position by Governor Hunter solely on the grounds of his family connections. The fact that the man was running from debt and had absolutely no training in the legal profession seemed to be of no concern, but it confounded Bligh who saw him as a constant source of frustration and the reason for his most recent bout of migraines. With his hand pressed tight to his temple, he wrote to London:

I am pleased to report that order has been restored in the colony and that the English pound is now currency. I am, however, in dire need of a judge and attorney general the people respect. Atkins is a disgrace to human jurisprudence, a drunkard, who is completely ignorant of the law …

He paused to take a sip of tea before dipping his quill back in the inkpot.

I also have my concerns about the NSW Corps. Seventy from its ranks have resigned to pursue business interests and their replacements are convicts which makes for a dangerous militia capable of rebellion. I recommend a change of troops to a regular army corps whose soldiers do not pose a threat.

Bligh was always able to think fast. But communication was so slow, and by the time his fears reached home, the worst of them would be realised.

Everything hinged on Macarthur, but Bligh refrained from sending a second letter of complaint about him.

"What was the use?" he reasoned, when back in England, both Macarthur's name and his rising fortune through fleece were held in such high esteem. Blind eyes were bound to be turned where money was concerned.

Instead, it was Macarthur who took up the poison pen and registered a series of complaints. In his first letter to London, he cleverly made no mention of Bligh's name, but undermined it, just the same, by attacking Andrew

Thompson, who Bligh had hired to run his demonstration farms.

In all good faith, I lent Mr Thompson money which he refuses to return in kind. That anyone should sponsor such a man is surely a mistake, but to abuse power in order to protect him is a travesty of justice.

It certainly was, if it were the truth. The full story was that along with his other profitable pursuits, Macarthur had taken up money lending, and to gain an advantage over Bligh, bought his protégé Andrew Thompson's 300-pound promissory note from another lender. It was an adroit move that put both men under obligation to him.

"But that's extortion!" Thompson exclaimed when Macarthur came to collect and demanded more. "When I signed the contract with Simon Carruthers, it was understood that its 300-pound value would be paid off with 99 bushels of wheat."

As Thompson was the most successful grain grower in the colony, the repayment was well within his means, even more so since the disastrous floods had made wheat prices sky-rocket. Ninety-nine bushels were now worth three times as much as when he signed his promissory note, which meant that Macarthur was demanding triple what he was owed.

"*Here,* you can have your 300 pounds in cash," Thompson said as he emptied his leather pouch of notes and coin onto Macarthur's desk.

Instantly, Macarthur swept them off its mahogany surface onto the floor.

"I won't accept it."

"And *I* won't pay more," Thompson countered.

"In that case, sir," Macarthur got up aggressively to say. "I shall sue you."

He always fancied himself a barrister, but in this instance, Macarthur's gift for oratory and persuasion failed to win over the magistrate who ruled in Thompson's favour.

It was the first time Macarthur had lost a case, but it was exactly what he wanted.

"I don't understand," Johnston said, bemused by his friend's glee.

"It *means*," Macarthur explained, slowly and succinctly, "that I've won the right of an appeal to the Governor. Bligh will have no choice but to hear the case. If he finds against his friend and employee, Thompson, he will look to have meekly bowed to my will. If he dismisses the appeal, he'll seem to be favouring his emancipist friend over the interests of a highly regarded free citizen. Either way, he loses."

Unlike Johnston, Bligh knew precisely what Macarthur was up to and was alarmed.

"I have no acquaintance with the law beyond Admiralty's," he confessed to Thompson. "Macarthur is bound to walk all over me."

"Then get advice from someone who does."

"You can't possibly mean Atkins!" Bligh scoffed.

"No, I mean a man who actually *knows* what he's talking about, George Crossley."

Bligh winced at the logic. There was no doubt of Crossley's legal credentials and his brilliant use of them, but he was a felon. After 20 years as an attorney at the

Court of King's Bench, he had stretched the parameters of the law and for forgery been transported to New South Wales. Although pardoned, he could no longer practice legitimately and for the past few years was earning a living by giving advice and drafting documents.

"The irony is that he's the only *trained* lawyer in the colony," Thompson continued.

Weighing up his options and the insufferable prospect of letting Macarthur win, Bligh took Crossley's advice to reject the appeal.

"I have considered all the evidence and uphold the magistrate's findings," he stated. "Mr Thompson's debt shall be discharged on payment of the original amount. It would be contrary to natural justice if the amount payable were allowed to be inflated by the consequences of a natural disaster which has had such a serious effect on the farms of the colony."

Bligh's decision put an end to conjecture and what slender threads of cordiality still existed between all concerned. If Macarthur did not like Crossley *before* the trial, he hated him now with a vengeance and added him to his list of vendettas. Bligh, however, who topped that list, had just given Macarthur the means to bring him down for having perverted the course of justice to favour a friend.

In the eyes of the law, the Governor had done nothing wrong, but Macarthur was a law unto himself and would deal with Bligh as he saw fit.

"I've never failed to ruin any man who crossed me," he boasted before having his motto stitched on a sampler to hang in his study – there to ward off anyone who might try.

His sour feelings flowed throughout the NSW Corp and soon after, Lieutenant D'Arcy Wentworth and Captain

Abbott, set up a mock trial to vent their disdain of Bligh's ruling in regard to the corps' arbitrary use of convict labour.

"It must stop!" Bligh decreed, which had a serious impact on the officers' cash flow.

So they used the trial as a forum for every unsubstantiated claim against him, with Whittle, among a host of others, giving evidence. The farce went on for days and at the end of it, Johnston sent a dispatch to England with written proof of their Governor's alleged mismanagement.

Bligh was relieved when they received no official reply, but for right or wrong, a case was building against him. Added to which was the arrival of Macarthur's two illegal stills in Sydney. Their confiscation came as no surprise to Macarthur, but he used it as a ruse to tackle Bligh in court once more.

"You won!" Johnston said, giving Macarthur a congratulatory slap on the back, but knowing it hadn't been fair and square, Macarthur shrugged off the compliment.

"It was a foregone conclusion," he admitted. "Atkins owed me money. His ruling in my favour resolved all debts."

That was obvious to everyone and they all wondered why Bligh did not object.

"There's no point," he explained. "I've resigned myself to Atkins' incompetence and am just waiting for his replacement to arrive."

It was completely out of character for him to keep his temper, but he vented it instead in a letter, alerting his friend Banks to the situation.

It's all but anarchy down here and increasingly hard for a man to stand alone against it. Why do I always attract trouble? I try my best, but I seem ever to be at war. I tell you, though, that I'd rather be facing the French Fleet where the fight is fair, than to battle the likes of Christian and Macarthur. With the first, the line of conflict was grey, but with the latter, it's of the darkest black. This man Macarthur is truly the devil, working fast and hard at my undoing.

Keen to save his friend from another disaster, Banks wrote straight back:

Dear William,

Do not let him win by arguing with him. You are your own worst enemy when you do so with all who question your opinion. I know you well and understand that your intentions are good, but those who don't will take advantage of them.

You've been dealt a bad hand twice over with your command of the Bounty and the Colony. Both difficult assignments were given to you without the required support and the blame is not yours to shoulder alone.

I beg you, though, not to fret any longer about Christian. The mutiny was a mistake from every point of view and if he were alive today, as an older and wiser man, I am sure he would agree and put your mind at rest.

Macarthur, however, is a different and far more dangerous kettle of fish, fully matured in mind and method, who knows exactly what he's about. Please do not risk your reputation by playing into his hands.

With all respect and wishes for your well-being,

Joseph

But even as he wrote his words of wisdom, Banks knew that Bligh would not abide by them. Although he would see their truth, he was incapable of letting go of any bone.

TWENTY-NINE

Christian had long since let go, having suffered four times over: First, over his guilt for inciting the mutiny; second, for having deserted his island family; third, due to the multiple lashes his 14 years of hard labour inflicted; and last, but not least, because he had betrayed his friend.

A better man, he told himself, would give his life for the chance to explain to Bligh; to tell him that the rash emotions of youth which stirred him to the inexcusable act of mutiny were long since gone and regretted.

It was cowardice, Christian was sure, which made him cling so tenaciously to a vile life ruled by whip and chain, rather than reveal himself to the authorities. To his never-ending shame, it appeared that his base instinct for survival surpassed all else.

He told himself that Bligh, living on the other side of the world, made the privilege of seeing him again impossible, but he did not reckon on the strange fate which would soon put him back within reach.

"The old Bounty Boy's been made Governor of New South Wales," was the news that ran the length of the chain gangs on Norfolk Island just two days before its inmates were transferred to Van Diemen's Land.

Shocked, Christian dropped his pick axe and broke into a cold sweat. It had been 11 years since he'd heard Bligh's name and felt the fear of death by association. More surprising, however, was that his initial panic was quickly followed by a feeling of elation at the prospect of having his friend close once more. What, after all, were the mere 600 miles between Van Diemen's Land and Sydney, compared with the 10,000 lonely knots to London that had separated them?

It was ludicrous, though, to imagine such a reunion when Bligh was as much bound by justified bitterness, as Christian was to his chains. As a mutineer and deserter, he was destined to die in them and when first moved to Van Diemen's Land, prayed it would happen sooner than later.

"*Dear God*, release me!" he had sighed in dismay when he first saw the uncivilised wilderness which awaited.

For two years, under the sting of the cat-o-nine tails, it was his hard labour that helped clear it. But then came a miracle, by courtesy of his old schoolmaster who, back on the Isle of Man, taught him Latin. In the process of reading it, Christian caught the attention of commandant, Lieutenant-Colonel William Paterson.

As administrator of the colony, Paterson was astonished by what he saw and went straight to the sentry guarding the chapel's front door.

"Who is that man?" he asked pointing to the convict on cleaning duty inside.

The prisoner in question had no idea that the commandant had been in the vestry. Thinking himself alone, Christian put down his mop to climb into the pulpit and read from the scriptures. That was surprising in itself, but became doubly so when he rejected the King James Bible in favour of its Latin version. The ancient text was there purely for display, but he read from it with a fluency and familiarity which exposed him as a man of quality.

In answer to the commandant's inquiry, the sentry flung the chapel door wide open.

"*Chapman!*" he roared at the prisoner.

At the sound of his adopted name, Christian slammed the Bible shut and scooped up his mop and bucket. For his audacity in having stopped work to browse through the good book, the guard slammed the butt of his musket down hard on his skull.

Stunned by the blow, Christian dropped to his knees and would have blacked out had the commandant not helped him back to his feet.

"*Imbecile!*" Paterson reprimanded the guard. "I told you to *bring* him to me, not *kill* him."

Beyond the blood that trickled between years of unshaven whiskers, it was hard to discern any signs of a gentleman on Christian's face, but intrigued by the mystery, Paterson gave him the support of his shoulder and walked him to his headquarters. There, he unlocked Christian's leg irons and offered him the luxury of a hot bath, razor and soap. What was revealed behind the ingrained grime from 13 years of torture was a man in his early 40s, with a face lined beyond its years and piercing blue eyes reflecting an eternity of suffering.

"Is that the name of your ship?" Paterson asked, pointing to the tattooed name of *Isabella* on Christian's chest.

Quick to cover it up, Christian grabbed for the linen shirt he was offered and tucked it in to the clean pair of brown trousers Paterson had provided. The feel of fresh fabric against his flesh was an extravagance he'd never thought he would experience again.

"No, sir," he answered with a simple courtesy in keeping with the kindness Paterson was extending.

At the sound of his cultured voice, Paterson's eyes narrowed. He had been looking through the records while Christian was cleaning up and wasn't convinced by the scant details their faded ink offered.

"Francis Chapman ... that's not your real name is it?"

Christian hesitated before running the proffered, whale-bone comb through his hair. It was still a rich black, but now sported thin streaks of grey and with one deft movement, he bound its excess length with the leather band Paterson handed him.

"Does it matter?" he replied. "Whoever I am and for whatever I did, I have paid the price."

To Paterson, that was evident. What danger he once represented had long since been knocked out of him. What was left was a man maimed and half starved in body, but still astute in mind – a mind, Paterson decided, he could put to good use.

"I'm transferring you to my household staff," he said. "Most of them need tutoring and my wife, goodness knows, will be delighted to have someone at last with whom she can discuss the classics."

For a fleeting moment, the look of relief on Christian's face took him back to the buoyant young man he used to be, his eyes full of hope and expectation of tomorrow.

"Thank you, sir," he said when Paterson showed him to his quarters at the back of the house. It was a tiny timber room with nothing but a stiff bed, washbasin and towel. But to Christian, it was a palace.

THIRTY

Back on the mainland, Macarthur had won his most recent court case, proving that at the click of his fingers and with clever rhetoric he could sway any jury. Proud of his achievement, he published his closing argument in the *Sydney Gazette* for all to read in wonder.

"The conceit of the man," Bligh said on seeing the headline.

He was not impressed, nor was the much-revered Robert Campbell, whose nephew Macarthur had used as bait to reel Bligh back into battle. The young man had been prosecuted and found guilty of unlawfully taking possession of Macarthur's stills.

"At my order, I'm sorry, Robert," Bligh apologised, still astonished that a command given by the Governor was questioned and ruled against in court. But more so, that Macarthur's audacity reached new heights in tackling Campbell, the one man in the colony he actually held in esteem.

"But then what did we expect with Atkins making the ruling?" Campbell replied. "He's a weak man at best, but Macarthur has him shaking in his boots."

Bligh strolled over to his drinks cabinet and poured some port.

"So he's won round one," he said, handing Campbell a glass. "But one day Macarthur's going to push his luck too far."

That day was fast approaching and throughout the colony rumour had it that there was soon to be a showdown between Bligh and Macarthur. The corps had already placed bets on the latter and was throwing around unveiled threats of taking vengeance on Bligh. All it was waiting for was the opportunity.

It came in a letter to Bligh from Tahiti, its contents scrawled in black ink by an irate missionary.

> *How dare you send a convicted murderer to our shores where we are attempting to convert natives to Christianity!*

The question was: *How* did the notorious convict John Hoare get there?

"On Macarthur's ship," was the answer provided by Robert Campbell, who as Collector of Taxes, was responsible for doing as much and of enforcing the law in the Port of Sydney.

"I've impounded it," he continued.

Bligh smothered a smile at the devastating impact this would have on Macarthur.

"He's not going to like that."

But then nor did Bligh when, as Governor, the buck stopped with him.

The impounded schooner Parramatta was jointly owned by Macarthur and trader Garnham Blaxcell, both of whom knew the punishment for facilitating stowaways.

To ensure that ship owners took every precaution to prevent such convict escapes, bonds had to be lodged with the colony's administrators; large amounts of money forfeited if felons got away.

Shortly after the Parramatta set sail for Tahiti it was discovered that convict John Hoare was missing, and as soon as the schooner docked back in Sydney, its cargo and crew were put under orders.

"Nothing is to be taken from the ship and no one is to leave it until the bond is paid in full," Campbell decreed.

He posted a contingent of constables on the wharf and, with a spring in his step at the prospect of payback, went to inform Bligh.

It was a touchy subject, however, and aware of Macarthur's open hostility towards him, Bligh tried to be fair by setting up an objective committee to bring down judgment.

> *We find that no particular member of the crew is at fault, but all failed to detain the fugitive in Tahiti, which enabled him to escape to America. We rule that the Parramatta and its cargo remain impounded until the bond is paid.*

The irony was that for a man who could talk his way around any crime, Macarthur had now been penalised for one in which he was genuinely not complicit. Too angry to speak to Bligh, he put his rage in writing and sent his son Edward to deliver it.

> *I am requesting that you reverse the committee's decision. As owners of the Parramatta, Mr Blaxcell and I have contributed much to the prosperity of this colony and have taken every reasonable step to ensure that no convict could stow away on our ship. It is contrary to natural justice to blame us for Hoare's escape and extremely unfair that we should be so heavily penalised for it.*

That penalty for Macarthur weighed in at a whopping 800 pounds and although secretly acknowledging the unfairness, Bligh could not help himself taking revenge for past injustices Macarthur had inflicted on him.

> *I will not overturn the decision of the committee,*
> he wrote back.

This left Macarthur no choice but to put his pride on the line once more and petition Campbell. It was an interview he dreaded, given that he'd offended the man twice over. Not only had he abused the regard in which he held Campbell, but he had dragged his young nephew through court purely for the sport of it.

With no way to make amends, he had to use every ounce of his charm to win Campbell over. But the man was unmoved.

"Put out your bond and you can have your ship," he said with implacable calm.

But as Scot against Scot on the subject of money, Macarthur fought back, shedding his facade in favour of the facts.

"The schooner itself should be security enough for the bond. At least, I should be allowed to salvage the perishables."

"You can have them when the bond is paid," Campbell reiterated, turning his attention back to the paperwork on his desk.

Seething, Macarthur drew a sharp breath.

"I shall not pay one penny! You can *keep* the ship and all its cargo. I'll write it off as a loss and claim compensation from my underwriters."

His declaration was followed by another he wrote to Parramatta's captain:

> *I have abandoned the schooner. Neither you nor the crew are henceforth to look to me for pay or provisions.*

The sailors were stranded. Unable to leave the ship, they slowly ate their way through its food, and to stop from starving, dared venture into Sydney's streets for supplies.

"You're under arrest!" they were immediately told by the constables, but then Campbell relented.

"You can buy some food," he told them. "But you must return directly to your ship."

When Campbell informed the Governor of the situation, Bligh was ill at ease.

"I don't want to give Macarthur any more ammunition to complain," he said. "It's not right to put the onus on the captain and crew. We'll refer the matter to Atkins, so it's *he* who lets Macarthur off the hook. Not us."

"Lord knows, the old boy's practised at it," Campbell replied contemptuously.

And that's why he was just as surprised as Bligh, when like a rabid dog, Atkins turned on his master.

Pursuant to your actions in having ceased to supply your employees with food," the judge advocate wrote to Macarthur, *"I request your attendance in Sydney at ten o'clock tomorrow morning to show just cause for your conduct.*

Macarthur wrote back:

I have no intention of explaining my conduct to you!

As the colony's wealthiest citizen, whose pride and success no governor had been able to contain, Macarthur certainly wasn't going to be brought to heel by his own lapdog. But sick of playing that role, Atkins stepped out of character and took umbrage. Without consulting the Governor, he drew up his own complaint accusing Macarthur of illegally stopping payment and provision of food for those on the Parramatta and sent him a formal summons to appear in court.

"It must be delivered to Macarthur at Elizabeth Farm tonight," Atkins instructed Constable Francis Oakes, who was none-too-delighted with the duty when Macarthur was renowned for his fiery temper and fascination for fighting duels.

By the time he arrived at the estate, it was dark, and not wanting to confront the great man at his own front door, Oakes knocked at the back.

"Constable Oakes," Macarthur said with candle in hand. "What on earth brings you here so late?"

"This, I'm afraid, sir," Oakes answered, handing him the summons.

He watched Macarthur read it and saw for himself the surge of hot blood which erupted red on his face.

"You may tell that *coward* Atkins," he hissed through clenched teeth, "that if he, himself, has the guts to ever deliver a *second* message of the like, it'll mean bloodshed. I've already been robbed of 10,000 pounds by those people. Push me further and just see what happens!"

What happened was that Macarthur was promptly put under arrest for "*contempt of court* and *sedition for making threats of bloody rebellion*".

"Macarthur's defiance cannot be overlooked," Bligh conceded after learning of Atkins' actions, "but I hand the issue over, in its entirety, to our judge advocate."

Things were getting out of hand and Bligh wanted no part of it. Not for fear of Macarthur, but because he was still in the throes of mourning his son-in-law. Frankly, he didn't care whether Macarthur lived or died, just so long as he kept his distance.

Macarthur, however, was not one to be brushed aside.

"Not Guilty!" was his belligerent answer to the charges at the preliminary hearing.

He was granted bail and his trial was fixed for January 15, 1808, by the four magistrates presiding.

He objected to Robert Campbell being one of them,

but was shocked when two of the others – his great friends majors Johnston and Abbott – said not one word in his defence. Instead, they agreed that he was a turbulent character who would do well to moderate his interests.

"Well thank you very much," he said scornfully to them afterwards.

Johnston explained in a guarded whisper.

"If we are to help you in the long run, we must at least *appear* to be objective."

Although calmed by the explanation, he was more astonished by its calculated cunning, a gift for which neither man had shown the slightest propensity in the past. It flashed a warning for him to watch his back.

Right now, it was flat to the wall. He knew he was guilty as charged and had to make sure that those judging his trial were prejudice in his favour. The Criminal Court of the Colony required that all cases be heard by the judge-advocate and six military officers. The majority ruled and so Macarthur needed only four of those officers to be on side.

Child's play, he reckoned, because since selling his commission, he had remained on very friendly terms with the NSW Corps and was sure of its keen-edged animosity towards Bligh. If no British ships were in Sydney at the time of the trial, there'd be no naval officers to vie for a place on the bench. The power would rest with the army and Atkins' vote would be immaterial.

But just as a point of principle, Macarthur wanted him out.

You still owe me ninety pounds, he wrote in a letter of demand to Atkins.

It's forty-five! Atkins wrote back indignantly, having all but forgotten the debt incurred six years before.

According to the Statute of Limitations it should have been null and void, but with a view to the upcoming trial, he appeared prepared to pay it.

It <u>was</u> forty-five, Macarthur penned back, *but with interest accrued and compounded, it's now ninety.*

Macarthur went to Atkins' house to collect.

"Tell him I'm not at home," Atkins instructed his butler.

So Macarthur waited all day in his garden for his return. Enraged, Atkins finally flung open his front door and confronted him.

"I'm not paying!" he yelled.

"Well in that case, sir," Macarthur replied coolly, "I shall take it to the Governor."

Playing middleman was the last thing Bligh wanted.

"I have no desire to get involved in a spat between you and Atkins," he said when Macarthur showed him the judge-advocate's old promissory note. "You'll have to take it to Civil Court."

"Well that will hardly be fair," Macarthur replied, enjoying every minute of putting Bligh on the spot, "when Atkins himself will be presiding over it! If you refuse to intervene in this issue, which by rights is your duty, I shall be forced to detail my case to His Majesty's Secretary of State to the Colonies."

"Damn that fool, Atkins!" Bligh swore when their meeting was over. Macarthur was right and he didn't have a leg to stand on.

All he had wanted Atkins to do was to reprimand Macarthur over the *Parramatta* business and the idiot, without consulting him, launched into a full scale accusation of sedition! Now Bligh had no option but to let the law run its course if he were to have any chance of stopping Macarthur reporting him, by default, to the authorities.

Nothing in life was fair.

Here, Bligh was wrong, for the very next day a petition arrived at Government House, its 16 pages signed by more than 830 of the colony's settlers:

> *We want to thank you, Governor Bligh, for improving our lot in life. Your courage under difficult circumstances and against such strong opposition is exemplary and we wish to assure you of our loyal support, even at the risk of our lives and properties.*

This alarmingly dramatic oath put Bligh on the alert. What did they know that he didn't? And why would he be in need of their protection?

"There's been talk of an armed revolt," one of those settlers told him.

But Bligh discarded the idea outright.

"They're a rowdy, undisciplined corps, to be sure, but its officers are gentlemen pledged to the King. They wouldn't *dare* lay a hand on his representative."

That was true, so Macarthur had to work hard to devise a scheme which would take the corps to a place of no return where hating Bligh was concerned. Instead of lifting a sword to wage war, he picked up his pen.

> *I am asking your permission to build on Sydney's Lot 77,* he wrote in application to Bligh. *The block of land was granted to me on a fourteen-year lease by Governor King.*

Here lay trouble and Bligh dealt with it as tactfully as possible.

> *I'm afraid that Lot 77 has been designated as a site for a church but I am happy to offer you another block of land in recompense.*

Macarthur smiled. Now he had Bligh just where he wanted him. With every courtesy, he replied:

> *Very well, I would like the block right on the waterfront.*

Bligh now realised that he had fallen into the trap, but rejecting the role of victim, he took back the whip hand.

> *That will not be possible. The erection of wharves on that site is already on the agenda. I will, however, apply to London on your behalf, to see if any amendments can be made in regard to your Lot 77, but in the meantime, you are to make no moves to build on it.*

The scene was set and the battleground selected.

When Bligh, the next day, saw soldiers of the corps erecting a fence around Lot 77, he leapt from his carriage to confront them.

"What on earth do you think you're doing?"

"Mr Macarthur is paying us double the normal rate to build a barrier around his property, sir," Corporal Colin Boyd explained, as he wiped his brow and quickly buttoned his tunic.

Staggered by Macarthur's brazen defiance, Bligh's temper exploded in a whirling, star-studded fury.

"Rip it down!" he ordered and in doing so, played right into Macarthur's hands by stoking the corps' smoldering hostility into a raging inferno.

In one swift maneuver, Macarthur managed to implicate the military in his private battle with Bligh. Now that *their* hard sweat and toil was involved, they were fit to kill and Macarthur had ensured that he had an army behind him.

THIRTY-ONE

Step Two towards rebellion had Macarthur organise a dinner party for all corps' officers on the eve of his trial. It was a lavish affair at his cost, with an abundance of wine supplied to loosen tongues and whip weak men into a frenzy. He, in the meantime, absented himself from the festivities. Were they not so drunk, the officers might have been offended that their host preferred to wander the city streets alone. But he had his reasons.

"I wanted to dissociate myself from the trouble zone," he explained to his wife, "and make sure that I was seen elsewhere by everybody, just in case plans go awry."

Elizabeth lifted her head from the pillow and re-lit the bedside candle.

"What plans?" she questioned, alarmed by her husband's need to provide himself with an alibi.

The reflection of the candle flame danced gold in her green eyes. In them he suddenly saw fear and, thinking better of making her a party to those plans of his, he kissed her goodnight.

"Nothing to concern yourself about, my love," he replied, turning on his side.

He had done a good day's work and fell sound asleep.

– oOo –

As he had hoped, there was not a naval officer in sight when he arrived at his trial the next morning. Sitting in judgment were just a row of friendly faces: six of his closest associates from the corps. All were suffering the sick consequences of the previous night's revelry and were keen to settle the case quickly in their friend's favour.

With a view to that end, Macarthur struck out instantly to take control of proceedings:

"Before we begin," he announced as he strode arrogantly in the door. "I object to Judge – Advocate Atkins presiding over this case. He owes me money, has a known agenda against me and will profit from a guilty verdict. I demand that he stands down."

Macarthur always knew how to work a crowd and the one in the courtroom exploded in a foot-thumping round of cheers.

"*Out of order! Out of order!*" Atkins bellowed above the noise, furiously hammering his gavel on the bench. "Behave yourself, Mr Macarthur, or I shall have you committed for contempt of court."

At this, the presiding officer, Captain Anthony Kemp, turned with an overriding contempt of his own to address the judge advocate.

"*You*, commit Mr *Macarthur?*" he said. "No indeed, sir. We shall commit *you!*"

"This is outrageous!" Atkins leapt to his feet to say. "Court is adjourned."

He stormed from the assembly and was followed soon after by Macarthur; who walked free with an armed escort for protection. It took a few minutes for Atkins to pull himself together and realise that he'd left his confidential papers on the bench. He raced back to retrieve them, but it was too late. The presiding officers of the corps had taken them.

"Quick!" he instructed Provost Marshal William Gore. "Run over to the Magistrates' Court and make sure that a bench warrant for Macarthur's arrest is executed immediately. With no court verdict he should remain in custody, but he's walked free without renewing his bail. You do that and I'll go to the Governor to let him know what's happened."

It was imperative that Bligh was briefed by both sides. However, not keen to deal with their Governor face-to-face, the six corps officers from the court sent him a note.

> *We consider Macarthur's objections to Atkins valid and believe that we, as commissioned officers, have acted correctly and shown the appropriate respect to the representative of the King.*

The magistrates' account of the court proceedings differed and Bligh had a crisis on his hands. The judicial system had collapsed and a man charged with sedition was walking free.

"Fetch Crossley," he ordered, knowing that he needed legal advice fast.

Crossley came and gave it, recommending that Bligh write a note straight back to the officers:

All criminal cases in the colony's Criminal Court must be presided over by a Judge-Advocate and six officers. The choice of that Judge-Advocate is not at the discretion of the latter and as Colonial Governor, I am not authorised to replace an appointee of the King.

The officers' answer came straight back:

We will <u>not</u> sit with Atkins.

"And they've stolen my court documents," Atkins chimed in, mopping his brow after his red-faced rush to Government House.

You must give them back, Bligh wrote to instruct the officers.

We will not! they replied.

It was deadlock with neither side prepared to budge. Ironically, Bligh had already applied for a replacement for Atkins, but his request, via sea mail, had still not arrived in England and he wasn't willing to defer the case until it did. Nor were the officers, in the meantime, prepared to officiate with Atkins.

Just to add to the chaos, there came an urgent letter to Bligh from Macarthur.

You must act immediately to protect me for I am under threat of my life from that dismembered limb of the law, your friend and legal advisor, George Crossley. I have had it from a reliable source that he, in association with Atkins, has arranged for a group of thugs to dispose of me.

"What nonsense!" Bligh scoffed.

It was absurd to believe as much when Crossley had done nothing but offer legal advice and certainly wasn't stupid enough to threaten another man's life. But realising, at last, that he was being played for a fool, Bligh wrote back:

I can hardly grant you armed protection, Macarthur, when a contingent of constables is already on its way to arrest you.

The situation was turning to farce and when the court officers realised that Macarthur needed to be granted bail if he were to remain free, they rushed back to the courthouse to organise it.

"You can't do that," Crossley informed them. "Your attendance without Atkins does not constitute a court and your ruling will be illegal."

"That's enough!" Bligh bellowed through the bickering, before he sent a written order to Sydney's Corps Commander, Major Johnston, demanding that he come straight away and take control of his men.

I cannot, the bedridden Johnston wrote back. *I fell from my carriage last night after Macarthur's dinner party and my arm is in a sling.*

At this pathetic excuse, Bligh was fit to break every other bone in the man's body, but his hands were tied. Macarthur was running rings round him and he'd been openly defied by the corps. All he could do was to sit in dread of tomorrow.

THIRTY-TWO

It came with a burst of summer rain, which did not augur well for their Australia Day celebrations. Yet, as the 20th anniversary of Governor Phillip's founding of the colony, Bligh was duty bound to commemorate it.

"Well I'm not doing it publicly," he said, having heard rumours of his own assassination plot.

Instead, he hosted an intimate dinner party, extending an invitation to those high-minded in the community, rather than the politically correct.

"By rights, Macarthur and his wife should be seated at your table," he was advised by those used to catering to the sheep breeder's prominence in their society.

But Bligh took advantage of the unstable circumstances and demurred:

"I will not entertain a felon in my home."

A lie when he was happy to share his meal with Crossley, who as a convicted criminal came to Sydney's shores in ball and chain. Sipping on his wine, the now liberated lawyer was still mulling over the situation, smug for having stumbled over its temporary solution. He had put it to Bligh two hours before.

"The court officers' actions amount to a usurpation of powers of His Majesty's government and should be treated as treason."

That was a crime punishable by death and Crossley warned the officers of as much in a dispatch.

On reading it, Lieutenant William Minchin panicked at the prospect of culpability and rode like the wind to Johnston's house to drag him out of bed.

"All hell's breaking loose in the city," he told his superior officer. "Macarthur's been arrested and the corps needs you *now!*"

Johnston groaned and flipped back his bedcovers.

"For God's sake, can't a sick man be left in peace?" he cursed, knowing that the previous night's accident had deprived him of a carriage and the use of one arm.

It was difficult saddling his horse with only the other arm and harder still to ride at a gallop to the city, but Macarthur needed him and had to be obeyed at all costs. Much as he loathed playing the part of the man's puppet, Johnston hadn't the strength of character to stop. So as soon as he arrived at the army barracks, he signed and sent an order to Macarthur's gaoler:

> *Release him!* it read.
> *By command of*
> *Major G. Johnston,*
> *Lieutenant – Governor.*

Minchin was concerned when he saw Johnston scratch his signature above that title.

"Do you think that's wise?" he asked. "I thought that rank belonged to our commanding officer, Lieutenant-Colonial Paterson."

That was true, but emboldened by the fact that Macarthur would soon be free to back his actions, Johnston replied:

"Yes, but *he's* in Van Diemen's Land and I am here. Who's on hand to question me?"

No one, it appeared, and with great fanfare Macarthur was released. Surrounded by sycophants and brothers of the corps, he strode triumphant through the city streets to the barracks, pausing only to write a declaration of war. With no table available to accommodate it, he put pen to paper on a parade-ground cannon and encouraged all present to sign it. Only six were brave enough to put their name to rebellion, but Macarthur was undeterred.

"I'll manufacture a few more after the deed is done," he said when he handed Johnston the petition. "You can be sure there'll be plenty to justify the rebellion after its success."

Johnston had complete faith in Macarthur's initiatives and read this one with a smile because he was its main beneficiary:

> With the alarming state of the colony putting every man's property, liberty and life in danger, we implore you, Major Johnston, to place Governor Bligh under arrest and assume command of the colony.

It was a mystifying state of affairs for those civilian bystanders who were going about their normal daily business. As far as they could see, there was no disturbance of any sort to incite a revolt.

From his pulpit, only the day before, Reverend Henry Fulton remarked that he had never seen the colony so content and that all confidence was in Bligh. Later, murmuring under his breath, that if the troublemaking New South Wales Corps would just do its job all would be well.

But by now the officers of the corps had blood in their eye and were beyond keeping the peace. To them it amounted to boredom, which for fit, fighting men was as much a catalyst for war as a foreign invasion.

Oblivious to the brewing danger, Bligh's dinner party went ahead, but mid-entree, he looked up with a start at the sound of a drum roll in the street. He recognised it as a call to arms and excusing himself from the table, went to the window.

All seemed in order, but he had an uneasy feeling of *déjà vu,* reminiscent of the day before the Bounty mutiny. Suddenly, at a mental flash of Fletcher Christian's face melting into Macarthur's, the hairs on the back of his neck stood to attention and he looked for reassurance to the two cannons guarding his residence.

"When all else fails, we can always put our faith in artillery," he quipped as he retook his seat and continued his meal.

He would have choked on it had he known that those guns positioned to defend him were soon to play a part in his destruction: that Lieutenant Minchin had secretly armed them with cannonball and gunpowder in readiness to turn and fire on Government House.

In rank and file, the entire New South Wales Corps was now marching up the hill towards it. Their show of force not so much needed to contend with Bligh, his daughter and nine guests, but with the 800 settlers who had earlier pledged their support to him and could come good on their promise.

Suddenly from the dining room window, the soldiers' red ranks were visible, and seeing the alarm on his guests' faces, Bligh calmly finished his glass of wine and folded his napkin.

"There's little we can do but welcome them," he said, getting up from his chair. "No need to panic. It's only me they're after. I'm sure that the rest of you won't be harmed. If nothing else, Johnston is a gentleman and will see to that."

"Papa …" Mary cried in dismay as she moved quickly from her seat to his side.

"There's no need to be frightened, dearest," he comforted. "Now I want you to calmly continue your meal and make every effort to maintain your composure while I go upstairs and dress for the occasion."

That, to him, was of paramount importance given his sad state of undress at his last mutiny. But having lost their appetite, Mary and guests went to the verandah to watch the enemy advance.

There they were at the crest of the hill with bayonets shining silver in the sun. Johnston, arm in sling, lead the way, he and his men marching out of step with fife and drum because of the imbibed rum Macarthur supplied to supplement their courage – while he, impressive and cold sober, headed the contingent of citizens that followed, each enjoying being part of the parade and feeling safe in his shadow.

All that stood between them and Bligh were the cannons and sentries positioned to protect him. Both now did an about-face; those guards on duty turning the guns on Government House before they deserted their post to join their comrades of the corps.

In full dress uniform, Bligh moved quickly downstairs to his study to destroy all incriminating documents. He grabbed as many as he could and carrying them back upstairs, locked himself in a back room to sort through them. All he needed was time, but he was fast running out of it.

The enemy was at the gate and being her father's daughter, Mary took the offensive and advanced on them before they had a chance to open it.

"Traitors!" she accused them, as she brandished her pink parasol and leant her light weight against the iron-picket barrier. "You have just walked over my husband's grave to murder my father, but you'll have to kill *me* first!"

Her brave gesture was met with an amused chuckle as two soldiers lifted her, like a feather, out of the way.

"Where's the Governor?" Johnston demanded of the dinner guests when his troops stormed the house.

At their failure to answer, the search of the mansion and its outhouses began. Hearing the soldiers approaching his small back room, Bligh swept his papers off the bed and hid behind it. For a tense moment, secreted behind the four-poster's drapes, he dared not breathe and exhaled with relief when the soldiers refrained from opening the door.

It was a close shave, but there was no longer any possibility of escape. The small window which was his one way of facilitating it now only offered him a view of the soldiers surrounding the house. They had been there for half an hour and Sergeant Whittle was fed up with their fruitless search.

"Blast you useless idiots!" he swore at his men. "*I'll* find him. Follow *me.*"

He had a personal score to settle with the Governor and this was his only chance to do it with some semblance of legality. When Bligh heard them coming along the corridor a second time, he stuffed what papers remained under his jacket and slipped back behind the red, velvet drapes, but his luck had run out.

"There he is!" Whittle shouted at the thrill of discovery. "Drag him out!"

"And that's where we found him," the sergeant later reported to the *Sydney Gazette*, "squirming like a cringing coward under the bed."

To which Mary hit back in burning-hot defence of her father.

"*If* my father were a coward, he would have taken his opportunity to escape, but instead, he stayed to see to his duty, just as he did with Lord Nelson who hailed him as a hero. *That* he is, so don't you *dare* defile his name."

Sadly, that's what they continued to do, if for no other reason but to justify their seditious actions. To destroy Bligh's reputation was their most effective way of doing it, so the newspaper ran with the 60-point banner:

FOUND HIDING UNDER HIS BED!

Even though Bligh could not possibly have squeezed under its four-inch-high feet, it was a good yarn destined to span the centuries and belittle him.

In reality, he gave himself up when the soldiers broke down the door. Seeing that he was unarmed, Lieutenant Minchin ordered his men to relinquish their hold on him as they escorted Bligh to his own office. There, already sitting at the Governor's desk, was Johnston, who without the courtesy of getting to his feet, read the riot act.

You are no longer the Governor of NSW. At the request of its citizens, I have taken command of the colony. We are now under martial law and I will act as Governor until replaced by another appointed by His Majesty. You are to leave for England on the first available ship and until then, you will remain under armed house arrest, seeing and communicating with no one.

"Well that was done with remarkable regularity," Macarthur said of his Rum Rebellion's success.

Having confiscated and read the papers that Bligh failed to destroy, he was now in full possession of the facts and would make sure they were never used against him.

Bligh's guests were unharmed and allowed to return home.

"You know that you can always count on our support," commissary general, John Palmer, shouted to Bligh over his shoulder as he was pushed out the front door.

But it was shut firm in the face of any such help from his friends.

THIRTY-THREE

Bligh had only served 18 months of his four-year term as Governor and was determined to see his contract out. What did it matter that he'd been overthrown; or that during a wild night of revelry, the rebels burnt his effigy and crowned Macarthur king?

"I'm not worried," Bligh confessed to Mary as much to put his own mind at ease as hers. "There's still a substantial percentage of the population on my side."

For that reason, the rebels were keen to get rid of him fast. They ordered him to leave for England on the first available ship, but as one after the other left port, Bligh refused to board.

In a fit of frustration, Whittle stepped out of ranks to demand an answer from his superior officer.

"Why don't we just *throw* him on one and be done with it?"

While Johnston dithered over a reply, Macarthur provided it.

"Because we don't want to manhandle the King's representative and have the charge of assault added to that of rebellion."

It was a stalemate destined to last 12 months, with Government House under armed guard and Bligh permitted only to stroll in its garden with his daughter where their conversations were closely monitored by soldiers walking five paces behind.

The rebels' tight reins had to be loosened, however, when it came to affairs of the navy. As Commander of His Majesty's Ships in the South Pacific, Bligh had to be allowed access to all Admiralty communication and the visits of naval officers, both of which facilitated contact with London.

Those officers in their blue coats saw for themselves the graffiti scrawled on the city walls that read *"Kill the Tyrant"*, and no doubt reported as much back to English authorities. But Napoleon and his war took precedence over the concerns of their colony on the other side of the world.

This, Bligh understood, as much as he did the fact that a counter revolution staged by his pledged 800 was impractical, given their inexperience of war. He, however, had a will stronger than any sword and was prepared to sit it out until Britain disposed of the little French Corporal and sent fresh troops to restore his rights.

Occasionally, Mary was permitted to visit her friends, but for the most part, she chose to stay with her father.

"I'm afraid you must find my company very tedious," Bligh said when he saw her sitting alone at the window.

She turned with a reassuring smile.

"Not one bit of it," she replied. "We are under siege and holding out against a numerically superior force. What exciting stories I'll have to tell my grandchildren."

She was his strength and joy and he never ceased to be proud of her courage. It bolstered his own enough to ask a favour.

"May I be allowed to see my secretary, Mr Griffin?" he asked Johnston.

"No," Johnston replied. "He'd be of no use to you because he's been relieved of his position. Macarthur is now Secretary of the Colony."

It was hard for Bligh to contain his dismay.

"Good Lord, the man's made himself Dictator!"

"So be it," Johnston confirmed, seemingly content with the disparity between himself and his friend. On paper the power was his, but in reality, Macarthur ruled supreme.

It was an interesting exercise in psychology and Bligh studied Johnston's face.

"You know, nothing Macarthur does ever surprises me," he said. "But I often wonder at *your* eagerness to play second fiddle. I mean, what's in it for you? He gets all the perks of power, but you'll be sure to suffer the same punishment for your part in usurping it."

Johnston often asked himself the same question and at a loss for an answer, walked from the room leaving Bligh to enjoy his moment of triumph.

Macarthur, meantime, was too busy to care, having put *himself* on trial to have his charge of sedition dismissed. It was a contrived forum to further discredit Bligh and to stand himself centre stage where, for days, he reveled in the sound of his own voice and the influence it had over others.

He was so thrilled by the audience response that he followed with an encore of trials aimed at innocent men against whom he held nothing more than a grudge.

"Seven years hard labour in the coal mines!" was the sentence handed down to George Crossley for giving Bligh legal advice.

And seven more for provost general William Gore, who under Atkins' order, procured a bench warrant for Macarthur's arrest.

Sir Henry Browne-Hayes, prominent owner of the Vaucluse Estate, was to serve the same for committing the unpardonable crime of speaking up in defence of Gore; and Reverend Fulton was suspended from his religious duties for simply saying a prayer for Bligh.

Having tampered with one of God's men, however, Macarthur stopped short of condemning Robert Campbell; still in awe, as he was, of his exemplary Arthurian aura.

But all in all, bringing down men of substance was heady stuff and intoxicated by Macarthur's free reign and flow of rum, the people were his for the taking, all of them drunk with power and too foggy-headed to interfere with his administration.

That was until the morning-after effects set in and the reality of retribution hung heavy on the horizon. An English ship would soon appear on it, carrying warrants for their arrest and their southern seclusion would no longer protect them. Desperate to pass the buck, the officers of the corps tried to hand Macarthur full responsibility. They did it with a smile and thick slathering of flattery in the hope that it would stir him to fall on his sword.

"You must go to England to explain the reasons for our

Rum Rebellion and our rightful claim on the colony. You are the only one of us with the eloquence to do it."

Seeing straight through the charade, Macarthur played their game.

"I will when I'm ready," he agreed, giving them a false sense of security while stalling for time to finish feathering his own nest. As far as he could see, he still had a few good months up his sleeve.

"What about me?" Johnston dared protest, having had *his* feathers ruffled by Bligh.

"What *about* you?" Macarthur casually replied as he signed off on a shipment of government supplies for his own use.

"Well what do I get out of this?"

"Whatever you can, so long as it doesn't clash with me and mine."

That seemed fair enough, and shrugging off Bligh's inference, Johnston slipped happily back into the role of underdog, consoling himself with a few more land grants while randomly handing out more to friends and suspect associates who had proved themselves unworthy. But those recipients soon wanted more and in their growing greed, turned on their benefactors with fang-bearing ferocity.

"Why should *you* and Macarthur get the prime cuts?" they demanded with an underlying threat of violence that Johnston found disturbing.

But to Macarthur it came as no surprise.

"Just human nature," he explained, knowing the time-limit on temptation and making the most of his while it lasted.

It was not for long.

"So he's coming back is he?" he said on reading the news of Lieutenant-Governor Foveaux's return.

Macarthur handed the English dispatch back to Johnston and with tongue in cheek continued:

"Looks like you're out of a job, Johnston. He'll outrank you."

It was a slap in the face for Johnston, but the smile was also wiped from Macarthur's when Foveaux made it his first order of business to remove *him* from power.

"That cunning bastard," Macarthur sneered, realising that Foveaux had his measure and that their feigned friendship had fallen forfeit to Foveaux's ambition -- an ambition which outstripped his own.

To soften the blow, Foveaux threw him a bone by way of another sizeable grant of land. It wasn't enough to make him happy, but Macarthur knew when to back off, his shrewd sense of survival telling him to temporarily kowtow to a man more ruthless than himself.

"And to think," he said with a sigh to Johnston, "what extraordinary measures I took to make sure that Paterson didn't come back from Van Diemen's Land when Bligh tried to recall him. I thought the weak sot would get in my way, but in his stead, Foveaux's obliterated it."

Reduced to a private citizen of limited power, Macarthur had plenty of time to mull over the problem and to polish his dueling pistols.

"The only way to get rid of Foveaux is to shoot him," he mused, as his expert hand smoothed gun-oil over their long barrels.

This was going to extremes and he laughed at his own expense. He had only himself to blame for underestimating the man's capacity. He'd assumed, that as a man disposed to evil, Foveaux would slide comfortably under his control.

But unlike Johnston, he aspired to nothing less than being number one.

Foveaux was smart in the way he went about it, keeping it all above board by quickly establishing a more conservative administration and depriving the people of nothing Macarthur had given them so they didn't miss him. For an army man, Foveaux had a flair for making things shipshape. His only mistake was to favour the rebels' side of the story over Bligh's and to treat those still loyal to him with contempt.

It was a very big mistake, when as a government appointee, it was his duty to stand by Bligh until he was formally relieved of his position. Foveaux, however, was pre-disposed to hate him.

He had sailed back from England on the same ship which carried a letter from Betsy Bligh to her husband:

My dear, please be wary of Foveaux for he is not your friend.

Foveaux had made that clear before he'd left London. He did not approve of Bligh's treatment of Captain Short during the HMS Porpoise affair and of course, there was always his questionable Bounty reputation. So as soon as Foveaux set foot in Sydney, he embraced the rebels' cause with its concocted accusations of Bligh's corruption and refused to even grant the man, himself, an interview.

It was outrageous and supremely unfair.

"But more so, disappointing," Bligh said to Mary, having thought Foveaux would be his salvation.

To accommodate his arrival, Bligh and the former first

lady were moved from the comfort of Government House to the spartan facilities of army barracks.

When two guards came to escort Bligh there, Mary ran to his side.

"Where are you taking him?" she asked.

"Never you mind, m'lady. There's no need for you to go with him," Corporal Barnes replied, gently moving her out of the way, but she stepped straight back in it.

"Do you honestly think I'd allow you to take him without me?' she replied.

They were not in the mood to argue the point. Grabbing Bligh's arm, they pushed past her.

She rushed after them, to the amazement of everyone watching in the street, running behind the carriage that carried her father all the way to the barracks. It was a good mile in the hot sun, dressed in long skirt and ruffles and she arrived fit to drop.

"For God's sake, man," Bligh demanded of Johnston. "Give my daughter some water!"

"Go home, Mary," he then turned to tell her as the soldiers dragged him away, but she called after him.

"I choose to stay with you."

Her mind was made up and from experience, Bligh knew better than to try to change it. So he slept on the barrack room's stiff sofa to allow her the luxury of its army-issue cot. Gone was their privacy and privilege, but they were determined not to complain or to condone the damning allegation that Bligh enriched himself at others' expense.

"It's certainly not apparent," said Foveaux's secretary, Lieutenant John Finucane, when on inspection of the colony their carriage drew up in front of Bligh's country estate.

They had been told that he lavished stolen funds on its construction and doubled its harvests to the detriment of other settlers. But here before them, in a field of untended weeds, was nothing but a derelict, timber shanty with tin roof rusted through and toppling down on one side.

Having accused Bligh of all bad things, Finucane felt ashamed. It was a shame heightened by the shine he'd taken to his pretty daughter, who through thick and thin, stood stoically at her father's side.

For Foveaux, shame was overshadowed by stark panic. He had made a major mistake and needed to quit the scene before being named an "accessory to the fact". It was imperative that he get back to England before he was formally called there to answer charges. For renowned as an exceptionally efficient, intelligent man, he had no excuse for being led astray by lesser men and liars.

He had been in charge for only six months, but was now keener than Bligh to see his superior officer, Lieutenant-Colonel Paterson return from Van Diemen's Land to relieve him of command.

"What in the hell's taking him so long?" he asked, echoing Bligh's own question.

Primarily for Paterson, it was laziness and a reluctance to leave his life of leisure in the penal colony. He had made it his kingdom where he reigned in peace and devoted himself to his garden, daily wandering its impressive acres to catalogue new species of flora for the Mother Country's reference. After a long life of war and adventure, he had settled into a more gentle way of life and was loathe to exchange it for the trouble in New South Wales.

And there was always the fact that he was afraid. Not of his NSW Corps, but of Bligh, who had threatened to tear him limb from limb for having disobeyed an order.

> *Come to Sydney immediately. I am under siege and need you,* Bligh had scribbled in a frantic note a few months before, to which came Paterson's reply:

> *You should go to England and sort it out with their Lordships in London.*

It lit Bligh's short fuse, and not knowing that his temper tantrums were always fleeting, Paterson was worried that Bligh, even after all this time, might punish him for putting plants above preserving his Governor's life.

THIRTY-FOUR

"I wonder how long he'll hold it against me?" Paterson said to Christian.

After all these years, it still seemed strange answering to his alias of Chapman, and hesitating, Christian put the volume of Cicero back on the shelf. He and Paterson had been discussing it, but for all its philosophy, he was at a loss.

"I suppose it depends on the depth of his anger and hurt," he replied, being the last person on Earth to be asked such a question. For him, securing Bligh's forgiveness was a pipedream.

Paterson got up awkwardly from his chair, his gout-ridden legs aching at the effort.

"Dash it all," he yawned. "I suppose I'll have to go back up north."

"It would seem so, sir," Christian replied.

They were accustomed to talking together in the

evenings, Christian having established himself in the household as a man of intellect, worthy of every confidence. Of course, to think of him as an equal was out of the question, but despite Christian's convict status, Paterson was more and more tempted to do so. He enjoyed the man's company and no longer wanting to be without it, he said: "You shall come with me as my valet."

Christian had not yet served his full sentence, but had long since been out of convict garb. To fit his adopted role as tutor and personal servant, Paterson provided him with suitable clothes and a small wage, both of which removed him from the ranks of prisoner and permitted him to travel to New South Wales, relatively unnoticed, in the company of the Lieutenant-Governor.

At Paterson's insistence, they arrived in Sydney without fanfare.

"Drop me off at Watson's Bay," he ordered to avoid the crowds at Sydney's main port and the political strife that awaited.

Delaying the inevitable, he remained in hiding there for a few days, but nothing stayed secret from Macarthur and Foveaux for long. For varying reasons, both men were keen to have him back on board: Macarthur, so that he could control him; and Foveaux, so that he could hand over the reins and get back to England as quickly as possible. As soon as they found him, they arranged for his staff and luggage to follow later and whisked Paterson away in a fast carriageride to the city to formally announce him as Lieutenant-Governor of the colony.

"But as commandant of the corps, Foveaux, you are still in charge of the inner city until you leave," Paterson quickly stipulated. "In the meantime, I shall take up residence at Parramatta and perform my government duties from there."

"Perfect!" Macarthur concurred, refraining from rubbing his hands with glee.

Paterson selected a Parramatta mansion, far from the public eye, in the hope that its private grounds would leave him free to garden and drink at will. Unfortunately, it was within a very short walking distance of Macarthur's Elizabeth Farm and he intended to drop in every day to make Paterson's hideaway the hub of political activity from where he, Macarthur, would once again rule the colony.

Despite the fact that Foveaux planned to leave it, he had to keep a close watch on their collaboration and several times a week made a point of turning up at Paterson's home at the same time as Macarthur; both men coming with their own agenda and a sudden overriding desire to be served morning tea.

"One lump or two?" Paterson asked belligerently as he signaled his maid to pass the porcelain cups of hot brew to his two guests.

Both declined the sugar, but accepted the piece of pound cake on offer.

"You know, Foveaux," Macarthur said, settling back comfortably in his chair. "You still haven't formally signed off on that grant of land you offered me."

With Paterson present as arbiter, Macarthur was primed to provoke Foveaux into coming good on his promise.

"I shall see to it soon," Foveaux replied, suddenly too tight-lipped to take another bite of his cake.

Annoyed by their regular visits and constant goading of each other, Paterson was keen for a diversion and found it when Christian walked into the room to leave documents on his desk.

"Ah Chapman …," Paterson said brightly. "Come over here will you, I want to introduce you."

It was unprecedented to say as much to a convict, but given his civilian attire, neither visitor saw him as one and stood up to greet him.

"Gentlemen," Paterson said taking over the formalities. "Mr Chapman here, has become my greatest help and closest of companions of late. He has an excellent mind which I'm sure you'll both appreciate."

Macarthur shook hands, polite but not particularly impressed; perhaps piqued a little that the man was as handsome as he and in that way, presented competition. His subservient status, however, precluded it and marked him as a person of no concern.

But Foveaux's reaction, Macarthur noted, was most peculiar, shaking Chapman's hand, as he did, with a knowing smile which inferred that this stranger and he shared a secret.

"It's a pleasure to meet you, sir," Foveaux said. "Mr *Chapman*, you say?"

And Christian, stony-faced and pale at recognising his old Norfolk Island commandant, answered "*yes*" before excusing himself from the room.

THIRTY-FIVE

Captain John Porteous had orders from Admiralty to take command of HMS Porpoise and was sitting impatiently in Sydney waiting for the ship to return to port. As a naval officer dedicated to following the rules, he was Bligh's one ray of hope.

"There's just a chance," Bligh said excitedly to Mary, "that when he's at the helm, he'll feel obliged to take orders from me, as his commodore, rather than the army rebels."

To this end, he wrote a note, its authoritative tone designed to bully Porteous into submission.

> *I am ordering you to desist from obeying military commands ashore and to fly my Commodore's flag from HMS Porpoise.*

When he received no answer, he wrote once more:

I am most disappointed that a Royal Navy Officer has chosen to betray his own kind <u>and</u> his superior officer in order to follow rebel army commands.

The subtle insinuation of court-martial changed everything and Bligh beamed with satisfaction when Porteous formally refused to accept any further orders from the rebel regime and hoisted Bligh's broad pennant to fly proud atop Porpoise's mast.

Zooming in on it through his telescope, Bligh let out a yelp of triumph.

"And so it begins!" he announced to his daughter. As a veteran of many a sea skirmish, he sniffed the shift of fair wind in his direction.

The situation for the rebels was starting to unravel and seeing the rot set in, Foveaux, Macarthur and Johnston were chaffing at the bit to leave for London. Johnston no longer had any interest in running the show and along with the other two, was keen to clear his name of all responsibility for the Rum Rebellion.

It was a case of who got there first and whose presentation of the facts was finest. But while they waited for their respective ships to arrive, the animosity among them was intense. The civilities Macarthur and Foveaux struggled for so long to maintain between them, disintegrated to a dog-eat-dog fight for survival.

"What's this?" Macarthur demanded in outrage when Foveaux presented him with a bill for 500 pounds.

Foveaux sat his corpulent self down at his desk and shuffled through his papers for the one he was after. Finding it, he answered:

"According to my bookkeeping, there's a discrepancy in your accounts back when you were secretary of the colony. It appears that you appropriated 500 pounds for your own use from government funds. You must pay it back to the Colonial Treasury."

Macarthur, fuming with indignation, strode across the room towards him.

"Who are *you* to speak of fraud when after all these months you still haven't signed off on that land grant you officially promised me?"

Unperturbed by his show of aggression, Foveaux looked up with a patronising calm to say:

"Mr dear fellow, one can hardly compare absent-mindedness with theft."

At this, Macarthur ripped the piece of paper from Foveaux's hand and challenged him to a duel.

– oOo –

"Turn at 10 paces," they were instructed by Lieutenant Finucane, when standing back to back in the early-morning mist.

It should have been quick and simple, with Macarthur the marksman and Foveaux's rotund figure making the perfect target. But when, for the first time in his life, Macarthur fired and missed, Foveaux had plenty of time to focus on the kill.

Like the proud man he was, Macarthur turned to face him front on, unafraid to die. He was not prepared, however, to be humiliated.

I do not consider my opponent worthy of the shot, Foveaux inferred when without firing, he lowered his gun in pretense of being the better man.

For that, Macarthur would never forgive him. One way or another he was determined to bring him down.

Lieutenant Finucane did such a fine job as go-between during the duel that he was sent to negotiate terms with Bligh. Given that he now treated his deposed governor with respect and had a soft spot for his daughter, Bligh was amenable to talk.

"Mr Macarthur and Colonel Johnston are soon to sail for London on the Admiral Gambier," Finucane informed him as he accepted the cup of tea Mary offered. "I've been asked to put it to you, sir, that you might like to go with them."

Bligh resisted the impulse to laugh out loud and courteously replied:

"I'm sorry Lieutenant, but travelling in such company would be untenable. If it were Colonel Johnston alone, I should not mind so much, but the presence of Macarthur would be most unpleasant for me and Mrs Putland."

Finucane nodded his understanding and smothered a smile. He could not have hoped for better because his and Foveaux's berths on the ship had to be sacrificed if Bligh wished to make use of them. For his part, Finucane could not wait to get home to Ireland and Bligh's stubbornness had just made it possible.

It was imperative, however, that he and Bligh kept up the charade. Finucane's mandate being to get the ex-governor on any ship at all, and Bligh's: to make sure that ship was his own HMS Porpoise on whose deck, as commodore, he would rightfully claim command.

The beauty of it was that Bligh had no need to swing the deal because Finucane did it for him. The young lieutenant was so keen to keep his berth on the Gambier, that he happily put the Porpoise forward as the sensible solution. He had no idea of the impact Bligh setting foot on it would have – that once on board, he and his warship would become a formidable fighting force.

"May I suggest to you, sir," he continued naively, "that Governor Paterson is a most amenable man and wants to accommodate you as best he can. May I have your permission to propose to him that you and Mrs Putland return to England on the Porpoise instead?"

Bligh made much of considering his opinion as he offered Finucane a biscuit.

"You may indeed," he then replied. "And thank you, Lieutenant, for thinking of it."

THIRTY-SIX

Acting Governor Paterson clearly stipulated the rules for the voyage in a written agreement with Bligh.

You must promise to leave on the HMS Porpoise on February 20. You must go directly to England and not return to New South Wales or interfere with its politics. It is expected, that as an officer and gentleman, you will honour this contract.

As Paterson dictated, Christian penned the words, musing all the while at how strange it seemed for him, albeit second hand, to be legally making demands of Bligh. Still sight unseen, however, he could not bring himself to personally deliver it.

"Would you excuse me from the duty, sir? I'm not feeling well," he lied to Paterson, who in his good humour, let him off and sent him home to bed.

When Bligh received the document from another's hand, he had no qualms about signing it. As far as he was concerned, all obligations of honour were made null and void by their crime of sedition.

So within a week, the Porpoise weighed anchor and was waved farewell by friends and family from the shore. But their tears stopped short, as did the Porpoise, just before sailing out of the harbour's headlands.

"Drop anchor!" Bligh ordered, surprising his crew and the crowds waving from the wharf.

For there, for a month, his ship was to stand sentinel at the cliff-faced gates of Port Jackson – its flag flying high and gun-ports open, ready for action.

"I told you so!" Macarthur ranted to Paterson. "I *told* you never to trust him. Now he's going to stop every ship that comes and goes and control the colony by sea."

This was of particular concern to Macarthur because he was due to leave on the Admiral Gambier within days and was convinced that Bligh, in his lawful role as Commodore, would intercept his ship and have him arrested.

On all counts he was correct. Bligh did stop every ship going through the Heads and handed their respective masters a proclamation forbidding the transporting of any individual, either civilian or of the corps, connected with the rebellion.

The colony went into a state of panic and Paterson took to the bottle. There was nowhere to look for help but to Foveaux, who was temporarily put back in command, charged with saving New South Wales from anarchy.

The *Sydney Gazette* printed the news of this switch of power, calling Bligh an outlaw and adding in bold type:

All those found guilty of aiding and abetting
him on shore will suffer the consequences.

It was a hedonistic paradise for Foveaux, who now had a free run to increase his fortune. Well aware of the pressing time constraints, he threw caution to the wind, imposing fines and sentences on Bligh's land-bound supporters, while making a last-ditch effort to enrich himself and his friends at their expense.

> *Oh we are living through the most charming of times here in the colony,* Sir Henry Browne-Hayes wrote to England before being sentenced, once more, to the coalmines for no sin greater than being Bligh's friend.

> *Foveaux hands out punishment to the innocent, while granting pardons and free land to whores and thieves. Justice should see us hang half his worthy lot, for they are the worst of robbers and rogues.*

It was at this point, oblivious to his friends' suffering on his behalf, that Bligh abandoned his harbor patrol and set sail for Van Diemen's Land. He was disappointed about having to forego his plan to waylay the Admiral Gambier, but family came first.

"You must try to eat something," he implored his daughter, who was deathly ill.

White as a sheet and painfully thin from her four weeks of chronic seasickness and retching, Mary lay limp on her cabin bunk, no longer able to tolerate their ship to shore standoff.

"Never mind, my dear," Bligh relented. "We shall head for Hobart to get you back on solid ground."

It was the end of March when their ship sailed into Sullivan Bay, and recognising Bligh's broad pennant, Hobart's Lieutenant-Governor, Colonel David Collins, rowed out with his entourage to greet them.

"I can't believe it!" he said in disgust when Bligh related the details of the rebellion.

Relieved, at last, that he had someone of consequence on side, Bligh gratefully accepted Collins' invitation to dinner and his offer to give Mary use of the main bedroom at his Government House. For her further security, a sentry was placed at her door ensuring her privacy, along with the promise that she would soon feel her old self again.

Bligh, in the meantime, was happy to stay on his ship and happier still to have Collins see to its provisions. It made for a pleasant hiatus that soon ended when Bligh sighted a frigate coming at full-sail from Sydney. On it, he was sure, was news from Foveaux, who surely knew by now that the Porpoise had sailed to Van Diemen's Land rather than England.

From its prow, Bligh watched anxiously as the frigate's captain went ashore to greet Collins. All stayed deceptively quiet for the first half of the day, but the fact that Collins remained silent for the rest of it, spoke volumes, as did the sudden absence of the sentry at Mary's bedroom door.

Before dawn the next day, Bligh stealthily went ashore and knocked lightly on it. When Mary answered with her fair hair in disarray and bed robe wrapped hastily around her, he put his finger to his lips, warning her to stay silent as he slipped into her room.

"Quickly!" he whispered. "Get dressed. We must return to the Porpoise immediately."

She knew better than to waste time questioning him and within the hour, they were safely back on board, having made their precarious way through the dark streets of Hobart Town.

As Bligh guessed, Collins had read Foveaux's dispatch the day before and was totally taken in by its unproven prejudice against him. Based purely on its circumstantial evidence, Collins took the rebels' side and finding that Mary had abused his hospitality by leaving without thanks, refused to further provision the Porpoise. He punished those who did with arrest and sentenced one man to 500 lashes for making the fatal mistake of sending the ship a small supply of chickens and potatoes.

"I have to give credit to that criminal, Foveaux, for getting Collins so quickly on side," Bligh said sarcastically.

Yet sickened as he was by the speed at which weak men were won over, he wasn't beaten and fought back instantly by blockading the Derwent River. It positioned him to stop all ships for supplies and to seize every dispatch to and from Colonel Collins.

One of them, at last, put a smile on his face.

"*Thank God* … the 73rd Regiment's advance troops have arrived in Sydney."

England had finally sent reinforcements, but sadly without a leader. For the time being, all they were good for was to pitch a few tents and watch Foveaux and his corps go about their shady business. More of their ranks were due, however, and Foveaux knew it was time to cut and run. So, in a frenzied final grab of land for himself and his friends, he divvied up 30 times the acreage that Bligh ever granted and he sliced off a large slab of 500 acres for his mistress, who for years he had kept hidden and to whom he was soon to say goodbye.

The tide was turning in the nick of time, for those on board the Porpoise were fed up with playing their nine-month-long waiting game. Mary was sick, but its officers were sicker still of the stalemate, every one of them refusing to speak to either Bligh or his daughter unless absolutely necessary.

It was January 1810 when Bligh finally admitted that he, too, had had enough. More than that, he was incensed. He had done and given up *all* for the sake of crown and country and yet the coup had lasted two years without England's personal response to his desperate dispatches. Fortunately, the tardy trickling in of the 73rd troops was enough to boost his confidence.

"That's it!" he suddenly said to Mary slapping his knees as he stood up. "It's time to move. Macarthur and Johnston *must* have reached London by now. That is if their ship didn't sink."

It was wishful thinking on his part when Macarthur's stranglehold on luck made it a chance in a million. One way or another, their Rum Rebellion case was soon to hit the English courts and it was imperative that Bligh defend himself against all accusations. So he set sail for Sydney, ready for whatever was to come and to fight if he had to.

THIRTY-SEVEN

Macarthur's luck hadn't changed. For him, Bligh sailing off nine months before and suddenly tacking south to Hobart, came as a welcome reprieve. It gave him time to gather all the information he needed to bring Bligh down, but before dealing with that prime objective of his, he had a score to settle with Foveaux.

The night before boarding the Admiral Gambier for England, he stopped off to say goodbye to Colonel Paterson and to play a friendly game of cards with his other party guests. He counted on the fact that Foveaux would be among them.

"If you want your 500 pounds, you'll have to *win* it back," Macarthur taunted, knowing that for all Foveaux's ingenuity, he was a fool at gambling.

Never one to resist temptation, Foveaux lifted his glass of champagne to toast the challenge.

This should be interesting, Major Johnston thought, begging off joining them in favour of sitting it out as a spectator with a front-row seat to the show. For this night Macarthur was out for revenge and the performance was destined not to disappoint.

Johnston's absence from the game left only five at the table. Although Paterson and Major Abbott played a fair hand of cards, they posed no real competition. The fellow Chapman, sitting next to Paterson, was an unknown quantity, but Johnston could lay bets on the fact that he, like most others, would fall victim to Macarthur's skill.

Already the man looked ill at ease and *had* done since Paterson insisted that he join them. Small beads of sweat were on his brow and he appeared grossly uncomfortable in the group – evidence, no doubt, that Macarthur's reputation preceded him.

He's as nervous as a cat, Johnston said to himself with a smirk. *And so far, not a single card's been dealt!*

Johnston never trusted a man who didn't look him in the eye and guessed that Foveaux felt the same way when this Chapman fellow refused to meet his. When they took a seat opposite each other and Foveaux smiled his welcome, Chapman lowered his eyes in response and hadn't lifted them since, intent instead on fiddling with the few pennies he had to bet.

All of this escaped Macarthur's attention, as with the cool expertise of a hustler, he shuffled the cards.

"Aces high," he then said, calling the name of the game and dealing with slick assurance.

Hours of hard play followed, Foveaux having a series of bad hands and ever worried that Macarthur would call his bluff, while Christian was petrified that Foveaux would call his. By midnight, a great deal of money had crossed to Macarthur's side of the table. A small portion of it still lingered in front of Abbott and Paterson, while just a few coins sat before Christian. Throughout the evening, he made a point of not winning or losing enough to stir suspicion or sympathy.

Used to Chapman's sharper game, Paterson was perplexed.

"What's going on?" he leant across to quietly ask him.

But Christian merely shrugged, concentrating on not drawing attention to himself in any way.

All eyes, fortunately, were on Foveaux who was out of money. He had lost steadily throughout and in his determination to out-manoeuvre Macarthur, played right into his hands. Short of giving him the shirt off his back, he had nothing left to wager and would have called it a night had he not just been dealt three Kings.

For this last chance to redeem his money and pride, he put it all on the line, betting with a promised IOU.

I've yet to see Macarthur hold a bad hand, but he'll have a hard time beating this one, he reasoned, having to gulp down hard when the man laid his winning royal flush on the table.

"You owe me 500 pounds," Macarthur said, echoing Foveaux's satisfaction when he had said the same two weeks before.

With a sigh of surrender, Foveaux quickly cast round for a way to pay and found it when his eyes settled on Christian. Nothing, he knew, meant more to Macarthur than to hold a trump card over Bligh and, in turn, nothing meant more to Bligh than to come face to face with his old Bounty nemesis once more. It would be a clash of titans and *he* held the key.

Considering Foveaux's dire circumstance, Macarthur was baffled by his slow, triumphant smile.

"I have no more cash on hand," Foveaux admitted, "but I'm prepared to pay with something more valuable."

With one of his losing cards in hand, he got up from the table and went over to Paterson's desk. There with ink and quill, he scribbled a few words on its patterned surface, walked back and slammed the card face down in front of Macarthur.

"*This* is the greatest ace *you'll* ever have up your sleeve," he said.

And mystified, Macarthur turned it over to read what was written:

Fletcher Christian lives and sits at Paterson's side.

THIRTY-EIGHT

When Macarthur's eyes drifted in his direction, Christian knew the game was up. Yet, rather than feel alarm, he was overwhelmed with relief. It had been 20 long years since the mutiny and there was nowhere left to run. For better or worse, he was ready to face the consequences.

Instead of exposing him, however, Macarthur put a proposition to Paterson.

"What will it cost to buy your man from you?" he asked.

Paterson was outraged.

"I am not in the practice of bartering with another man's life," he replied, not for the first time astounded by Macarthur's effrontery.

Realising that Paterson was ignorant of the facts and well within his rights to take umbrage, Macarthur reconsidered his approach.

"Forgive me, but I must speak to you in private," he insisted with an urgency which gave Paterson no choice but to excuse himself from his other guests and escort Macarthur into his library.

"Well?" he then turned on him to demand, riled as he always was by Macarthur's high-handed ways. "If you're after the benefit of Mr Chapman's services, I'm afraid that's impossible."

His morally superior tone left Macarthur unmoved.

"It is not only *possible*, sir," he replied, "but imperative if you are to clear yourself of having committed a crime."

"I don't know what you mean."

Macarthur came right out with it:

"Yes you do, for you are knowingly harbouring a criminal. I, however, am prepared to take him off your hands and say nothing of your involvement to the authorities."

Macarthur had made it crystal clear. He knew that Paterson was aware of Chapman's convict status and that he was guilty by association in having camouflaged the fact. Tempted as Paterson was to take advantage of the "out clause" Macarthur was offering, he had a sudden attack of conscience. He was fond of Chapman and not wanting to throw him to the wolves, spoke up in his defence.

"He's not who you think he is," he said, firmly believing in Chapman's innocence.

But to this, Macarthur merely smiled.

"I'm afraid, Paterson, that he's not who *you* think he is. Your friend out there whose cause you so nobly champion is none other than the infamous Fletcher Christian, who I intend to bring to justice in London. I'm simply sparing you the shame of having your good name linked with his."

Paterson reeled back in shock and with no further explanation necessary, returned to the main room and handed Christian over to Macarthur's care.

From habit, Christian signed his release papers: *Francis Chapman.*

"That will no longer be necessary," Macarthur told him, before turning to say to Paterson: "But I must impress upon you, sir, how imperative it is that Mr Christian's true identity be kept strictly between us."

"You need have no concerns about that," Paterson agreed, too ashamed to look his friend, Christian alias Chapman, in the eye.

He had deserted him to save his own skin and loathed himself for it. It was only Macarthur's kind tone that came as some comfort, for it marked his intention to treat Christian with the respect he deserved.

The reality was that Macarthur had no interest in bringing him to justice. Fascinated by the man and his myth, he had always imagined him not wholly guilty of the mutiny, and after his own dealings with Bligh, was convinced of his innocence.

All he wanted was to use him as a weapon. With the world thinking Fletcher Christian dead, it would cause a sensation to bring him home alive after all these years. Guilty or not, that world would be at his feet and Bligh, who had been haunted by his ghost for so long, would be devastated to see him again in the flesh.

With the famed mutineer, himself, present to tell the Bounty tale, Macarthur reasoned, *there'll be no more hiding from the truth.*

That, Bligh had never done. He swore himself innocent of the mutiny at the time and never veered from that belief. He was not afraid of others' false versions of the facts and would forever hold Christian accountable. Yet, having been hurt to the heart by his betrayal, there still skulked under his thin skin, a bubbling brew of raw emotions set to explode. It was this suppressed mix of nostalgia and rage that Macarthur intended to tap. He was sure that seeing Christian again would bring Bligh undone.

THIRTY-NINE

Bligh sailed into Port Jackson to find two British ships moored in the harbor. At last, the rest of the 73rd regiment had arrived and he let out a sigh of relief.

Their senior officer, Lieutenant-Colonel Maurice O'Connell came aboard to greet them with apologies to Bligh for taking so long, and a lingering smile for his lovely daughter.

"You must let me introduce you to Lieutenant-Colonel Macquarie," he said, ushering them both into his rowboat.

"Macquarie?" Bligh repeated, having a recollection of meeting a young army officer of that name, years before when the Bounty had stopped off in Cape Town. "Is he your commanding officer?"

"He's the new Governor of New South Wales, sir."

Stunned, Bligh sat down heavily in the boat and grabbed hold of the gunwale to steady himself.

"But that can't be," he replied. "*I* am Governor."

Thinking that it may have been better to break it to him gently, O'Connell sat down opposite to explain.

"Macquarie's mandate from the Secretary of State, sir, was to formally reinstate you as Governor for a day and then replace you. Please know that the British government has nothing but praise for your administration and handling of this very difficult affair, but because of its volatile nature, they felt a change in command was best.

"You should know that they shoulder much of the blame for putting a naval officer in command of army personnel. It was to your distinct disadvantage from the start and Macquarie, as an army officer, is their solution. Unfortunately, you weren't here when we arrived and with no one in control of the colony, he had no option but to take over from you immediately. I'm sorry if it comes as a blow."

That it did, but it was balanced by a bit of good news. The New South Wales Corps was recalled to England in disgrace and the rebel administration declared invalid. Everyone unfairly arrested under its regime was released and all lands granted by Johnston, Paterson and Foveaux were confiscated.

"And of course," O'Connell continued, "Macquarie came with orders to arrest Macarthur and Johnston for high treason."

This came as music to Bligh's ears. A note of resounding success that soon turned discordant when O'Connell added:

"It's just a pity that they left for London before we arrived."

For his part, Governor Macquarie was glad they'd gone. As fellow Scots, he and Johnston trained together as army cadets and he didn't want the man's death on his hands. Much as he wanted to back the army rebels' cause, the facts proved it unconstitutional and a crime for which both Macarthur and Johnston were sure to hang.

In the meantime, for the good of the colony, Macquarie knew it was important not to choose sides, but promptly broke his own rule by taking an instant shine to Foveaux, whose advice and administrative expertise he found invaluable.

"How can you *praise* such a man?" Bligh complained bitterly to the new Governor. "Foveaux openly disobeyed the Secretary of State's orders to go straight back to Norfolk Island and without authority, strode in to assume the lieutenant-governorship of New South Wales while keeping me illegally under arrest. The man's a criminal, plain and simple."

"Be that as it may, I think it's better to let bygones be bygones, Bligh, now that the man is proving himself such an asset to the colony."

Bligh swung round on him sharply, pointing an accusing finger.

"Who thought *nothing* of breaching the law and human rights at his every turn. You know as well as I, that he's every bit as guilty as Macarthur and Johnston and should be arrested along with them."

His argument was valid, but Macquarie had stopped listening. He was tiring of his predecessor's temper tantrums and was keener now to entertain those from the rebel ranks, along with *their* side of the story. In line with his new-found sympathies, he thought it wise to break down Bligh's initiatives in the colony and to reinstate rum bartering.

I don't know why I bothered, Bligh wrote to Betsy despondently. *I gave my heart and soul to the welfare of the colony, but it appears its inhabitants are happy to throw it back in my face.*

He was relieved, therefore, when Macquarie suggested that he take charge of the convoy transporting the shamed New South Wales Corps back to London.

"In consideration of its officers' upcoming court-martial," Macquarie said, "you can take as many witnesses as you like along with you to support your case."

Reading Bligh's hesitation as a bid for more, he added:

"All at the government's cost, of course. And naturally, all pertinent documents will be put at your disposal."

It was an after-thought to ask Bligh and his daughter to dinner.

"Oh, I'm afraid we can't," Bligh replied. "We've already accepted an invitation to dine with your Colonel O'Connell."

In adhering to social etiquette, Bligh did not intend to offend Macquarie, but could see that he had when the man sat bolt upright in his chair, insulted that his second-in-command was given precedence.

Bligh apologised once more, but it marked a turning point in their relationship. Macquarie had been feeling guilty about his growing dislike for Bligh. On the whole, it was unfounded and he was glad to grab hold of this small incident to justify it.

"The sooner Bligh leaves, the better," he confided to his wife, and was disappointed when the ex-governor's departure was delayed an extra few weeks because of a fire that broke out on one of the convoy ships in the harbour.

All desperate bucket-slinging attempts to extinguish it failed and the inferno was out of control.

"Slip her cables and scuttle her at Government Wharf!" Bligh ran from his house to order. Used, as he was, to such sea emergencies.

And for the first time, those army men battling the blaze were relieved that Bligh took command. Foveaux among them.

BLIGH AND FOVEAUX
FIGHT ON THE SAME SIDE!

It was the headline in the *Sydney Gazette* the next day which neither man could deny, when at the peak of the conflagration, they stood shoulder to shoulder. In the emergency of the moment, with buckets in hand and rolled up sleeves, they had turned to each other in recognition of their respective efforts, their faces streaked with soot and sweat and a smile of shared combat.

But it was a little love too late which soon gave way to Foveaux's pressing need to get back to London before Bligh, if he were to stand any chance of exonerating himself.

Without ceremony, he and Lieutenant Finucane slipped out of Sydney on an American whaler in the dead of night. The excuse for his swift departure was left in a letter on Macquarie's desk stating his intention to travel home to lobby for the position of lieutenant-governor of Hobart. It was a job which had recently fallen vacant due to late Lieutenant-Governor Collins' heart attack, a fatal condition brought on by his terror of the hangman's noose for having embraced the rebels' cause at Bligh's expense.

Bligh, too, was homeward bound and about to suffer a near-as-strong blow to his heart. It came when Lieutenant-Colonel O'Connell climbed on board their HMS Hindostan, minutes before it sailed for England.

"I would like to ask for your daughter's hand in marriage," he said to Bligh, who along with Mary, was on deck ready to set out for home.

Initially just irritated by the delay in departure, Bligh was now dumbfounded.

"I hardly think this is an appropriate moment," he blustered, but then one look at Mary's face told him otherwise.

With her cheeks flushed pink and eyes lowered shyly, it was obvious that they were in love and that he, her father and hitherto favoured confidante, had been kept completely in the dark.

He had known someday this would happen, but hadn't expected it to be today. Because of his all-consuming obsession with Macarthur, he hadn't said all he needed to say to her and could only ask the question:

"Is this what you want?"

At her nod of assent, he knew it was time to step aside for the new man in her life.

It was not *that* he minded so much as the prospect of being left alone. He had never been good at it and suspected that her absence would weigh heavily on him forever. She was his dearest daughter and friend and when she waved goodbye from the wharf, he had to bite back tears. He would never see her again.

FORTY

Macarthur thoroughly enjoyed his voyage back to England. With him were his two eldest sons, who he wanted educated in England; Johnston, ever his right hand man; but best of all, Christian, who lived up to the interesting image Bligh painted of him in his pre-mutiny days. Not only was he good company, but for Macarthur, there was the added bonus of appropriating a friendship which by right and sentiment belonged to Bligh.

Initially, Christian was no more to him than a means to an end, but after a shared four months at sea, Macarthur was won over and only sorry that he had to put him in harm's way. When their ship docked at Southampton, he said a few words in consolation.

"Don't worry about what's in store for you. After all these years, you're more celebrity than criminal. Bligh's part in *both* mutinies cannot be ignored and will work in your favour. You're folklore now, my good fellow, and there'll be a public outcry if you're condemned."

Whether it was to be life or death no longer concerned Christian. He'd had enough, and unafraid of what was to come, followed Macarthur's directive to keep a low profile while staying in the small Chelsea house he rented for him; there, to await the court case of the decade being held in The Great Hall at Chelsea's Royal Hospital.

Forget Napoleon's War and General Wellesley's dazzling Iberian Peninsula campaign. Both ran a poor second to this real-life drama being played out between the notorious Captain Bligh and the senior British army officers who mutinied against him. The outrage in Australia was the talk of the town and it seemed that the whole of London turned out to be part of it.

Their number, too large for The Great Hall, spilled into the hospital corridors and out onto its impressive grounds; senior navy and army representatives claiming the prime seats, while a liberal sprinkling of the uniformed lower ranks coloured the crowd red and blue.

Having to wait months for the trial to begin, Bligh had time to recoup from the insult of being summarily replaced by Macquarie. The Secretary of State's betrayal, he believed, was worse than that of the rebels in New South Wales. He had stewed over it for five months at sea and arrived back in England in a foul mood; one which was exacerbated by the fact that, for a second time, he had to defend his reputation before the nation.

"Johnston *must* be found guilty," he said to his old friend Joseph Banks, who, as ever, made a show of his support by regularly visiting the Bligh family home in Lambeth. "If by some travesty of justice they declare him *not guilty,* there's no doubt I'll go down in history as a tyrant and all that I went through to clear my name after that Bounty business will count for nothing."

"Calm down," Banks replied. "You have a solid case and I'm sure all will work out well."

It was comforting comments like these that helped Bligh take himself in hand. Those, and the frequent visits from other good friends Robert Campbell and John Palmer, who came with him from New South Wales to speak in his defence.

And then, of course, in Mary's absence, there was always the consolation of his other five daughters and his darling Betsy who, as ever, made him rest easy. Even though his wife was terminally ill in bed, she still exuded a strength that sustained him and by the time he was called to present himself at court, he felt far more composed.

At least until the counsel for the defence pursued a line of questioning he didn't expect.

"In hindsight, Governor Bligh, how early could you have demanded that Colonel Johnston be court-martialed?" lawyer John Adlophus asked, addressing him by his former title which remained his for life.

"Not until I arrived back in England in October 1810."

Bligh's answer was clipped, because he believed that this three-year Statute of Limitations Law to which Adolphus alluded, had already been resolved during his own counsel's interrogation. Smelling a rat, he continued warily:

"That is, unless I ordered Colonel Paterson to try him back in New South Wales."

He had taken the bait and with upturned hands, Adolphus asked:

"Well wouldn't that have been the most sensible thing to do? You would have saved yourself and our English courts two years by simply writing him a letter."

"Do you presume me a *fool?*" Bligh fired back, bristling with rage. "I couldn't write to the man because he was a *blasted* rebel! Even to *you,* that should be *bloody* obvious. How could I, as His Majesty's Governor, officially communicate with the man when he *damn well* had me under arrest!"

Macarthur had instructed his counsel to pursue Bligh in this way.

"Don't be daunted by him. Just push him till he cracks," he had advised. "He's got very thin skin. You'll only need to scratch the surface to make him explode."

He knew that Bligh's bad temper would work against him and, in an instant, give the court the full picture.

The judge, however, was not swayed by ploys of the like and seeing Bligh's mounting distress, instructed the counsel for the defense to desist in its pursuit of this issue, before saying to Bligh:

"And perhaps, sir, it would help proceedings if you were not as liberal with the lesser side of the English language."

The defence happily backed off. Right from the start, they knew they had no chance of winning this particular argument, but they'd made their point.

Had he heard, Macarthur would have smiled with smug satisfaction, but at that moment, he was busy rallying further support for himself. Most of the men waiting with him as witnesses in the antechamber were old friends-turned-foe on whose testimony he could not rely. Many of them, both civilians and members of his old corps, had an axe to grind in regard to his treatment of them. Most of their complaints were valid, but feeling only contempt for their pettiness, Macarthur turned his attention to the only man among them more forgiving.

The one thing he always liked about Foveaux was that he was a good loser who saw no value in holding a grudge until he could use it to his advantage. Right now, waiting to give testimony at the trial, he and Macarthur were in the same boat, both wondering if either could gain from the other. As Foveaux walked across the room to discuss it, Macarthur only hoped the man had got over the fact that he'd once tried to kill him.

Fortunately, to Foveaux, their duel was old news and sitting down beside Macarthur, he casually crossed his legs and got straight to the point.

"So where have you had him stashed for the last few months?"

There was no need to mention names.

"Just down the road in a small terrace I rented," Macarthur replied, knowing he could trust Foveaux with his secret because the man had so many of his own to hide.

"He didn't attempt to run?"

"He hasn't as yet and I've no reason to believe he ever will. Our Mr Christian," Macarthur then lowered his voice to say. "appears to be a man of integrity."

"Then let's hope that he'll do us both some good."

With their conversation over, Foveaux got back to his feet. He had feigned friendship long enough to apprise himself of the situation and get from it what he could; a fact that Macarthur didn't hold against him, being a man after his own heart.

It was the consensus among the British hierarchy that, at the very least, Johnston and Foveaux should be prosecuted for instigating and perpetuating the Rum Rebellion. The same would have applied to Paterson had he not conveniently died during the voyage back to England.

The prospect for Macarthur looked a little less grim. Not only did he have the Bounty mutiny and its instigator on hand as back-up, but he believed that Johnston's fine connections in London would stand them all in good stead. It was imperative that they did, for if Johnston were found guilty, he, Macarthur, would be implicated as a conspirator to commit treason.

It was a complex affair that had all of England intrigued; all but the new Secretary of State, Lord Liverpool, who had no vested interest in the outcome and was thoroughly bored by proceedings. He had more to worry about with Napoleon and his war, and the wayward behavior of colonials was of little consequence. Determined to make short work of it, he was frustrated when the counsel for the defence tried to put Bligh on trial, rather than those who illegally deposed him.

"Such stuff and nonsense," Liverpool scowled, "when Napoleon's threat to the proposed alliance between Russia and England should be taking priority."

But still, Bligh was in the witness chair and Adolphus was showing no signs of relenting.

"Please explain to the court," he demanded of Bligh, "why, in an act of duplicity and dishonour, you took control of the HMS Porpoise in breach of your promise and signed word as an officer and gentleman."

After a full day's grueling interrogation, Bligh reply was resigned.

"Sir, *once again,* I will state for the record that I, along with my daughter, was locked in a subaltern's barrack for seven days because, as Commander of His Majesty's Ships in the South Pacific, I rightfully refused to give up control of the Porpoise. This unlawful close confinement imposed by an illegal regime was unacceptable and I believe that no bargain with traitors is worth the paper it's written on. I stepped aboard the ship considering myself the legal Governor of New South Wales and continued to do so till the last."

Adlophus took another tack.

"How many times have you been involved in courts-martial for mutiny?" he questioned, swiftly changing the subject from the one he'd just lost.

"You refer, I presume, to the Bounty," Bligh replied, knowing its mention was inevitable. "But if you're trying to also tie me to the mutiny at The Nore, then you are wasting your time. Although I was certainly present, I was not a key player. Therefore, it has no pertinence to this case and should be of no concern to the court."

Here, the defence made a mistake because Bligh's role at The Nore was a positive one and worked in his favour.

"As for the Bounty," Bligh continued, drawing a deep breath before launching into a long account to once more justify himself. But he was stopped, mid-sentence, by the judge-advocate.

"This is immaterial to the case at hand."

A member of the audience disagreed and in contempt of court called out:

"Captain Bligh has a *right* to defend himself now that they've brought up the Bounty to incriminate him. Let the man speak."

It was an unauthorised interjection, but the judge allowed it.

"Very well, but make it fast."

Bolstered by this support from strangers, Bligh continued, rounding off his synopsis by saying:

"And please make note that it was not *I* who brought the mutineers to court, for at the time I was on the other side of the world completing what should have been the Bounty's mission. I am proud to say that while I was in command of the HMS Providence, there was never a sign of discontent."

Fast losing ground, Adlophus switched his argument to Bligh's controversial governance of the colony.

"I think that all here have sampled your temper and colourful language, Governor. Whereas the judge was gracious enough to overlook it, I'm sure the Secretary of State would object strongly to being its subject. You are reported as having publicly damned him in regard to land granted to Mr Macarthur. I quote:

> *Damn the Secretary of State. He is but a clerk in office. In today, out tomorrow.*

"Were these not your exact words?"

Grim-faced, Bligh replied:

"I state, unequivocally, that they were not."

Fed up and with his memory having failed him, he wasn't sure whether or not he had just lied. How could he possibly remember, verbatim, words spoken years ago in the heat of the moment? God knows, Macarthur, who was no doubt the one who had reported them, said far worse over the course of their acquaintance. For this reason, he had no intention of retracting his statement and was too tired to care.

Thankfully, when the prosecution was allowed to cross-examine him, the pressure was off for a short while. Within a few slick statements, his lawyer established that Bligh had been honourably acquitted by the Bounty court-martial and had never gained personal advantage from any of the measures he imposed on the colony.

"I object!" Adolphus leapt from his seat to say. "We have it on account that Governor Bligh illegally ordered the destruction of private property on government land as an act of perversity. Not only that, but on many an occasion, through pure personal jealousy, he actively sabotaged the productive efforts of the colony's leading businessman, John Macarthur, to better the New South Wales economy."

Bligh was at the end of his tether. Midway through the litany of further farcical complaints, he suddenly got to his feet and thumped his fist down hard on the court table.

"*Enough!*" he declared and the court fell silent.

"I may be guilty of possessing a bad temper, but my loyalty to the crown goes without question. It is a crime, in itself, that this case has turned from a trial for traitors to one targeting me and my integrity. Over the last few days, my *whole life* has been searched for occasions of censure with not one mention of my achievements."

The court's attention was his, so he continued.

"Perhaps the good people here might like to hear, instead, that in dire circumstances I navigated a lifeboat through 3000 miles of unchartered waters and saved my men's lives or that I fought at Nelson's side and for my major part in winning him his battle, received his personal commendation. I tell you now, that if that great man were still here to speak on my behalf, you should all be ashamed."

This call on their conscience brought an end to the penultimate day of court-martial. Its participants left contrite with Bligh's words ringing in their ears as if he had physically cuffed each and every one of them.

When court resumed the next day, it was clear that Bligh's past acts of valour and his close ties with the revered Lord Nelson gained him the advantage.

Macarthur missed the prevailing mood, still waiting as he was in the antechamber to give testimony. Through its thick timber door, he could clearly hear the hammering of the gavel and roars of discontent from the court, but had to strain to make out Bligh's words when he struck out hard with his closing argument:

"This was no ordinary mutiny in New South Wales, but one unprecedented in the annals of history!"

Macarthur pressed his ear flush to the door when, for a muffled moment, Bligh paused to rest his hands on the leather-ingrained table that separated him from the military jury.

"*So* dangerous in its example," he then leant forward to continue, "that it's threatened British military discipline worldwide."

"Well *you* should know," Macarthur muttered sarcastically.

But with Bligh making an impact, he was worried about Johnston. Without his support the barristers in there were going to eat him alive.

The same prospect awaited him, and for the first time in his life Macarthur wasn't sure that he was up to the challenge. For all his courtroom flair, he had lost a little of his confidence since being in the Mother Country; a fact that his former friend Major Abbott was happy to report back to the colony. Having been rubbed the wrong way once too often by Macarthur, he reveled in putting him in his place.

> *Contrary to Macarthur's prominence in New South Wales, he cuts a very small figure on this side of the world. Here, he's a nobody and all the worse in temper for knowing it.*

Used to lesser men's jealousy, Macarthur sloughed it off; biding his time before presenting the long-lost Fletcher Christian to the public. The sensation of it, he hoped, would shift the focus from himself and put the onus for both mutinies back on Bligh. As a man of little consequence in London, Macarthur knew he hadn't a hope of swinging the nation's vote in regard to either rebellion, but he had complete faith in Christian's extraordinary ability to win and influence all.

"Ten minutes until you're called, Macarthur," the court officer opened the door to inform him.

This was his cue to make his move, and slipping out the side door, Macarthur went to fetch Christian from the hospital chapel where he instructed him to wait. Half expecting him to be gone, he was relieved to see him still sitting alone in the pew, his eyes fixed on the altar.

"Are you ready?" he asked.

Without a word, Christian stood up and walked down the short aisle to join him. But at the sound of footsteps in the corridor, Macarthur quickly closed the chapel door, making sure that he and Christian were out of sight when he re-opened it an inch to see Bligh, of all people, sitting on the hall bench outside.

It was a breath-stopping, moment for Christian. It had been 20 years since he'd laid eyes on him and having repeatedly rehearsed their reunion, he expected to be swamped by burning revenge. Instead, he felt nothing but sympathy for Bligh, who having aged considerably was nursing his head in his hands, seemingly in enough distress to strip Christian of any sense of triumph.

Without the benefit of time to soften *his* wounds, however, Macarthur did not share his compassion.

"Look at him ... the old fool," he sneered, "Doesn't he know his day is done? He's lost his daughter, his wife's dying and now here *you* are to bring him to his knees."

But at this poignant piece of news and Christian's swift flashback to his happy years spent among the Bligh family, he could not do it. Betsy, he knew, was Bligh's life. Without her he'd be lost and worse still ... alone. *That* for Bligh was a punishment worse than death and one far more severe than any Christian could inflict.

At this revelation, the burden of rage dropped like a cloak from Christian's shoulders and he turned to Macarthur to decline his offer of revenge.

"Are you *mad!*" Macarthur shot back. "After all these years, here's your chance to settle the score and you're throwing it all away."

"I won't be a part of the witch-hunt," he replied. "When

all's said and done, what does it matter who was right or wrong? Either way, I've served my sentence and Bligh's served his. I only hope that for all the kindness you've shown me, Macarthur, you won't have to serve yours."

Stung by Christian's astonishing loyalty to his old friend and his own inability to sway it, Macarthur took a moment to collect his thoughts. The reality was that without Christian's surprise appearance and testimony, the courts would probably find against him and his Rum Rebellion.

If he chose, he could expose Christian to the authorities against his will, but that would be the act of a small man – something he never was nor ever would be. So with the courage and presence of mind he so often had to muster, he put his hand on Christian's shoulder and said:

"Leave. Walk away fast and don't look back."

FORTY-ONE

The trial was over. Bligh won, but the victory left him feeling drained and unsatisfied.

He had never disliked Colonel Johnston, and pitying him as Macarthur's dupe, didn't wish to see him hang. The man, however, had been found guilty of high treason, which was punishable by death, and the fact that he was merely cashiered from the army was a very light sentence. To Bligh, it smacked of the government's lack of confidence in *him* and its suspicion that he was not entirely innocent of the crime.

That question mark, he knew now, would forever hang over his head, but with his Betsy on her deathbed, he was beyond caring. Distraught at the thought of her deserting him and his devastating solitude to come, he walked into the street, dazed by the milling crowd and cacophony of frenzied voices that surrounded him.

"Are they going to hang him?" one woman asked him in excitement.

Refusing to dignify her ghoulish inquiry with a reply, Bligh pushed past her, further into the throng.

And as for Macarthur, he thought bitterly, as he knocked another's shoulder with a force mentally intended for his sheep-breeding nemesis. *I swear the man must have nine lives!*

Macarthur, every bit as deserving of a death sentence as Johnston, had been let off scot-free.

"Only for the time being," the judge-advocate clarified. "As a private citizen, no longer a member of the military, he must be tried in the country where the crime was committed."

Well, I'll look forward to that! Macarthur mused, making up his mind, then and there, to stay in England for the next eight years until things cooled down – right in believing it was his best way to avoid his crime and punishment.

"To the devil with him!" Bligh cursed under his breath, unaware that only hours before, Macarthur had held his fate in his hands; that in a magnanimous gesture many would call kindness, he set Christian free and spared Bligh from disaster. For beyond the devotion of an old friend there was nothing Macarthur respected more than a dedicated enemy.

Sick of himself and the rest of humanity, that 56-year-old enemy, Bligh, was still battling his way through a sea of unknown faces when his gaze fell suddenly on one so familiar that it stopped him dead in his tracks. Dazed by the sun's glare, he blinked to refocus on what he was sure was an hallucination. But his clear eyes fixed firm once more on the man standing at the street corner.

There, not 50 feet away, was Fletcher Christian's spitting image.

Bligh's world stood still, its logic disintegrating into a vacuum of ear-piercing silence. In that instant, nothing existed but the two them and magically, no longer impeded by the crowd, Bligh walked towards him in a trance, convinced that each step would make the mirage disappear.

Instead it stayed steady, his every footfall consolidating its form; but, when almost within reach, Christian turned to walk away, his pace picking up as did Bligh's in pursuit.

"Christian!" Bligh called out after him, as his quarry turned a corner.

Desperate to catch up, he broke into a run, rounding the bend, out of breath, to find Christian waiting for him just a few feet away.

"Follow no further Bligh!" he said, holding up his hand. "I came only to make sure you were all right and to put your mind at rest about me."

Bligh stood stunned, panting hard from exhaustion and disbelief.

"It can't be," he gasped, still struggling to convince himself that he wasn't seeing a ghost.

Yet, this man before him was flesh and blood, having aged just as had he, with his familiar thick crop of black hair now grey at the temples.

Christian spoke:

"Is it too much to ask that we both forgive and forget?"

Hesitantly, and for the first time in his life, Bligh put pride aside and nodded his assent.

"Then all seems to have turned out as it should, so I'll say goodbye," Christian replied, throwing him a casual salute and the youthful smile Bligh remembered, before he turned and disappeared around the next corner.

Not wanting to know whether or not it was real, Bligh saw no point in following.

For if it were the man himself, he reasoned, *seeking him out would only condemn him to the gallows.*

And if it were a vision, then it had appeared for his benefit and he expected no less of his friend, Christian.

THE END

EPILOGUE

THE FATE OF FLETCHER CHRISTIAN

Acting Lieutenant – Bounty

Whereas the bulk of this book is based on fact, the story of Fletcher Christian, beyond Pitcairn Island, is fiction and a matter of conjecture.

In 1808, The American seal-hunting ship Topaz visited Pitcairn Island and found only one Bounty mutineer alive. John Adams and nine Tahitian women had survived, along with the children fathered by the rest of the mutineers. Both Adams and Christian's wife Maimiti claimed that Christian was murdered on "Massacre Day" during the bloody conflict between the Tahitian men and the mutineers.

"Christian was shot while working by a pond next to the home of his pregnant wife," one of the other Tahitian women reported.

Four other mutineers and all six Tahitian men were killed in the clash. Of the four who survived, William McCoy fell intoxicated from a cliff and was killed. Matthew Quintal was later murdered by the remaining two mutineers, Adams and Ned Young. The latter died soon after of asthma, leaving Adams in charge of the island.

Adams gave conflicting accounts of Christian's demise to others who visited Pitcairn. Christian was variously said to have died of natural causes, committed suicide, gone insane and been murdered.

Christian was survived by Maimiti and their son, Thursday October Christian (born 1790), a younger son,

Charles Christian (born 1792) and a daughter, Mary Ann Christian (born 1793). Thursday and Charles are the ancestors of almost everybody with the surname Christian on Pitcairn and Norfolk Islands, as well as the many descendants who moved to Australia, New Zealand and the United States.

Rumours have persisted for more than 200 years that Christian's murder was faked and that he made his way back to England. That hearsay was inspired by Samuel Taylor Coleridge's *The Rime of the Ancient Mariner*, which was believed to be based on Christian's life and only made possible by the poet's interviews with the man himself.

It was not, in fact, Bligh who thought he saw Christian in a London street, but Christian's friend and fellow shipmate from the Bounty, Peter Heywood, who swore he saw him on the streets of Plymouth. The account was reported by Sir John Barrow in his book: *The Mutiny and Piratical Seizure of HMS Bounty:*

> *Captain Heywood found himself one day walking behind a man, whose shape had so much the appearance of Christian's, that he quickened his pace. Both were walking very fast and the rapid steps behind him roused the stranger's attention. He turned, looked at Heywood and then immediately ran off. His face was Christian's spitting image and in excitement, Heywood ran after him. The stranger, however, had the advantage and after making several turns, disappeared.*

The chance of it being Christian, Heywood thought,

was most unlikely, but the stranger's efforts to elude him said otherwise. Although Heywood was tempted to make further inquiries, the thought of what pain and suffering such a discovery might cause convinced him to drop the matter. The memory, however, stayed with him for the rest of his life. Heywood's was the only documented account of such a sighting, but there was already something of an urban legend of Christian's survival in place.

There was a strong belief that Christian was living in the neighbourhood of the lakes of Cumberland and Westmoreland, where he frequently visited an aunt.

Coleridge's colleague, William Wordsworth, was a childhood classmate of Christian's. When the Bounty mutineer was tried in absentia, Wordsworth joined Christian's brother Edward in his defence. So well known was the association of Coleridge and Wordsworth to Christian that it was proposed the two famed poets collaborated to have Christian somehow brought back to England. No evidence has ever been provided of this, but it remains the most popular rumour of Christian's fate.

With no portrait of Fletcher Christian in existence, we can only rely on his myth and what was said of his character by a member of the Bounty crew:

> *He was a gentleman and brave man who every officer and seaman would have gone through fire and waterto serve. As much as I have lost and suffered by him, if he were restored to his country, I would be the first to go without wages in search of him.*

PETER HEYWOOD

Acting midshipman – Bounty

Born on the Isle of Man, Heywood was of excellent lineage and recommended as a midshipman by Bligh's father-in-law, Dr Richard Betham. As one of the men of greatest interest on the Bounty, it was he on whom the fictional *Byams* was based in Hall and Nordhoff's novel *Mutiny on the Bounty*.

Being of similar age and background to Christian, they became close friends, but when he ran up on deck during the mutiny, he was ordered below. There, he was kept under guard and played no active part in the uprising. Given his and Christian's close relationship, however, Bligh was convinced that he had a hand in planning it.

As a loyalist, Heywood was kept on board the Bounty against his will and when Christian set out to find sanctuary on Pitcairn Island, he elected to stay in Tahiti. He loved the island and said as much in a letter to his mother.

The natives treat us with a friendship, generosity and humanity unparalleled by any civilised nation; such as to disgrace all Christians.

He was found guilty at the Bounty trial, but acquitted because of the very favourable impression he made on the judges. A short time after, he thought he saw Fletcher Christian on a street in Plymouth. It was a sighting never forgotten and one which was added to other rumours that Christian had survived and returned secretly to England.

Heywood went on to lead a distinguished naval career, retiring from active service in 1816 and dying on February 10, 1831, only days before reaching the rank of admiral.

JOHN FRYER

Sailing master – Bounty

Born in 1753, John Fryer had served as master in the Royal Navy since 1781. He was considered highly competent when made sailing master of the Bounty.

From all accounts, he was a sober man of strong opinions who was not as sensitive to criticism as Fletcher Christian and let Bligh know that he would not take insults lying down. He was the only officer on board who tried to talk Christian out of the mutiny and mediated between Bligh and Christian to that end. He was also among those who insisted that Bligh be given the launch rather than the other unseaworthy boat with which he was first presented.

Not afraid to stand his ground, Fryer posed an impediment for Christian at the time of the mutiny because he stood by Bligh as was his duty. He was, however, as much anti-Bligh as the mutineers and when on the loyalist launch, he headed the faction of men who wanted him in command rather than Bligh.

Although he and Bligh crossed swords regularly, Bligh did not bring charges against him at the trial. And despite the fact that they both had a genuine axe to grind in regard to each other, Fryer's testimony was fair and weighed in Bligh's favour.

After the trial, however, Fryer looked up Joseph Christian, a distant relative of Fletcher's, to tell him of issues which were not divulged at the court case. Later he was also instrumental in helping Fletcher's older brother, Edward, gather the facts omitted by Bligh, which Edward published in 1792 in his *Appendix to Stephen Barney's Minutes of the Proceedings of the Court Martial.*

Fryer went on to have a notable naval career reaching master of the first rate in 1798.

At the Battle of Copenhagen, he was sailing master on Admiral Sir Hyde Parker's flagship, London. His son Harrison Fryer was midshipman on Nelson's flagship, Elephant, and his brother-in-law Robert Tinkler, also a member of Bounty's crew, was a lieutenant on the Isis.

Contrary to Bligh's opinion, his competence was recognised by other commanders and his character summed up by biographer Rolf Du Reitz in 1981:

> *John Fryer was not a so-called historically important figure and will never warrant a full-dress biography. Nevertheless, as far as we know, he was a loyal and professionally competent officer and an honest man who served his country well during the greatest and most critical point of Britain's naval history.*

He died on May 26, 1817, at the age of 64.

THOMAS HAYWARD

Midshipman – Bounty

Born in 1767, Hayward (not to be confused with Peter Heywood) was the son of a minor official in Hackney. His older sister was a close friend of Betsy Betham, and it was through her that he obtained the position of midshipman on the Bounty.

His service on the ship was lacklustre, but he remained loyal to Bligh and a staunch opponent of Fletcher Christian, who, along with Peter Heywood, disliked him intensely. Heywood referred to him as a *"worldling raised a little in society with affected airs and graces beyond his station"*.

As a loyalist, he was forcibly put on board the launch with Bligh. He survived and after returning to England, set out as third lieutenant under Captain Edward Edwards on HMS Pandora to track down the mutineers. Although they succeeded in finding some of the mutineers on Tahiti, and Hayward evidently performed well, it was an unfortunate voyage that ended with the Pandora being shipwrecked.

For the second time in as many years, Hayward found himself without a ship, in an open boat making for safety. Again, he stayed alive and eventually returned to England with other survivors from the Pandora, after which his career is uncertain.

It has been suggested, based on nearly illegible papers, that Hayward commanded HM Sloop Swift. If so, he drowned when the ship was lost with all hands in a typhoon in the South China Sea in 1798 aged 31. One way or the other, the sea seemed intent on taking him.

JOHN HALLETT

Midshipman – Bounty

Born in 1772, John Hallett was a British naval officer and midshipman on the Bounty. Coming from a respected family, he mustered onto the ship in 1787, at the age of 15 as its youngest officer.

He became friends with midshipman Thomas Hayward and aped the older man's arrogant behaviour, which made him very unpopular with the rest of the crew. Like Hayward, he was forced into Bligh's launch. He survived the open boat voyage to Timor and returned safely to England.

He gave false testimony, however, at the 1792 trial against innocent officers Peter Heywood and James Morrison, which ensured their convictions. Later, he defended Bligh against the more offensive allegations published in Edward Christian's and John Fryer's accounts of the mutiny.

Hallett rose to the rank of lieutenant, but died in the sinking of the HMS Penelope, aged only 26.

EDWARD CHRISTIAN

Lawyer and older brother

Born in 1758, Edward Christian was an English judge and law professor. He studied at Cambridge and was admitted to the Honourable Society of Gray's Inn in 1782. In 1788, he was appointed Downing Professor of the Laws of England. He held that professorship at Cambridge University in conjunction with a fellowship of Downing, and was also law professor at the East India Company College from 1806-18 and Chief Justice of the Isle of Ely in 1816.

In 1794, at the urging of Edward Christian, Stephen Barney, counsel to the mutineer William Muspratt, published his version of the *Minutes of the Bounty Court-Martial*, with its appendix written by Edward Christian. In it, at Bligh's expense, Edward attempted to justify his younger brother's conduct by citing his own private interviews with several of the people involved (none directly) and listing the names of prominent people who witnessed the conversations.

Due to Edward Christian's prominent position in society, his appendix turned public opinion against Bligh. Bligh had no choice but to respond in kind by publishing *An Answer to Certain Assertions Contained in The Appendix to a Pamphlet, entitled…* etc, to which Edward Christian promptly published *A Short Reply to Capt. William Bligh's Answer*. All of which only served to fan the flames.

The process was aided by the efforts of Peter Heywood's family and to this day, many attribute Bligh's bad reputation less to Fletcher Christian than to his big brother's interference.

Edward Christian died in 1823, aged 65.

PITCAIRN ISLAND

Refuge of Bounty's mutineers

It became increasingly difficult for the small island of Pitcairn to sustain the lives of its settlers. Of its one and three quarter square miles, only 88 acres is flat land and by 1855 there were nearly 200 mouths to feed. A violent storm in 1845 compounded the problem, resulting in a scarcity of fish and massive landslides.

It was at this point that the elders of the island wrote to Queen Victoria, humbly begging for help. In one of the most generous gestures in the Empire's history, she offered them Norfolk Island.

The entire Pitcairn community of 194 people sailed on the Morayshire to settle on Norfolk Island on June 8, 1856. A re-enactment of this landing is celebrated annually and known as Bounty Day, because its date is shared with the commissioning of the famous ship.

JOSEPH FOVEAUX

Acting Lieutenant-Governor – Norfolk Island

Born in 1767, Foveaux was an ensign in the 60th regiment and then joined the New South Wales Corps in 1789 as lieutenant. When he reached Sydney in 1791 he was promoted to major and, as senior officer between August 1796 and November 1799, controlled the corps at a time when the senior officers were making fortunes from trading and extending their lands. He soon became the largest landholder and stock-owner in the colony.

In 1800, having established a reputation as an able and efficient administrator, Foveaux sought to improve his status by offering to go to Norfolk Island as Lieutenant-Governor. Finding the island run down, he built it up, paying particular attention to public works for which he earned the praise of New South Wales' Governor King. He was described as brutal in his dealings with the convicts; a fact corroborated by the island's gaoler, Robert Jones.

Governor Macquarie, however, was impressed with Foveaux's administration and put him forward as David Collins' successor as Lieutenant-Governor of Van Diemen's Land. But after the trial, Foveaux was considered as something of an embarrassment to the army and was posted to an Irish backwater as an inspecting field officer.

When Major (later Lt Colonel) George Johnston was cashiered from the army for his part in the uprising, Secretary of State Lord Liverpool felt that the army was unhappy at doling out further punishment to its own for the overthrow of a navy man. Therefore, he closed the book on the NSW Rum Rebellion and Foveaux escaped prosecution. His superiors were not fooled by his excuses for having taken over the colony, nor were they impressed by Governor Macquarie's extraordinary support of him. It was just that luck was with him.

He pursued an uneventful military career from that point on, rising to the rank of lieutenant-general in 1830 before dying in London on March 20, 1846, at the age of 79. He was buried in Kensal Green Cemetery.

The suburb of Surry Hills in Sydney was once a farming area owned by Foveaux, his property named *Surry Hills Farm,* after Surrey Hills in England. Foveaux Strait in New Zealand is named in his honour, as are many streets in New South Wales and the Australian Capital Territory.

ROBERT CAMPBELL
Merchant, pastoralist and politician

Born in Inverclyde, Scotland, in 1769, Robert Campbell was a member of the first New South Wales Legislative Council.

As owner of the trading company Campbell & Co, he travelled to Sydney with his cargo from Calcutta and established a trading connection between the two countries. In 1800, he settled in Sydney, where he married Sophia Palmer, Commissary John Palmer's sister. He built private wharves and warehouses and by 1804 had them stocked with £50,000 worth of goods.

His high character led to Bligh appointing him treasurer to the public funds and collector of taxes. With no bank in Sydney at the time, the gaol and orphan funds were deposited with Campbell on his undertaking to pay interest at 5 per cent.

In 1825, Campbell was appointed a member of the first New South Wales Legislative Council and in 1830, he recommended that the King's School be founded at Parramatta. When the Savings Bank of New South Wales was founded in 1832, it was found that Campbell had deposited £8000 belonging to convicts and £2000 belonging to free people. He was allowing 7.5 per cent interest on these deposits -- a more generous rate than the one stipulated for the undertaking.

Campbell retired from public life in 1843, and in 1844 his name was included in a list of those considered eligible for a proposed local order of merit. He died in 1846 at the age of 77.

Campbell built Australia's first shipbuilding yards in 1807 at the site that is now the Royal Sydney Yacht Squadron, Kirribilli. A suburb in Canberra is named in his honour.

JOHN PALMER
Commissary of New South Wales

Born in Portsmouth in 1760, John Palmer arrived with the First Fleet in 1788 as purser on its flagship, Sirius. He was appointed Commissary General of New South Wales in 1791, and as such, he was responsible for the reception and issue of all government stores. He kept the public accounts and funds of the colony and was official supplier, contractor and banker to the settlement.

Palmer received his first land grant of 100 acres in 1793 which he named Woolloomooloo Farm. Here he planted an extensive orchard, built one of the colony's first permanent residences and elegantly entertained the first rank of colonial society. In 1795 he was one of the three principal farmers and stockholders. In his judicial capacity as a magistrate, Palmer was familiar with most of the disturbances that occurred in the colony. He was no friend of John Macarthur, or of most of the New South Wales Corps.

In 1809, as a supporter of Governor Bligh, he was briefly put in gaol on a charge of sedition for having declared New South Wales to be in a state of mutiny. Palmer denied the competency of the court and refused to plead, but was found guilty. He also continued to refuse to allow Lieutenant-Governor George Johnston access to his ledgers without the authority of the British Treasury.

In 1810 he was ordered to England with Bligh. He was one of Bligh's chief witnesses against Johnston.

When he died at Waddon, near Parramatta, on September 27, 1833, at the age of 73, he was the last surviving officer of the First Fleet.

HENRY FULTON
Irish clergyman in New South Wales

Fulton was born in Lisburn, Ireland in 1761 and educated at Trinity College, Dublin. He was a clergyman in the Diocese of Killaloe and became involved in the Irish Rebellion of 1798 for which he was sentenced to penal transportation to New South Wales. Though sometimes afterwards referred to as an ex-convict, he was really a political prisoner.

With his wife and son, he arrived in Sydney in 1800 and was conditionally emancipated in November of the same year and began to conduct services at the Hawkesbury. In 1801 he was sent to Norfolk Island as chaplain and in 1805 received a full pardon from Governor Gidley-King. He returned to Sydney in 1806 to take over the duties of Samuel Marsden, who was on a leave of absence.

At the time of the revolt against Bligh, Fulton stood by him and was suspended as chaplain because he did not yield to the corps officers. In1809, he wrote letters to the Secretary of State, Viscount Castlereagh, giving accounts of what happened to Bligh, severely censuring the conduct of the New South Wales Corps.

Immediately after the arrival of Governor Macquarie, Fulton was reinstated as assistant chaplain. He went to England as a witness at the court-martial of Colonel Johnston and returned to Sydney in 1812.

He was appointed chaplain at Castlereagh, New South Wales, and was made a magistrate. Fulton died at his parsonage on November 17, 1840, at the age of 79; a brave man, who lost his living in Ireland because of his sympathy for the Irish and in Australia again, for going against his own interests to support Bligh.

GEORGE JOHNSTON

Major (later Lieutenant-Colonel)
Acting Lieutenant-Governor of New South Wales

Born in 1764 in Annandale, Scotland, George Johnston was a soldier and farmer, the son of Captain George Johnston, aide-de-camp to Lord Percy, later Duke of Northumberland. He was chosen by Governor Arthur Phillip as the "most deserving" marine officer to raise a company that would be annexed to the incoming New South Wales Corps.

He was promoted to major in 1800 and during his service in the colony he often held positions of responsibility: as Phillip's adjutant of orders, as Hunter's aide-de-camp, and as commanding officer of the corps during the long absences from Sydney of Lieutenant-Colonel William Paterson.

A handsome and popular officer, he quarrelled with King and Bligh when those governors appeared to intrude in military administration.

The critical point in Johnston's colonial career was his decision on January 26, 1808, to assume the lieutenant-governorship and arrest Bligh. He was found guilty at the 1811 trial, but the leniency of his sentence indicated that the court was convinced that he was used as a tool by other people.

Johnston returned to Sydney as a private citizen and lived on his land at Annandale. He had no further dealings with John Macarthur and died, much respected, on January 5, 1823, at the age of 59, leaving a large family.

He was first interred in a private mausoleum on his Annandale property, until its subdivision to become an inner-city suburb. His remains were moved to a new mausoleum at Waverley Cemetery in 1904.

GEORGE CROSSLEY

Lawyer and convict in New South Wales

Born in London in 1749, George Crossley practised as a lawyer for 24 years. In 1796, he was charged with forging the will of Reverend Henry Lewin for the benefit of Lady Briggs, defrauding the heir-at-law. He was sentenced to be transported for seven years.

As a loyal and capable supporter of William Bligh, Crossley at times advised deputy judge-advocate Richard Atkins and finally assisted him to prepare the information on the prosecution of John Macarthur, preceding the Rum Rebellion. For this support, Crossley was tried by the rebels for having practised as an attorney after a conviction for perjury. He was found guilty and sentenced to the Coal River Mines for seven years.

When Governor Macquarie arrived, he was released and he sued the rebels for damages for trespass and false imprisonment.

He was a successful farmer, trader, moneylender and lawyer and continued to practise in the Judge-Advocate's Court, while also advertising his business in the *Sydney Gazette*. In 1816, however, Governor Macquarie was informed that emancipated men were only allowed to practise when there were less than two free lawyers in the colony.

He was a colourful, if somewhat shady character, who may not have possessed the virtues expected of his vocation, but a man unnecessarily maligned. With his career marked by pressure from creditors, Crossley died on March 19, 1823, at the age of 74. He was buried in the old burial ground in Sydney and the headstone was later removed to Bunnerong Cemetery.

RICHARD ATKINS
Judge-Advocate in New South Wales

Born in 1745, Richard Atkins was the fifth son of Sir William Bowyer, baronet. He assumed the surname Atkins in recognition of a legacy from Sir Richard Atkins of Clapham, Surrey.

He procured a military commission and in 1780 became adjutant to the Isle of Man Corps. Addicted to liquor, immorality and insolvency, he led a thoroughly dissolute life, riding on the back of his brothers' good name: Sir William Bowyer, Lieutenant-General Henry Bowyer and Admiral Sir George Bowyer.

Principally to evade his creditors, he resigned his commission and sailed for Sydney in 1792. There, he impressed the string of New South Wales governors with his connections. Despite his lack of legal credentials, Governor Phillip made him a magistrate at Parramatta and appointed him registrar of the Vice-Admiralty Court. Behind these influential titles, he sheltered from existing creditors while engaging fresh credit locally on the security of his family name. It was soon common knowledge that his bills were never met.

John Macarthur declared Atkins *"a public cheater living in the most boundless dissipation"* and, after exchanges of equal warmth between them, requested that Governor John Hunter prosecute Atkins for libel. The application clashed with Hunter's instructions from England to appoint Atkins acting deputy judge-advocate while David Collins was on leave.

The most prominent of Atkins' adventures on the bench was the trial of John Macarthur in 1808. When Major Johnston took command of the colony, Atkins was immediately suspended, but soon made his peace with the rebels, though it was from necessity alone that Lieutenant-Governor Joseph Foveaux, having canvassed unsuccessfully for a replacement, reinstated him as judge-advocate Lord Castlereagh finally ordered his recall to England, censuring his *"want of professional education and practice which had caused great inconveniences".* This was a mild appraisal of the decrepit old man who Macquarie thought unlikely to survive his passage home in the Hindostan.

However, he reached England safely and went into retirement. For a time, he could not be found to give evidence at Johnston's court-martial, but he ultimately gave his testimony in a fawning fashion demonstrating his wavering loyalties and feeble character. He remained insolvent until his death in London on November 21, 1820, at the age of 72.

SIR HENRY BROWNE-HAYES

Merchant, industrialist, convict and adventurer

Born in 1762, Sir Henry Browne-Hayes was the son of Attiwell Hayes, a reputable and opulent citizen of Cork, Ireland.

Browne-Hayes was transported to New South Wales for kidnapping the Quaker Mary Pike, heiress to a fortune of £20,000. He forced her to undergo a spurious marriage at his home at Mount Vernon, but she was rescued soon afterwards.

He was sentenced to death, but the sentence was commuted to transportation for life and he arrived in New South Wales on July 6, 1802, on the Atlas. He paid handsomely for a privileged passage, which was just as well for him, for the voyage was the worst in the history of transportation. During it, he antagonised the surgeon Thomas Jamison, which earned him and additional six months imprisonment after his arrival.

Browne-Hayes' sojourn in New South Wales was noteworthy largely for his war against authority. He lived comfortably in a house he built in Vaucluse, Sydney, until 1808 when he expressed sympathy for deposed Governor Bligh, and George Johnston sent him to the Newcastle coal mines as punishment.

He was released after eight months, but was back there in May, 1809, for attempting to bring the rebel government into ridicule. That temporary government was on its way out, however, and a pardon made out by Bligh in 1809 was honoured by Governor Macquarie.

Browne-Hayes left for Ireland in December 1812, surviving a shipwreck at the Falkland Islands. He retired to Cork and died in 1832 at the age of 70.

His first positive contribution to the colony was his attempt in 1803 to found a Masonic lodge, for which he incurred the displeasure of Governor King. It is doubtful that he had a warrant to establish a lodge, but his meeting on May 14, 1803, is regarded as the Foundation Day of Freemasonry in Australia.

His second contribution was Vaucluse House, the home he built near South Head. Here, when not on his travels, he lived in remarkable style and freedom for a convict. It has become a national monument, passing to John Piper after Browne-Hayes' departure and in 1829 to William Charles Wentworth, who extended it considerably to make it even more grand. The mansion was rented for some years from Sir Henry Browne-Hayes by Colonel O'Connell and his wife Mary Putland (nee Bligh).

ELIZABETH MACARTHUR
Anglo-Australian pastoralist and merchant

Elizabeth Macarthur (nee Veale) was born in Devon, England, the daughter of provincial farmers. She married Plymouth soldier John Macarthur in 1788. Travelling as part of the Second Fleet in 1790, she, with her newborn son Edward, accompanied John and his corps to New South Wales. She was the first lady of quality to set foot in the fledgling colony.

From nine pregnancies, seven of their children survived childhood and for the early years, she concerned herself only with social and domestic duties. However, during John's two long sojourns in London to avoid trials, Elizabeth oversaw the huge family estates at Parramatta, Camden, Seven Hills and Pennant Hills. This included the management of household and business accounts, the employment of convict labour, the supervision of wool washing, baling and transport and the selection of rams and breeding to improve the flock.

Her hands-on contribution to the Australian wool industry and its international trading was essential and astounding, while her husband, in England, used his flair to promote their wool produce worldwide.

After John's return to New South Wales in 1817, she retired from active participation in the business to look after her family. She was saddened by her husband's mental deterioration, his deep fits of melancholia and unfounded obsession that she had been unfaithful to him. His feelings of persecution became so violent that he could not bear to see his wife and sent her from his house.

Though she suffered terribly from this rejection, her strength of character and extreme good sense kept the family together. Despite his bad treatment of her in later life, she remained devoted to her husband until his death and encouraged her sons to deal with the difficult situation of caring for their father without allowing them to experience any sense of conflict in their relations with her.

She died on February 9, 1850, at the age of 84, having survived John by 16 years. She lived to see the phenomenal success of Australian wool exports in the mid-1830s and the fulfilment of every one of her husband's predictions concerning the economic development of the colony.

Her influence on her sons cannot be overestimated. Both James and William were deeply devoted to her and owed their conservative, aristocratic temperaments less to their father's driving economic ambition than to the educated example of their mother.

The Elizabeth Macarthur Agricultural Institute is named in her honour. It is the largest centre of excellence operated by the New South Wales Department of Primary Industries, employing 200 scientists and located at Camden Park. Elizabeth Macarthur is commemorated on the 1995 Australian five-dollar coin which was struck for inclusion in a special *Masterpieces in Silver* collectors' set entitled *Colonial Australia*.

JOHN MACARTHUR

Soldier, entrepreneur, pioneer, pastoralist
Father of the Australian Wool Industry

After the Rum Rebellion trial and his eight years of exile in England, Macarthur arrived back in Sydney in 1817. In his absence, his wife had carried on the great success of his pastoral and commercial interests.

As he had done with prior New South Wales Governors, Macarthur was at odds with Governor Macquarie. As part of his enmity, he cultivated a friendship with visiting commissioner John Thomas Bigge, whose written assessment of Macquarie, no doubt influenced by Macarthur, brought an end to his governorship.

In the1820s Macarthur owned more than 100 horses. He established Camden Park Stud and was a major provider of thoroughbreds. But growing madder by the day, he outfitted his household staff in grandiose royal blue livery and threw himself into architectural designs for Elizabeth Farm and sumptuous houses for his other land holdings. He owned 60,000 acres, but in growing rich, he became increasingly unstable.

He established Australia's first commercial vineyard and was a founding investor in both the Australian Agricultural Company (London 1824) and the Bank of Australia (1826) His involvement in the Rum Rebellion blocked him from being appointed as a magistrate in 1822, but in 1825 he was nominated to the New South Wales Legislative Council.

In 1825, Governor Darling appointed Macarthur to the colony's new Legislative Council, but in constant dispute with the Governor, he rarely attended meetings. He was appointed to the reconstituted Legislative Council in 1829, but in three years, Governor Bourke had him removed.

Macarthur had gone mad. He had thrown his wife Elizabeth out of their house accusing her of infidelity and turned her room into a room for royalty, from whom he expected a visit any day.

Elizabeth moved into their Sydney house. His three daughters were commanded to stay at Elizabeth Farm and were banned from his sight, accusing them and the household staff of stealing his clothes, while raving that his sons were planning an armed insurrection in a remote part of the colony.

Declared insane, he was confined to his bedroom at Elizabeth Farm for the last years of his life, finally dying in a cottage at his Camden Estate on April 11, 1834, at the age of 67. His death barely rated a mention in the press, but was summed up by colonist Robert Scott:

> *A man of the most violent passions, his friendship strong and his hatred invincible.*

Nonetheless, he was a man in a million whose legacy lives on.

MACARTHUR'S SONS

Edward Macarthur

Sir Edward Macarthur KCB (16 March 1789-1872) was a lieutenant-general in the British Army, an administrator active in Australia and Commander-in-Chief of Her Majesty's forces in Australia from 1855.

James Macarthur

James Macarthur (1798-1867) was an Australian pastoralist and politician. He was a member of the New South Wales Legislative Council and Legislative Assembly.

William Macarthur

Hon Sir William Macarthur (1800-1882) was an Australian botanist and vigneron. He was one of the most active and influential horticulturists in Australia in the mid-to-late 19th century. Among the first viticulturists in Australia, Macarthur was a medal-winning winemaker, as well as a respected amateur botanist and noted plant breeder.

Macarthur's descendants still live and prosper in Australia, proud to bear his name.

MARY PUTLAND O'CONNELL
née Bligh

The second of Bligh's six daughters, Mary was born 1783 and accompanied her father and husband Lieutenant John Putland to New South Wales in 1806. Her young husband died soon after from tuberculosis.

After marrying Lieutenant-Colonel Maurice O'Connell, they stayed in New South Wales, but not for long. Governor Macquarie found their pro-Bligh presence in the colony disruptive and lobbied hard for the 73rd Regiment and thereby, the O'Connells, to be transferred to Ceylon in 1834.

Maurice O'Connell was knighted and Mary became Lady O'Connell. With Maurice now a general, the O'Connells returned to Sydney in 1838 where Maurice became Commander of British Forces in all Australian Colonies. Mary did charity work, including being on Caroline Chisholm's committee with immigrant women.

When Maurice died in 1845, Mary returned to London where she died in 1864 at the age of 81. Several of her children and grandchildren remained in Australia.

WILLIAM BLIGH

Vice Admiral of The Blue

Soon after the Rum Rebellion trial, Bligh received a backdated promotion to rear admiral. Although he was in Australia for only three years and four months, he received the promised pension for a four-year term as Governor. With no more frontline commands, he was assigned to engineering and mapping and was in the navy for only three more years, during which time he was promoted to Vice-Admiral of the Blue.

In 1812, his wife Betsy died, her years of sickness made worse by the stresses of Johnston's trial.

Bligh was never the same again. He and his daughters moved from their much-loved home in Lambeth because the memories of Betsy once being there were too hard to bear.

Nonetheless, ever mindful, as was his mentor Captain Cook, of all the knowledge he needed to impart, Bligh continued to guide his protégé, the famed explorer-to-be Matthew Flinders.

I was his disciple in surveying and nautical astronomy while sailing around the world with him on the Providence, said Flinders. *Throughout the many years of our acquaintance, he never ceased to be remarkably obliging and attentive to me.*

Bligh was sick for some time with an intestinal cancer and in 1817, at the age of 63, collapsed and died in Bond Street, London. Related to Admiral Sir Richard Rodney Bligh and Captain George Miller Bligh, his descendants include the former premier of Queensland, Anna Bligh, and the former Australian Liberal Party leader Malcolm Bligh Turnbull.

He died, ironically, in the same year that Macarthur returned to Australia. With his nemesis gone, Macarthur probably thought the coast was clear, but the South Seas will never be free of Bligh, for they are his forever.

In a little Lambeth churchyard rests a tombstone engraved Captain Bligh, but his true memorial lies on the other side of the world. There, where the Trade Winds rustle the fronds of tall palms and the swell of the blue Pacific beats incessantly on white coral reefs, lie the landmarks that still bear his name. They remind us that here sailed a man who for all his faults was a great Englishman, a gallant officer and one of the greatest navigators the world has ever known.

– Kenneth S. Allen.

ACKNOWLEDGEMENTS

THAT BOUNTY BASTARD
Kenneth S. Allen
St Martin's Press Inc., 1977
NEW YORK, USA.

BLIGH IN AUSTRALIA
Russell Earls Davis
Woodslane Press Pty Ltd, 2010
SYDNEY, AUSTRALIA.

WILLIAM BLIGH & EDWARD CHRISTIAN
THE BOUNTY MUTINY
(This edition with introduction by Robert D. Madison)
The Penguin Group (USA) Inc, 2001
NEW YORK, USA.

MUTINY ON THE BOUNTY
Charles Nordhoff & Norman Hall, 1932

CAPTAIN BLIGH'S OTHER MUTINY
Stephen Dando-Collins
Random House, Australia, 2007
SYDNEY, AUSTRALIA.

Fate of Fletcher Christian:	www.skeptold.com
Biography of John Hallett:	B. Edwards.
Biography of George Crossley:	*Australian Dictionary of Biography*: K. G. Allars
Biography of Richard Atkins:	*Australian Dictionary of Biography*: J.M. Bennett
Biography of Mary Putland:	www.abc.net.au
Biography of Sir Henry Browne Hayes:	*Australian Dictionary of Biography*: N.S. Lynravn
John Fryer: Master, HMAV Bounty Handwritten Account and Peter Heywood's letters:	www.fatefulvoyage.com

Printed in Great Britain
by Amazon